GONE
to the
DOGS
Mysteries

BOOK 6

NEW LEASH ON LIFE

GONE
to the
DOGS
Mysteries

BOOK 6

NEW LEASH ON LIFE

KATHLEEN Y'BARBO

BARBOUR
PUBLISHING

New Leash on Life ©2023 by Kathleen Y'Barbo

Print ISBN 978-1-63609-662-9

Adobe Digital Edition (.epub) 978-1-63609-663-6

Scripture taken from the Holy Bible, New International Version®. niv®. Copyright © 1973, 1978, 1984, 2011 by Biblica, Inc.™ Used by permission. All rights reserved worldwide.

This book is a work of fiction. Names, characters, places, and incidents are either products of the author's imagination or used fictitiously. Any similarity to actual people, organizations, and/or events is purely coincidental.

Cover illustration by Victor McLinda

Published by Barbour Publishing, Inc., 1810 Barbour Drive, Uhrichsville, Ohio 44683, www.barbourbooks.com

Our mission is to inspire the world with the life-changing message of the Bible.

Member of the
Evangelical Christian
Publishers Association

Printed in the United States of America.

DEDICATION

In honor of RMWD VVolt N629,
a real American hero and a very good boy.
Rest easy, soldier.

For those who serve,
who served,
and who are still fighting the battle.

To Folds of Honor (www.foldsofhonor.org),
an organization that stands in the gap
for the families of military and first responders
by meeting sacrifice with hope.

To Andrew, a.k.a. Carrot Star Man.
Your absence in our lives is deep and wide,
a distance that only God will someday remedy.

To the trio of much loved and adored Apostrophes—
Joshua, Jacob, and Hannah.
Long may you Barb.

And for Senior Master Sgt. Robert C. Turner,
USAF USANG, Retired,
my forever love.

But he said to me, "My grace is sufficient for you, for my power is made perfect in weakness." Therefore I will boast all the more gladly about my weaknesses, so that Christ's power may rest on me. That is why, for Christ's sake, I delight in weaknesses, in insults, in hardships, in persecutions, in difficulties. For when I am weak, then I am strong.

2 CORINTHIANS 12:9–10

CHAPTER ONE

Nora

Tuesday
Brenham, Texas

The sun had just dipped behind the collection of buildings that made up the downtown district of Brenham, Texas. In a few hours it would be sunset.

My friend Cassidy Carter sat beside me, a pitcher of my newest concoction—raspberry lavender iced tea—on the table between us. From the street one floor below, snippets of conversation from passersby mingled with the soft jazz music from my restaurant, Simply Eat.

Dinner service would start in an hour, and I really should have been in the kitchen supervising. However, I had a well-trained staff, and my new chef, Roz Holt, cooked my recipes better than I did, to be honest. She'd only been in my employ for a little over a month, but Roz had caught on quickly and was now firmly in control of the kitchen.

No. They wouldn't miss me a bit, and if needed they knew where to find me.

I closed my eyes and smiled. It was one of those moments I wish I could capture and put away so I could feel exactly like it whenever I wanted. It was, in a word, perfect.

Well, almost.

"Congratulations on adding another property to the Nora Hernandez real estate empire."

"It's hardly an empire," I protested, opening my eyes to look over at Cassidy. "Just two properties downtown and my little cottage. But thank you."

One year ago today, she and I had purchased this building where we now sat. Cassidy turned the upstairs portion into a loft apartment for herself, while the ground floor became Simply Eat, a farm-to-table restaurant.

I reached over to clink glasses with Cassidy, then took a sip of tea. Oh, that was good. If I could replicate the taste on a large enough scale, it just might go on the menu.

I sat back and exhaled. Life was good. So very good. The only thing missing from this moment was the man I loved.

But then, I'd gotten used to that.

Somewhere around the four-year mark, I'd decided I wasn't going to keep looking for the engagement ring that never seemed to be inside the gift box from Dr. Lane Bishop, DVM. Too many birthdays, Christmases, and Valentine's Days had passed without any sort of hint at steering our relationship toward marriage.

I had quit my job as a pet food rep and made a different long-wished-for goal come true. I opened Simply Eat. Lane and I bumped along, seeing one another when we could find time away from our careers. I told myself it wouldn't always be that way.

We'd settle down. We might even have a family before we were eligible for our Medicare cards.

Then, a little over a year ago, came what I had come to refer to as the moment of clarity. We were strolling along a path beside one of the pastures at my parents' ranch. Sunday suppers were a tradition with my family, and we were walking off fried chicken with all the fixings. I wandered ahead to pet one of the horses that had come to meet me at the fence.

When I turned around, Lane was behind me. On one knee.

My heart soared. My hand went to my mouth, I suppose to stifle the scream of happiness that might have ruined the moment.

This was it. The proposal I had waited for was about to happen.

Lane looked up and grinned. Then he tied his shoe and stood.

"That sure was good chicken. Do you think you could get your mother's recipe?"

To this day, I don't think he had a clue why I stalked off in tears. He's still apologizing and telling me my fried chicken tastes just fine.

A month ago, I told him we needed some time apart. The man actually had the audacity to remind me that we lived in two different cities and thus had time apart already.

That was it. I was done.

Again.

I broke up with him. I didn't say the words, exactly. I didn't have to. He wasn't there. But I stopped counting on a ring and a happily ever after.

Again.

Yes, I know. I'm working on not loving him, but it's definitely a process.

After a breakup—or whatever it was that happened—many women head to the salon to change their hair color or try a daring new hairstyle. Not me. I bought an antique shop.

It all started three weeks ago when Mr. Lazlo, a retired professor of English at Brenham College, walked over and knocked on the back door of Simply Eat.

Everyone in the kitchen loved Mr. Lazlo. He'd been our next-door neighbor as long as the restaurant had been around, and he would often pop in the back door to buy lunch or dinner.

"My family wants me to move to Florida, Nora, and I want to go. Make an offer on my store, and it's yours."

So I did. And as of today, it was.

My phone buzzed. I glanced down to see it was a text from my dad. CONGRATULATIONS ON THE BIG PURCHASE. WATCH OUT LATE TONIGHT. THE WEATHER LADY ON TV SAYS TORNADOES ARE POSSIBLE.

I grinned. Only my father would text a congratulatory message alongside a warning to beware of bad weather. THANKS, DAD. I'LL TRY

NOT TO BLOW AWAY.

He responded with a smile emoji. SEE THAT YOU DON'T. GOOD NEWS IS THE BUILDING IS STURDY.

I chuckled. "That was my dad."

"Weather forecast for tonight?" Cassidy asked.

"Storm coming. And he sent his congratulations on buying the store," I said.

"That sounds like Mr. H. He always did keep us updated on the weather, and he's your biggest cheerleader." She paused to check her watch. "Jason should be picking me up soon. I'm not sure what we're doing, but you're welcome to come along. Unless you have plans for the evening?"

"Do you mean am I seeing Lane tonight?"

She shrugged. "I figured you would be. It's kind of a big day."

I returned my glass to the table. "Lane has something going on with work. He said he'd try to see me after. Besides, we're kind of broken up."

"Have you told him yet?" Cassidy asked, knowing me too well.

"I didn't have to," I said. "He still thinks I'm mad at him for wanting my mother's chicken recipe. He's clueless."

I know how it sounded when I said that. Like I was a needy girlfriend who was lashing out because she was disappointed yet again. And honestly, that's how I felt.

Okay, maybe not the needy part. In the past year, I'd found so much joy in chasing the dream of owning my restaurant. It was a lot of work, but it was also exactly what I had hoped it would be.

Unfortunately, Lane did disappoint me. Repeatedly. Sometimes when work took precedence over me, like today. And other times when I got my hopes up only to have them dashed when he did that thing where he shut down. Or rather, shut me out of whatever was going on inside that beautiful, brilliant brain of his.

I wanted to be done with him. I really did. It was just so much harder falling out of love than it had been to fall in love. It was so much easier to just go along with the status quo—that is, except for the times I forgot I wasn't expecting the relationship to go beyond what it already was.

I looked over at Cassidy just in time to catch the expression on her face before it disappeared. "What?" I asked.

My red-haired best friend gave me her best attempt at an innocent look. "What?" she said right back.

"You know something."

Rust-colored brows rose. "I know lots of things, Nora. Be specific."

"You know where Lane is," I said, making a wild guess as to why she was looking so guilty.

She sighed. "Nora, why in the world would I know that?"

I stared at her a moment longer then shrugged. She was right. Why in the world would Cassidy know anything about my boyfriend's whereabouts? Or rather, my eventually ex-boyfriend's whereabouts?

LANE

Tuesday
Lone Star Veterinary Clinic

The only person who knew my whereabouts was Cassidy Carter, the office manager at the vet clinic. I'd told her very little of what I had planned, but I did have to tell her enough to get the information out about when to intercept Dr. Tyler Durham, current owner of Lone Star Veterinary Clinic.

I could have asked Tyler for a meeting, but I had a feeling I would do better to surprise him. He was Nora's friend, and considering the rocky status of our relationship, I wasn't sure how he would react.

Now here I was sitting in my truck in the employee parking lot of the clinic, waiting for Tyler to appear. Cassidy told me he'd be leaving late because he'd agreed to see a patient after hours. I'd staked out the place from a safe distance, and once the last of the employees were gone, I parked my truck next to Tyler's and sat back to bide my time.

The building hadn't changed since my father owned it. I smiled at the recollection of following Pop, a.k.a. Dr. Elvin Bishop, DVM, in that very door and stepping into a world I would one day join.

My career as a veterinarian had led me to one of the premier veterinary programs in the country at Texas A&M University. I was on the fast track

NEW LEASH ON LIFE

to big things at the university and possibly beyond.

Pop, however, had been happy seeing patients here in Brenham and making house calls to homes and barns all over the county. Even after he retired and sold the clinic to Tyler, he'd stayed busy working with animal shelters and rescues, including Second Chance Dog Rescue.

My father was busier now than when he had practiced here at the clinic. He was also happier than he'd ever been.

Than I'd been lately, if the truth were told.

I held on to that thought as I played a half dozen rounds of solitaire on my phone and then scrolled over to check out what the sports pundits were saying about the Texas Aggies' chances this season.

I'd just started reading an article written by my favorite TexAgs columnist when the back door of the clinic opened and Tyler stepped outside. I turned off my phone and tucked it into my pocket then climbed out of the truck.

Tyler saw me and waved. "Lane, I didn't expect to see you here."

I closed the distance between us and reached out to shake his hand. "Got a minute?"

He gave me a confused look then checked his watch. "Sure," he said, looking up. "We can talk in my office." He unlocked the door then held it open for me. "Has something happened with Dr. Bishop?"

"Pop's fine," I told him. "Actually, there's something else I'd like to discuss."

The familiar antiseptic smell of the clinic hit my nose along with a landslide of memories, all of them good. I followed Tyler down the hall to an office that had changed very little since my father sat behind the cluttered desk.

Photos of my sister and me had been replaced by framed pictures of Tyler and a pretty blond on a beach, on a snowy ski run, and all smiles at an Aggie football game. Otherwise, the space looked like Pop had just walked out.

"My fiancée," Tyler said, nodding to the pictures. "Kristin is a veterinarian here at the clinic." He paused. "Sorry, I forget you've met her. Anyway, what can I do for you, Lane?"

The moment of truth. I sat back in the chair across the desk from him—the same chair where I'd learned my multiplication tables and done a decade or more of homework—and smiled.

"Actually, Tyler, it's what I can do for you."

I told him my idea then sat back and waited for his response. It wasn't every day that I offered to take a two-week vacation from work—in fact, I'd never done that since I moved into the research position—just to play country veterinarian at my father's old clinic.

He matched my smile then nodded, his hands steepled in front of him. "Wow. That's, well, it's more than generous. When Kristin and I planned our honeymoon, we were both reluctant to be gone for two weeks, but we decided our marriage deserved it."

"Of course. I'm happy to do it," I said, leaving out the part where I had selfish reasons.

Two weeks here meant two weeks of being close to Nora. Even as I had the thought, I began tallying all the reasons this was a bad idea.

All the meetings I would have to catch up on after the fact.

All the research data I'd be reading every free moment.

The list went on, but I stopped thinking about it and said a quick prayer. If Tyler said yes, then it was meant to be. If he didn't, then I had my answer.

"And I would be happy to have you here," Tyler said. "I'd know the clinic would be in exceptionally good hands. I mean you almost literally grew up here." He paused. "Except. . ."

"Except?" I echoed.

"Except I've already hired your father to do it."

I sat back, surprise and relief washing over me. "Pop's going to fill in? He never said a word to me about it."

Tyler shrugged. "Maybe he wanted to surprise you."

I scrubbed my face with my hands then shrugged. "Well, it worked. I'm surprised."

Silence fell between us, then Tyler frowned. "You're not worried that he can't do the job, are you?"

"Not at all," I told him. "My father's as healthy now as he was when I was a teenager. I'm not concerned about that at all." I thought a moment. "I will admit that he scares me to death when he gets out in his yard with his saw to cut tree limbs. I've told him over and over he doesn't need to be climbing a ladder at his age, but he refuses to use the cutter with the extension pole that I bought him. Says he gets a better view of things up on the ladder."

We shared a chuckle. "Sounds like my future father-in-law. Kristin's dad isn't nearly the age of your father, but he's stubborn as it gets when it comes to doing things for himself that he ought to have help with. It drives Kristin crazy, and I guess, by default, me as well."

"Parents," I said, "who knew we'd be raising them?"

"Oh, I'm sure they had their share with their own parents," Tyler commiserated. "But that's the circle of life."

I nodded and rose. "I won't take up any more of your time. Thanks for talking to me about this. I'd appreciate it if you don't mention it to Nora."

Tyler stood. "Of course. I'm guessing you didn't want to get her hopes up that you'd be around more while you're working here for us."

"Something like that."

He shook my hand. "Right, well, how about I walk out with you? Kristin will be wondering where I am, and I'm sure Nora will be wondering where you are as well."

But she wouldn't. And not just because I hadn't told her about my plan to talk to Tyler tonight. She'd made a big purchase today—the antique store next door to her restaurant—and she would be celebrating.

She thought I was at a work event. I should have told her my plans and not been so vague. What was wrong with me? I adored that woman.

I knew the answer. She needed a man who didn't have to hide a part of himself from her. A part he had no control over.

The nightmares were something I couldn't fix. I consoled myself with the fact that some guys I served with had it much worse.

And some hadn't come home at all.

I climbed into the truck and drove. Telling Nora about my struggle would change everything. What I hadn't yet decided was what that change would be.

Likely she'd declare she loved me anyway, and that her love was greater than any struggle I—or we—might have. And she would mean it. At first.

But for how long?

It was the answer to that question that kept me up at night. That and the fear that once I fell asleep, the dreams would return.

I couldn't do that to the woman I loved more than life.

I wouldn't.

But until I could figure out a way to stop seeing her, to stop loving her, I'd stick around as long as she let me.

Who was I kidding?

I would be with that woman until she got fed up with waiting for me to pop the question and kick me to the curb. Every day that she didn't do that was a gift from God.

I should tell her that before I lost my nerve.

Again.

The clock on my truck's dashboard said it was half past six. Nora was most likely at the restaurant. I'd just made the turn onto the street leading to Simply Eat when my phone rang. I pushed the icon for hands-free talking.

"Hey, Pop," I said, slowing to allow a woman in workout gear and her dog, a Belgian Malinois or German shepherd—I couldn't tell from this distance—jog across the crosswalk. "What's up?"

"Are you at home?"

He only ever asked me that question if he needed something. "Actually, I'm right around the corner from your house. What can I bring you?"

"Just a couple of things from the hardware store. I'm trying to get my branches cut before the storm."

"Pop, no. It's almost dark. Just leave them."

"It's not dark when I'm wearing that light you gave me for Christmas. That was a nifty gift. I just can't find the right battery to replace the ones that just burned out."

I had given him a light that clipped on to his lapel and was bright enough to light his way as he walked around his property. "That wasn't meant for tree trimming, Pop. And tell me you don't have the ladder out."

Silence.

I groaned as I circled past Nora's restaurant and headed toward my father's house. "I'll be there in a few minutes. We can go to the hardware store together."

"Okay," he said grudgingly, "but it's only open for another hour, so we'll have to hurry."

When I arrived, Pop was just closing the door on the shed next to the garage. He looked up sharply, the lights of my truck catching him with guilt written all over his face.

"Did you just hide your ladder?"

My father's expression turned stubborn. "I don't have to answer that."

I looked behind him to where the floodlights from the back porch illuminated his pecan trees and the pile of branches beneath them. "You're right. You don't have to answer that."

His expression changed to something hopeful. "Have you had supper yet? I've got something warming in the Crock-Pot, and there's plenty for two. And there's a new episode out of that western show we both like. We could watch it together."

The possibility of seeing Nora anytime soon was getting slim. I should say no. This was a big day for my girl. But my dad was alone, and I was all he had.

"Sure, Pop," I said on an exhale of breath. "That sounds good. Just let me send Nora a text, and I'll be right in."

I reached for my phone. I WAS HEADED YOUR WAY BUT HAD TO DETOUR TO POP'S PLACE. HE'S OKAY BUT LONELY.

I would make it up to her.

CHAPTER TWO

Nora

Tuesday
Simply Eat

I tucked my phone back into my pocket, deciding not to respond to Lane's text. I understood. Unlike my big family with all the kids and grandkids who could look after aging parents, Lane's dad was a widower who only had Lane.

For a short while, it had looked like the elder Dr. Bishop might marry again. He'd certainly been sweet on my friend Marigold Jenson's grandmother, Peach Potter. But when Peach Potter married Pastor Nelson instead, he'd been stoic.

"She just wasn't the one for me," he'd said with a shrug.

And ever since, I'd been praying for the right one to come along for him. He was just such a sweetheart.

I took out my phone again. TELL HIM HI FOR ME. SEE YOU ANOTHER DAY, I texted then put my phone away again.

I didn't bother to check his response when it came. I already knew what he would say.

"Something wrong?" Chef Roz peered into the tiny closet I had commandeered as an office.

She wore a hot pink chef's coat with black striped linen pants and an array of colorful bracelets marching up both arms. Her shoes were neon orange high-tops with laces that matched her pink shirt. Not only had Roz brought elevated cooking to Simply Eat, she had also brought plenty of color to the kitchen.

"No, everything's fine," I told her. "Did you need something?"

"I figured we could go over the menu before the crazy hour starts. We had a few substitutions in the grocery order, and I've had to pivot."

When a restaurant was committed to a farm-to-table menu, there were always substitutions in the orders we placed. So far Roz had handled them beautifully. She went over the changes to the menu, and I approved them.

"I'll get those printed," I told her. "Is there anything else?"

"All good, boss," she said. "I'm watching that new waiter. He's good, but there's something off. I can't put my finger on it. And maybe I'm imagining it."

I considered asking which one. Instead, I decided to let Roz handle the situation and declined to request more information.

"Okay," I said instead. "Let me know if there's anything I need to deal with."

"I will." She crossed her arms over her chest. "You know I run a tight ship. I'm not going to let you down, and neither is my crew."

She'd said that when I interviewed her for the job. I'd been ambivalent about putting someone else in the driver's seat of this kitchen, but I knew it was time. Managing the place and trying to cook all the meals had become exhausting.

It also took away from any time I could spend with anyone but my kitchen staff. I had become just as big a problem in the relationship as Lane.

Dad had pointed this out, and I'd hated that he was right.

With the dinner service under control, I left the kitchen of Simply Eat in the capable hands of my chef and walked down the street to the store I'd purchased that morning. Dad, my brother Tony, and I had gone over every inch of this building while I was considering the purchase, so

I knew what would greet me when I opened the door.

But this was the first time I would be the owner. It felt good.

Maybe Cassidy was right. Perhaps I was on my way to owning a real estate empire.

I laughed at the thought. Given the choice, I'd follow in my mother's footsteps and share ownership of a ranch with my husband, cook for family, and love on children and grandchildren, but that wasn't the path for me right now.

So I guessed I'd just have to keep building my empire until God changed my path.

The old wooden door swung open on hinges that needed a good oiling. I made a mental note to put that on the list.

The very long list.

Starting with what I was going to call the place. Mr. Lazlo had simply locked the door and handed over the key. The building came with all furnishings, stock on the shelves, and a second floor that contained a storage closet filled with cleaning supplies and the furnished one-bedroom apartment upstairs.

Tony suggested I rent out the place, but Dad didn't like the idea of a stranger upstairs. I promised him he could interview anyone I decided to allow to live there.

But as I sat here alone in an empty store, I had to reluctantly agree with my father. I didn't think I would want a stranger in the building with me either, even if there was a door that could be locked to keep the tenant out of the store and an outside entrance for the upstairs.

My phone buzzed. I retrieved it from my pocket as I flipped the light switch. "Hey, Cassidy," I said, blinking to adjust my eyes to the abrupt change. "What's up?"

"Marigold just called and asked me to join her on a rescue. I thought you might want to come with us." She paused. "Since you don't have any plans."

"I thought you had plans with Jason," I countered.

She sighed. "He had to cancel. With the storm blowing in late tonight, he got called in to work. It's the hazard of dating a first responder, I guess."

I locked the door behind me and pocketed the key, balancing the phone between my chin and shoulder. Marigold Jenson was the owner of Second Chance Dog Rescue, an organization that rescued strays, got care for them, and then found them forever homes.

Cassidy often went with her, as did Mari's husband, Parker. All three of these valiant souls worked full-time at the Lone Star Veterinary Clinic and still managed to volunteer anytime a call came through with a tip about a possible stray.

I really should say yes. As I had the thought, I glanced around at the disarray, the chaos, and the work that needed doing to get the store back open—if that was what I decided to do. Mr. Lazlo had certainly held on to this property well beyond the time when he could keep up with it.

"Do you need me to?" I asked. "What I mean is, I will if you need the help. I know you'll want to have the animal back at the facility and be home before the weather gets bad."

"True. And if we don't need you to?" Cassidy said, her tone strangely cheery.

"If you don't, then I'm going to tackle some of the chores that need to be done at the store. Or at least make a list of them," I told her.

"Oh." Just like that, her tone changed. "No, we've got Parker driving, and Mari and I are here too. Enjoy your chores."

"Is there something wrong?" I asked.

"No. Everything's fine. I just thought you might want to get out and do something tonight."

"Since I wasn't celebrating with Lane?"

"You're not? I'm sorry." She paused. "I guess I hoped he might. . ."

Her voice trailed off. There was no need to continue.

"I'm fine," I told her. "I promise. And I'm actually excited about getting an inventory of stock done." I paused. "I may need the dog rescue crew to come help. Mention that to them tonight."

I laughed, but I was sort of serious. The more the merrier when it came to trying to get a count of all the things here. I decided to tackle the books first since that section of the store was smaller and better organized.

Snatching up the little three-legged stool from its place in the cluttered storeroom upstairs, I traversed the length of the narrow building to reach the back of the space. Row upon row of books—some leather bound and beautiful and others paperback and falling apart—were in need of attention. There seemed to be no rhyme or reason to the organization.

Actually, there was no organization at all.

The idea of taking everything down and putting it in order was overwhelming. So I did the next best thing and went back to the storage closet for a cleaning cloth.

I had only been at it a few minutes when I realized I needed a cleaning crew before I employed a counting crew. My sneezing was out of control, and I was covered with dust.

"Enough of this. I need a better plan."

From the other side of the wall shared with Pupcake Bakery, I could hear the soft thumping sounds of music. Then I heard a louder thump and a clattering sound that could only mean broken glass.

And an intruder.

Because that sound was coming from inside and not the other side of the wall.

I sat very still and formulated a plan. At this point, I wasn't worried enough about the inventory to consider defending anything in the store from someone who might want to take anything.

There were two exits on the first floor. The closest one led to the back alley. If there was one bad guy in the building, there could be more waiting in the dark out there.

So I stood slowly and looked around to be sure that whoever had broken something wasn't anywhere in sight. Then I snatched up the stool and began retracing my steps to the front door.

Something fell behind me, and I jumped. A mannequin dressed in a Brenham High band uniform complete with feathered cap lay on the floor where I'd just walked.

My heart was racing. Afraid to turn my back on whatever was hiding there, I walked backward toward the front entrance, wielding the little stool like a shield. Just as my back hit the wood and glass door, I heard it.

A meow.

"What in the world?"

And then again.

I kept the stool close to me but followed the pitiful sound until I spied the orange tabby peering down at me from atop an ancient yellow Kelvinator refrigerator. "Hey there, sweetheart," I said, setting the stool down. "Did I frighten you? Because you sure frightened me."

It took some coaxing and a bowl of milk I retrieved from the kitchen next door, but the skinny feline finally relented and came down. While the cat lapped up her milk, I called Mr. Lazlo.

"I'm sorry to bother you," I told him when he answered, "but I think I found your cat."

"I don't have a cat, Nora," he told me. "Perhaps he snuck in when we were moving my things out."

"I'll check with the other businesses," I said. "Maybe they'll know who it belongs to."

We chatted for a few more minutes then hung up. I could still hear the echoes of music through the wall, so I tucked my phone into my pocket and went outside. My first stop was the pet bakery where the ladies said they would ask around about the cat. Then I headed to the new ladies-only gym. The space was open and bright with pastel colors everywhere. Since no one was at the front desk, I walked down the hall to the room where the class was in session.

I couldn't see who was teaching, and I hated to interrupt. So I went back up front and used a sticky note I found on the desk to leave a message about the cat.

The wind was picking up as I stepped out onto the sidewalk. Back inside the store, I found the empty milk bowl but not the cat. I locked up and went next door to check on things at the restaurant.

"If things get slow, go ahead and close early," I told Roz. "Bad weather is predicted for later, and we may not have the usual late crowd."

"Roger, boss," Roz said. "I'll keep an eye on things, and I'll text you if we bug out early."

"Never say 'bug' in a restaurant kitchen," I said with a chuckle.

Roz laughed. "Yeah, no bugs here. Not on my watch."

With that assurance, I went next door to deal with the cat I'd just inherited. I braced myself for the battle that it would require to catch the feline and then somehow transport it to my place for the night.

To my surprise, when I stepped inside, the orange tabby came running toward me meowing in a tone that seemed to ask where in the world I had been. Then it proceeded to thread itself between my ankles while purring at high volume.

"Okay then." With that, I scooped up the cat and took it—or rather, *her*—home.

By the time my phone rang, I had rummaged around and found tuna to feed the still-hungry cat and was about to reheat leftovers for myself. I snatched up my phone from the counter and saw Lane's face.

"Looks like you're home," he said when I hit the buttons to begin video chatting with him.

I spied his father waving in the background. "And it looks like you're at your dad's. Hello, Dr. Bishop."

"It's not his fault he's here," Dr. Bishop called. "It's mine. So don't be mad at him this time."

This time. I could have had a whole conversation about those two words. Instead, I smiled. "Yes sir," I told him. "I'm glad you're enjoying him tonight."

Lane looked back at his father. "I'm going to step out and talk to Nora."

The cat had been staring up at me ever since the call began. I reached down to pet her, and she purred.

I love almost every kind of furry animal except a rodent—they are a restaurant owner's nightmare—but I had never owned a cat. Growing up on the ranch, there were always sweet barn cats around. But Mama never allowed one in her house.

The object of my thoughts jumped into my lap and made three circles before settling down.

A minute later, Lane reappeared. He had walked outside, and floodlights from his father's house illuminated the back patio and the fringe of pecan trees beyond.

"Okay, I'm back. I was on my way to see you when he called," Lane said. "I'm so sorry. He was on the ladder with a hacksaw again. You can see the pile of wood behind me. I don't know what I'm going to do with him."

In the distance, a dog barked, sending the cat's ears slanting backward.

"I guess the positive side of things is that he's still got his health. He wouldn't be able to climb that ladder otherwise." At Lane's "that's not funny" expression, I hurried to continue. "Honestly, I don't know. It's definitely concerning, but what are you going to do? Move in with him? Knowing how happy your father is here in Brenham, he's certainly not going to move in with you."

"I don't think we've reached that point yet," Lane said. "But if he thinks he's going to have that ladder hidden in his storage shed when I leave tonight, he's wrong. I'm taking it and the hacksaw."

"Can I suggest that you just take the ladder? Taking a saw that he might use for other things seems a bit much."

A dog barked again in the background, this time closer. "Does your dad have a dog now?" I asked Lane.

Dr. Bishop's dog had died of old age several months ago. Lane had been urging him to get another one, but his father was reluctant.

"Not yet," he said. "Pop is still saying it's too soon."

I nodded. "Okay, but it sounds like there's a dog right there with you."

Another round of barking sounded through the phone. This time the cat was not amused. Ears back, she peered up into the phone and hissed.

"Nora?" Lane said. "Did you buy a cat today?"

"No, Lane," I told him, my tone more sarcastic than it should have been, "I bought a building today. Apparently the cat came with it."

"About that. . ." Lane paused. "I'm sorry I wasn't there to celebrate with you. I meant to, well, after I did the work thing, that is."

I wasn't about to tell him I understood or that it was okay. Well, not about the work thing.

"I wasn't alone," I said instead. "Bryce Robinson walked me through the process."

As soon as I said the words, I regretted them. Never had I stooped to trying to make Lane jealous. That was a high school move at best. And worst.

"Right," Lane said. "Well, Bryce is helpful."

There it was. The slight change of tone that told me he was just a bit jealous. I did not want to feel as good about that as I did.

"He is a Realtor, Lane," I said. "Anyway, it's all done, and I've started looking over the inventory to see what's there. I don't know what I'll do with it all, but I do know I need a cleaning crew first."

"It's a lot to take on," he said. "Maybe you should just try to flip the place. You could have one of those estate sale places give you a price to haul off the contents and then have the interiors improved before putting it back on the market at a profit."

The suggestion made sense. Why, then, did it bother me that he'd made it?

Because once again I'd be doing all of this without him. It was a totally irrational thought, but it was exactly what I was thinking.

"I miss you," I blurted out.

"Oh honey, I miss you too," Lane said. "I really do. I know my track record of being a no-show doesn't back up what I'm saying, but if I had the choice, I'd choose to be with you instead of working all the time."

"That's a nice thought," I said.

"You're thinking that I have that choice already," Lane challenged.

I was, but admitting it now wouldn't fix anything between us. "No comment."

He opened his mouth to speak, but the barking grew louder. In the background, I spied something moving quickly toward him.

"Lane, behind you!"

The horizon tilted, and the phone landed on the deck. In the distance, I saw an animal—it must be a dog—dart into the woods with Lane following close behind. A few minutes later, Lane returned and picked up the phone.

"Sorry about that," he said, slightly out of breath.

"What in the world?" I asked.

"Big dog running fast," he said. "I didn't see a collar, but I lost it in the dark not long after it buzzed past. I hope he isn't injured."

"He wouldn't have run that fast if he was injured, Lane. From what I saw, he was zigzagging like crazy. There's a storm coming, and Dad says the weather does that to animals sometimes."

I realized after I said it that I had just offered my father's absolutely-not-an-expert advice to Dr. Lane Bishop, DVM. "But you'd know more about that than me," I added.

"All I know is someone's big dog is running loose tonight. It's a shame I couldn't catch him. I'll tell Pop to be on the lookout in case the animal shows up here again."

"I hate to think of an animal out in the weather," I said, looking down at the cat that had returned to sleep mode in my lap.

"Speaking of the weather," Lane said, "I don't like the idea of you at home alone if there is a big storm tonight. Would you consider coming over here and staying at Pop's place? He's got plenty of bedrooms, so you'd have your privacy and we'd definitely have a chaperone."

"I heard that," his father said from off in the distance.

Lane shook his head. "Pop came out to see what the yelling and barking were about."

"I appreciate the offer, but I think my cat and I will stay where we are tonight. Besides, it's already starting to rain over here."

As I said that, I saw the first plops of moisture hit the screen on Lane's end. "Here too," he said, ducking inside. "Okay, I'm going to step into the kitchen while Pop is in his room."

"I'm glad you'll be with your dad tonight," I told him. "He always looks so lost when I see him. I know he must miss your mom."

"Yeah." Lane ran his free hand through his hair. "So can we make a deal? Can we set aside some time to figure out how we can fix what needs to be fixed between us?"

"Of course," I said, trying not to get my hopes up.

"I didn't say that right." Lane paused. "I know what needs changing in me, or at least I think I do. You've probably got a longer list than I do, but you'd be right."

We shared a laugh.

"And Nora," Lane said gently, "in case you're wondering, I think you're perfect just the way you are."

I smiled. I wasn't, but it certainly was nice to hear him say it.

"Go see about your dad," I said, smiling. "We can talk about this another time."

"I love you, Nora Hernandez," Lane said. "I really do. Stick with me until I can make you believe it, please. I've got things I need to work through, but none of it has anything to do with you."

"Lane," his father called, "are you still on the phone?"

"Go," I told him. And this time he did.

I wondered if he noticed I hadn't told him I loved him back. I was pretty sure I still did—in fact, I know I did—but was it truly love when one was contemplating a breakup as often as I did? Or was I just hanging on to something that I was meant to let go of?

My phone rang again, shattering my thoughts. It was Cassidy.

"I'm making sure you're at home," she said. "Jason said things are getting intense out there, and we should all be watching the weather."

"Tell Jason he sounds like my dad," I said with a chuckle. "Seriously though, I'm fine. This little cottage is solid, and I've got my new pet cat to keep me company."

"Nora, I saw you a few hours ago, and you did not have a pet cat."

"Actually, I did, but I just didn't know it." I told her what happened and how the sweet orange tabby cat had come to live at my little stone cottage, at least for now.

"She needs a name," Cassidy declared.

"I know, but I haven't had time to decide on one."

"What about Tab? All the southern ladies of a certain age had cans of it in their fridges," Cassidy said.

I shook my head. "I don't follow."

"Tab, as in Tabby." Cassidy paused. "Or you could call her Peaches."

"I doubt that Lane's dad would want the reminder of the woman he thought he was in love with walking around in fur form," I told her. "But it is a cute name."

"True. I didn't think of that."

"The right name will come," I said. "If I'm supposed to keep her, that is. There may be someone looking for her. Mr. Lazlo certainly didn't know she was in his store, so I can't claim her as mine just yet. I need to find out if she's someone else's first."

CHAPTER THREE

Nora

Wednesday
Brenham, Texas

When the phone rang, I jolted awake, not sure where it was or, for that matter, where I was. I had fallen asleep listening to the rain pound my roof and scrolling online to see if anyone might be missing an orange tabby cat.

I grappled around in my blankets and found the noisy thing then silenced it by offering a sleepy greeting. A familiar voice said my name.

"Lane?" I glanced at the clock and saw it was nearly half past four. No wonder my bedroom was still dark.

"I'm at the door, Nora. Let me in."

Well, that woke me up. "My door?"

"Yes, let me in, please."

My cottage is tiny. Just a downstairs with a kitchen and living area and an upstairs with two minuscule bedrooms wedged under the eaves between a bathroom the size of a postage stamp.

However, I managed to throw on clothes and get downstairs with a pair of sneakers in my hand in less than a minute. Or at least it felt that way.

I opened the door, and Lane stepped inside along with enough rainwater to make my few meager houseplants happy for a week. "You're soaked! Let me go get a towel."

"No time," he said. "Grab those boots you wear out at the ranch and put on your rain gear. We need to get downtown."

"Downtown?" I froze. "Has something happened to the restaurant? Oh my gosh, and to Cassidy upstairs? I didn't get any messages from Roz other than to let me know they all finished their shifts and closed up on time." I checked again. "No, nothing from the alarm company either. Just a bunch of weather alerts."

"Nora, trust me. Just grab your boots. And seeing as it's after four in the morning, you'll want to text your dad when you get in the truck to let him know you're okay."

Lane knew my father's penchant for waking up at four on the dot every day. I never understood why the man insisted he could get so much done before the sun came up, although to his credit I had never tried it. I was solidly not a morning person.

My dislike for the wee hours of the day was on full display as I donned my boots and rain gear then made a pit stop in the bathroom to pull my hair into a ponytail. The person in the mirror looked as anxious as I felt.

"Okay, I'm ready," I told him, bounding back down the stairs.

He glanced down at the cat, who was now lapping at the puddles of water growing at his feet then back up at me. "Cute cat. Now let's go."

I followed him through the pouring rain and climbed into the truck. Once he pulled out of my driveway and onto the road, he gave me a quick glance.

"I got a call from Jason saying there's trouble downtown. If you didn't get anything from the alarm company and Jason didn't mention any issues with Cassidy, then it's not the restaurant building."

"But?" I said with trepidation, my heart pounding.

"But we'll find out when we get there." He paused. "Text your dad and tell him you're fine. If you don't, he will call you, and it'd be better if he thought you were at home and woke up because of one of those weather alerts."

I nodded. "Well, I did. In a way. From you. Did Jason tell you anything else?"

Lane reached across the truck to take my free hand. "No, but if I had to guess, there's been a tornado."

The breath went out of me, and I sat back against the seat. Tornadoes were rare in this part of Texas, but they weren't unheard of. We'd had a few nasty ones during my lifetime, and I sure hoped whatever happened downtown wasn't going to be like those.

"Text your dad," Lane reminded. "And remember that Cassidy is fine or Jason would have said so."

I nodded and did as he said. A minute later my father responded.

ALL RIGHT. STAY SAFE AND KEEP ME POSTED. WE'RE GOOD HERE. I'LL KNOW MORE AT DAYBREAK.

"Okay, that's done." I tucked my phone into the pocket of my rainsuit just as Lane turned onto East Alamo Street. Up ahead through the rain I spied a blur of red and blue lights in the middle of the road.

My heart sank. Lane drove slowly until he reached a police barricade. When an officer approached carrying a big black umbrella, Lane rolled down the window and a gust of rain blew in.

I recognized Officer Todd Denison immediately. He was an active supporter of Second Chance Ranch and even owned one of the success story rescue dogs.

"Can't go any farther," he told Lane. "There's debris all over the roads, and it's still an active scene."

Lane produced his driver's license from his pocket then nodded toward me. "Nora owns two of the buildings in that block. Game Warden Jason Saye called me earlier to let me know there had been some trouble down here."

"Nora, hey. I didn't recognize you in that rainsuit."

"Good morning, Todd," I managed.

He turned his attention back to Lane. "We had a tornado skipping around down here. Jumped right over the Blue Bell plant before heading this way. Took out places here and there and left everything else standing without so much as a scratch."

A Brenham Fire Department ladder truck made a U-turn in the middle of the road up ahead then drove toward the barricade. Office Dennison jogged over to move the barricade and allow the truck through.

My throat constricted. "A tornado, Lane. Oh my gosh, a tornado."

I sounded like an idiot, but I didn't care. Images of the whole block reduced to rubble came to mind, and it didn't matter that the lack of alarms on my phone meant Simply Eat and Cassidy's home upstairs were probably fine.

Leaning forward, I tried to get a better look at the scene up the street, but it was nothing but a blur of lights and rain. Even from here, though, I could tell that my side of the street had escaped the damage inflicted on the neighbors across the way.

The lights were on outside the pink and white brick building that held the Pupcake Bakery. All of the restaurant security lights appeared to be blazing as well. I hadn't had time to arrange for lights on the antique store, so it was dark.

I turned to Lane. "Just sitting here is maddening."

He reached across to squeeze my hand again. "Just give him a minute, Nora. Then we'll get through."

When Todd returned, he took the license and looked at it briefly then handed it back to Lane. "Nora," he said to me, "the restaurant and Cassidy's place upstairs are fine. Nothing was damaged that we can see. The alarm is still set, so we haven't gone inside, but I can't imagine that you'll find anything out of place."

I let out a long breath. "I'm so glad, Todd. That's a huge relief."

Todd adjusted his hat and swiped at the rain on his brow. "Now, the building next door. That antique store?"

"Yes, it's mine. I bought it this morning," I told him. "What about it?"

"Just this morning?" He whistled low under his breath. "I hope you had time to get some insurance on it, because you're going to need it. A fire like that could cause as much damage to the structure as it could smoke damage to everything else."

I jumped out of the truck and ran toward the lights. Fire? And a tornado? Rain pounded against my face as I raced ahead. Then, inexplicably, the horizon tilted and I went down hard.

LANE

Wednesday
Brenham, Texas

"I need to go after her," I shouted to the cop. "It's going to have to be either me or you, because we both know she shouldn't be inside the perimeter."

He gave me a look then nodded. "Pull the truck over closer to the curb and bring her back as quick as you can."

I did as I was told, all the while watching Nora sprint down the street. I'd just pocketed my keys and made my way around the barricade, my brain in full-on first responder mode, when I saw her fall.

After that it was all a blur. I hadn't run track since college, but I was sprinting around obstacles like I was ten years younger.

Possibly twenty.

I scooped her up just as a paramedic arrived. Blood flowed from a gash on Nora's forehead near the hairline, but otherwise she looked okay.

"Let's get her out of the rain," he said. "I can go for the gurney."

"No," I snapped. "Just lead the way so I don't fall on debris. I will not let any harm come to this woman under my watch."

"I'm the professional here," he said tightly.

"USAF, then a DVM," I told him. "I know my way around triage."

His eyes met mine. "Army medical corps. Multiple tours. Triage is what I'm paid to do."

I nodded. "All right, soldier. Nobody's shooting at us, and I doubt we'll be hit by bombs on the way to your truck, so this should be a breeze."

He gave me a look then nodded. Together we got her out of the rain and into the back of the ambulance for triage.

"I'm fine," Nora protested after we placed her on the gurney. "I just tripped. I need to go make sure the restaurant is okay. Then I need to look over whatever has happened to the antique store and let the adjusters know."

"This first then you can do all that." I paused, realizing the medic needed ID on the patient. "Her name is Nora Hernandez," I told the paramedic, whose badge said Ewing. "Her ID is in my truck. I saw her trip over something in the road."

"I was watching," he said. "I'd just finished up a report on a guy who didn't want treatment when I spied her heading down the street."

I helped Nora out of her rain jacket and tossed it aside. She swiped at her forehead then looked down.

Her lip trembled. "I'm bleeding."

"Looks like a gash just at her hairline," I told him. "She'll probably need stitches or a few butterflies until we can get her to her doctor."

"Stop talking about me like I'm not here," Nora demanded.

"Okay." Ewing wrapped a blanket around Nora's shoulders then reached behind him for a bag marked Triage. "Sit back, please, Nora."

She looked up at me. "I do have insurance, I promise. But I hope there's not a delay in it going into effect. That would be a disaster."

"Nora?" Ewing said. "A policy takes effect immediately. Now sit back."

"How do you know that?" she demanded as she complied with his command.

"I kind of work in an industry where I see a lot of folks who need insurance," he said, bending over her to get started on his assessment. "Now be still. I'm sure your husband can handle the insurance adjuster if he shows up before we're done here."

"That is not my. . .ouch!"

"Be still, Nora," he told her.

I leaned over Ewing's shoulder to see what was happening. The paramedic was assessing the wound with gloved hands while Nora's eyes were on me.

"It's going to be fine, sweetheart," I told her.

Ewing paused to glance back at me. "Hey, flyboy, it'd be great if you could just give me some space. Maybe take that umbrella over there and wait outside while the army handles the problem?"

I opened my mouth to respond then thought better of it. "Do what he says, Nora," I told her. "I'll just be over here."

Then I moved out of the ambulance and into the rain. My rain gear kept me dry enough without resorting to borrowing an umbrella from Ewing.

"Bishop, is that you?"

I turned to see Jason Saye jogging toward me. "Nasty night," he said when he arrived at my side. Then he looked into the ambulance. "Oh no, is that Nora?"

I nodded. "Just a bump on the head. He's putting some butterfly bandages on it. Where's Cassidy? Nora's been worried about her."

"She was out on a rescue with Marigold and her husband. When the storm hit, she decided to stay at their place instead of driving home." He paused and looked down at his boots then back up at me. "I'm glad she did that. I hate to think if she was here when all that went down."

"Definitely."

I was about to ask what "all that" meant when he spoke again. "Man, I hate that Nora's hurt. Will you be sure and message Cassidy so she knows? I don't know when I'll get the chance to do that, and if she hears it from anyone else but us, she's not going to be happy with me."

"Sure."

"I appreciate that." Jason lowered his voice. "And speaking of not being happy, Nora is not going to be pleased when she sees what happened to that building she just bought. The good news is the fire was put out before there was any damage to the roof or anything on the first floor. We can credit the rain and Brenham FD for that."

"Fire?" I shook my head. "I thought the damage was from the tornado. Was there lightning involved? If there's not much damage, it couldn't be a ruptured gas line."

"None of the above," Jason said. "I can't say that the fire was started intentionally, but it did originate in the apartment upstairs."

"I thought the upstairs was empty."

After I said it, I realized I'd only assumed that. Nora's father and brother were the ones who'd actually walked the building with her and inspected everything. I'd been too busy.

"Nope. Fully furnished apartment up there with a separate entrance into the alley." Jason paused. "She needs to be careful who she's renting to if she's going to be spending time in that building. I doubt Lazlo had any idea what was going on up there."

"Hold on," I said. "There was someone living up there?"

He nodded. "Cassidy told me Nora had just bought the place so she probably hadn't met her tenant yet. Or tenants. Hard to tell how many were living there."

"Jason, I don't think she had any idea she had tenants. She certainly didn't mention it to me, although she did say she found a cat in the building. It was hiding downstairs."

I looked over at the back of the ambulance where Nora was now sitting up, the silver blanket still gathered around her shoulders.

"Between you and me," Jason said, "make Nora understand she doesn't need to go in there alone until the locks are changed and a good alarm system is put in. I'm going to be telling Cassidy the same thing. Remember, she lives next door. Literally on the other side of the wall."

"Based on what, Jason?" I asked him. "It's possible that Lazlo thought he'd told her he had a tenant, and this guy, or whoever it is, is completely legit."

The game warden seemed to consider this for a moment. Then he nodded. "Sure, that's possible."

"But you don't think so."

Jason's radio squawked, and he responded. "Look, I need to get back over there. But no, I don't think so, or Lazlo would have told Nora about it. And Nora would have told Cassidy."

"True."

"For Cassidy's sake, I intend to get to the bottom of whatever is going on up there. I'm hoping she'll listen to me and not go back there until I do. But it's Cassidy, so that's probably not going to happen."

I nodded. "It's the price of loving an independent woman."

"We both know that well." He paused. "Let me know if you need anything. I want to talk more about this later. And don't forget to talk to Cassidy. It'll keep me out of the doghouse."

"Speaking of dogs." I told him about the animal I'd chased before the storm. "Pop's place isn't far from downtown, and the dog was headed this way, so it's possible he came through here."

Jason shook his head. "Not that I saw, but I'll see what I can find out.

An animal like that would be hard to miss." He paused. "You know what? I wonder if that's the dog that Cassidy and the Jensons were out looking for before the storm hit. I'm not sure where they were, but I do know they didn't find the dog that had been reported to the tip line."

I smiled. "Thanks for checking into it. If you get a chance, that is. I know you're busy here. I'll see what I can find out from the rescuers."

"I'm glad to," he said. "I wouldn't be much of a game warden if I wasn't concerned with the welfare of animals."

CHAPTER FOUR

Nora
Wednesday
Brenham, Texas

I'm fine, Lane."

I wasn't, not really. However, the last thing I needed was Lane worrying about a bump on my head and a few butterfly bandages when there were more important things to think about. And yes, I realized the irony of wanting Lane to pay more attention to me and then, when he was, not liking it.

I hit my head, all right?

The rain had let up enough to allow us to walk without feeling like we were being pummeled from above. Lane was holding tight to my arm, and he wore a worried look on his face.

"I texted Cassidy while you were getting treated," he said. "She wants you to call when you can."

Cassidy's decision to stay out at Mari and Parker's place instead of driving home in the storm had saved her from being home alone when the tornado hit. Looking at the damage to this street, I was grateful she made that choice.

Her home did look fine, as did Simply Eat. But she would have been in the middle of this mess all the same.

Lane took my arm and guided me around a piece of debris. I'd been so busy looking up that I wasn't remembering to look down.

"Thank you," I told him. "I'm just a little overwhelmed."

My phone rang, and I stopped and handed it to Lane. I wasn't up to speaking with anyone yet.

"Hey, Daniel," he said, giving me a look.

I shook my head then winced at the pain. "You talk to him," I whispered.

"No, she can't come to the phone right now." A pause. "Yes, we did hear that there was damage downtown, but the restaurant building is just fine. We're here now looking at it." Another pause. "No, she'll call you when she knows more."

Lane held the phone to his ear for another minute then managed to get in a quick, "I'll tell her," before he said goodbye and hung up.

"Thank you," I said, taking the phone from him and tucking it into my pocket. "Is he worried?"

"You know your dad. He will be soon enough."

I could see my father and brothers arriving on the scene with their advice and take-charge attitudes. That was the last thing I needed right now.

"Thank you for settling him down," I told Lane. "You've always known how to handle him."

"I don't know about that, but I'll always try for you."

He looked so tender, so worried about me. I leaned into him and allowed him to hold me in an embrace.

The crackle of a police officer's radio nearby broke the moment. Lane's hand remained on my back as I glanced around. Deep purple sky was beginning to fade to pink and pale gold at the horizon. It was just a matter of time now before the sun rose.

Channel 2 was setting up a news truck just beyond the perimeter. If one was here, soon there would be more.

The last thing I wanted right now was a microphone stuck in my face, especially considering I didn't know how my face might look after my visit to the ambulance.

"Okay, then let's get this over with. First I want to see for myself that the restaurant hasn't been damaged."

"Nora." Lane's tone held a warning that I ignored.

"I'm fine. Just humor me. I want to look at the properties, and then I'll go home and rest." I smiled. "That's what you were going to tell me I should do, right?"

"Okay," he said, "but just the restaurant. And please don't argue. There's been a fire in the antique shop. Until we know if it's safe to enter, let's not risk it, okay?"

I understood his logic. Truly I did. However, I needed to see for myself.

As we set off walking toward the properties, I spied game warden Jason Saye helping a Brenham police officer place crime scene tape across the antique shop's front doors.

"Can't go in, Nora," Jason told me. "Not now anyway."

"Come on, Jason," I pleaded. "Just let me go take a peek, and then I'll go."

He shook his head. "Not even for you, Nora. Come back when it's safe."

"Well, there you go," Lane said triumphantly. "We'll come back when it's safe."

"Fine." I left the men standing there and used my key to step inside Simply Eat.

Lane made to follow, but I turned to shake my head. "It'll just take a minute."

He made a face, but I ignored him to walk away. There was no need for him to follow. "I promise I'll call out if I need you."

After disarming the alarm, I made a quick inspection using the flashlight on my phone combined with the soft light of dawn outside. I certainly didn't want to draw attention to the fact I was there by turning on the lights.

When I was satisfied that everything was as it should be, I walked over to reset the alarm but heard the men speaking in hushed tones. I stuck my head outside, and Lane and Jason's conversation ended abruptly.

Too abruptly.

"What's going on with you two?" I demanded.

Neither would look at me and both were smiling. "Nothing," Lane said, his hands stuffed into his pockets.

"Just passing time," Jason said, his smile just a little too forced.

They both looked guilty. Of what, I had no idea.

An idea occurred. "Okay, I'm going to go back in for just a minute. Resume passing time."

I retraced my steps to the kitchen, this time using the light that was beginning to show through the windows. With the front door open, the back door made no noise on the alarm panel as I slid it ajar and peered out into the alley.

Trash cans were strewn around as if they'd been tossed like a child's toy. Limbs from the spindly trees on the other side of the alley were here and there, along with a dusting of green leaves that had presumably been shorn from their branches by the wind.

Stepping sideways through the opening in the door, I moved as quietly and carefully as I could toward the back door of the antique store. The lock was still securely in place, and nothing seemed amiss here.

I glanced up beyond the industrial black iron staircase that hugged the building and concentrated on the second-floor windows. How could a fire start up there? I frowned. There was no damage on this side of the street. Just beyond where I was standing, the pastel pink brick that covered the back of the pet bakery was perfectly clean.

I hadn't explored this part of the building—other than to raid the storage closet for cleaning supplies—since Dad and I walked through before I bought it, but if I remembered right, the window on the right was a bathroom and the one on the left was the kitchen.

I considered climbing up to see the damage for myself. I would have if a police officer hadn't chosen that moment to step into the alley. He was far enough away, and I was still in the shadows, but if I tried, I'd be spotted for sure.

Then I saw something small and dark on the landing about halfway up the staircase. I took a tentative step and then another until I could see it was covered in brown fur and completely still.

"Oh no," I said, thinking of the sweet orange tabby I had at home as I hurried to scoop up the little creature in hopes I could save it.

Only it wasn't a creature. At least not a real one.

I picked up what looked to be a much-loved and somewhat soggy dog toy. I held up what I realized was actually a stuffed squirrel to get a closer look.

"Lovely." I headed for the dumpster then paused. Second Chance Ranch was always looking for gently used pet toys.

Slipping back into the kitchen door, I was just in time to see Lane walking through the dining room. "I'm just locking the back door." I grabbed a towel and wrapped the toy in it then placed it on top of the tall wire shelf in the back of my office.

"Did you go out there?" Lane called.

I stepped into the kitchen and dried my hands on another towel then tossed it into the hamper. "Yes, but just to see what it looked like."

He stepped into the kitchen and gathered me into his arms. For a long moment, neither of us spoke.

"I've been an idiot, Nora," Lane finally said.

Silence fell between us.

"You're not going to argue with me?" he said with a chuckle.

I looked up at him. "Nope." Then I nestled my head into his shoulder, being careful to avoid the bandages on my forehead.

"I don't spend enough time with you. I could blame my job." He paused. "But I'm the one who chose that job."

"Not going to argue," I said.

"So I'm the one who has to change that."

I took a step backward, breaking the embrace. "And?"

Lane let out a long breath. "And I was hoping to surprise you with a couple of weeks of me here in Brenham. I offered to help out over at Lone Star while Kristin and Tyler are on their honeymoon."

Well now. That was unexpected. "You did?"

"I had already cleared my vacation time with the college." He paused. "Unfortunately, Pop got to the job first. He's going to be the fill-in vet."

"Oh." I sighed. "Well, that's too bad. But I'm really touched that you thought to do that, even if it didn't work out."

He shrugged then grasped my hand and lifted my fingers to his lips.

"I love you, Nora. I know I'm the one who has the burden of proof on that. I want to show you that I do."

I do.

It took all I had in me not to make some kind of joke about saying "I do." Instead, I answered softly, "Then show me, Lane. With your actions, not just with promises you don't keep."

"I hate to interrupt this moment," Jason Saye said from the door, "but you two might want to take off before they let the press in. Channel 2 has already gone live once. Stations from Austin and two more from Houston have just arrived. Standing on the other side of the barriers isn't going to sit well with them for long."

"Thanks," Lane told him then turned his attention back to me. "Let's get out of here."

I looked past him to Jason. "Will you let me know when I can go in?"

"Nora," Lane warned. "He's working. Don't ask him to contact you."

"It's fine," Jason told Lane. "Cassidy is asking the same thing. I'll figure out a way to let both of you know when we get the all clear. It'll probably be a text, not a call."

I thanked Jason then walked with Lane back to the truck. After shedding my rain gear, I climbed inside. Only then did the shaking begin.

Lane drove me home with one hand on the steering wheel and the other grasping mine. Exhaustion had replaced adrenaline, and I wanted nothing more than to fall back into my bed and sleep for days.

Unless I could get into the building. Then I wanted to do that before I took a long nap.

Although the drive was short, I found myself nodding off. When we reached my cottage, I opened my eyes and reached for my things. The sun was bright now, too bright to be comfortable for tired eyes.

"Before you go in," he told me, "there's something you need to know about the new building."

"About the fire?" I asked wearily. "I do want to know how it started, but I'm so tired, Lane. Can we talk details later?"

Lane seemed to be considering this. Then he checked his watch before returning his attention to me. "Absolutely. But I've got to go home and change for work. I'll be in meetings the rest of the day, so I doubt I'll be able to come back here until late this evening." He paused. "If I could take today off, I would. But we've got a team coming in from—"

"It's fine," I interrupted. "I'm fine."

"I know," he said on an exhale of breath. "You're a strong, independent woman, and you amaze me. But we need to talk about that building. And I don't want you going back there alone under any circumstances."

I frowned. What happened to me being a strong, independent woman who amazed him?

"I get it. A fire is bad, but once the building is declared safe by whoever it is that declares these things, then I'm going in to see what the damage looks like. It's ridiculous that you think I need someone to escort me into my own building that I bought with my own money. Since when do you treat me like I'm incapable—"

"Someone else has a key to the apartment, Nora," Lane blurted out. "We don't know who that is. This is information I got from Jason, so keep that in mind. Law enforcement is involved."

"Okay," I said slowly. "Then I'll get it rekeyed."

He shook his head. "You don't understand. The person with the key was living there. He didn't just go up and randomly set a fire. Jason wouldn't give me the details, but there's a reason that law enforcement is looking for whoever it was. Something was going on up there."

"In my upstairs apartment?" I said slowly. "No. Surely not."

But as I said the words, I thought of the sounds I heard just before I found the cat. Had the orange tabby made all that noise? Now that I thought of it, the sounds could have been coming from upstairs instead of the other side of the building. With the music coming from the Pupcake, it's possible that I only thought I was alone.

And what was going on?

I closed my eyes and shook my head. "Sorry, I'm not thinking straight. Who told you this again?"

"Jason," he said patiently. "He got it from either Brenham PD or Brenham FD. I can't remember if he said which. But whatever was going on up there came to light because of the fire."

My mind went to a dozen awful scenarios for what might be happening up there. I shoved them all away. There was no need to worry. I just needed to think practically. If I couldn't get inside yet, what was the next step?

My thoughts scattered and formed again. Then it came to me.

"Okay," I said, opening my eyes. "I'll call Mr. Lazlo. Maybe he made a deal with someone and forgot to tell me. At the least, he can tell me who else had keys. Or who might have had access to a key and copied it."

"Nora, you're exhausted, and there are butterfly bandages holding a wound together on your forehead," he said. "Text me Lazlo's number, and I'll call him on my drive back home. He's an hour ahead in Florida, so it won't be too early there."

I nodded and did as he asked.

"Okay, now we're going inside and you're going to rest. Do you want me to tell Roz she's in charge today, or will you be doing that?"

"If we're even able to open," I said, wincing when I turned my head and pain jolted across my forehead.

"True."

"You know what?" I said. "We've got food orders coming. I'll message Roz and tell her to prepare the menu as planned. We'll feed the first responders and anyone else who's cleaning up, reporting, or whatever. I'll come in when I can."

He grinned. "That's my girl. But would you please let Roz handle it? You won't be any good to anyone until you get some rest. Consider it a short-term choice toward a long-term goal."

I made no promises, but once I was back inside with the cat curled up beside me on the sofa, I knew he was right. I called Roz and arranged everything, and then, although I really didn't want to, I called my dad.

"I'm fine and so is the restaurant." I told him about the tornado and the fire but left out the part about my possible unwanted tenant. "I tripped in the dark and hit my head, but I got it checked out and I'm fine."

"So let me get this straight," my dad said. "You're fine. The restaurant is fine. You bumped your head."

"Yes to all of that, Dad," I said, stifling a yawn. "Lane was with me. And Cassidy's boyfriend, Jason, was there too. Oh, and I talked to Roz, my chef. Simply Eat will be open all day today to feed first responders and the others who are cleaning up."

Dad was quiet for a moment. "That's nice, sweetheart," he finally said. "Would it bother you if your old dad went down there and helped serve?"

"I would love that," I told him as I heard my mother saying something in the background.

He chuckled. "Okay, so Mama's going with me, and she's bringing food."

"Not a surprise," I told him. "Mama is always ready to feed a crowd. We could live off the contents of her freezer alone for weeks. I've been trying for years to get her to open a restaurant. When she refused, that made me want to open one even more."

We talked for a few more minutes then hung up. I must have fallen asleep, because the next time I opened my eyes, an orange tabby cat was staring at me and my phone was ringing.

I sat up gently, scooping the cat into my arms. Then I reached for the phone.

After a full minute of my mother expressing her concern, she paused. "Your father says you'll be fine, but you know I worry."

"It was just a little fall. I shouldn't have been out there to begin with, so it's not surprising that I tripped and fell. The EMT said there's no concussion or head injury. If there had been, I wouldn't have gone home alone to sleep."

"Well, praise the Lord for that," my mother said. "So, have you had your supper? I can bring something over."

I looked at the clock and groaned. It was half past six. Where had the day gone?

"Oh goodness, I can't believe I slept so long. I meant to get over there to help."

"You stay put," Mama told me. "We all did just fine. Your chef, she's a hard worker. We fed a lot of people today. Once we ran out of food we closed up for the day. Dad and I will be back tomorrow to help again."

"Thank you for that," I said.

"We're honored to serve, sweetheart. Now, about that dinner."

"I have plenty," I told her, knowing there was just enough left in my kitchen to make a grilled cheese sandwich plus two cans of tuna for the cat. Then a thought occurred. "You closed because you ran out of food? You must have served a lot of people."

"We did," she said. "But your chef did say there were some things missing from the grocery order. Anyway, it turned out just fine."

While my mother continued to talk about her day, I rose and walked into the kitchen with the cat still tucked under my arm. Other than the slightest twinge when I furrowed my brow, I felt no pain.

Just as I'd managed to get off the phone with Mama, my phone buzzed with a text from Lane. LIGHTS WERE OFF, SO I LEFT DINNER FOR YOU ON THE PORCH. CALL ME LATER. I LOVE YOU.

"Oh, Lane, I love you too," I whispered.

He did have his good qualities, I reminded myself as I padded to the door.

CHAPTER FIVE

Nora

Thursday
Brenham, Texas

The next morning, it didn't take a genius to understand that someone's food bowl was empty again. Apparently the orange tabby wasn't convinced, because she once again woke me up to let me know. At least this time the cat waited until half past eight. She had made two attempts during the night that I had ignored.

I opened the cabinet and reached inside. Since I still hadn't bought cat food, I emptied another can of tuna into a bowl and presented it to my purring house guest.

My head ached a bit, but after a shower and a couple of over-the-counter painkillers, I felt good enough to head down to Simply Eat to help. Seeing the street in the light of day was a shock.

All the debris had been cleared, but there was no mistaking that a tornado had come through. On one side of the street, windows were boarded, and roofs were missing shingles and, in some places, entire portions of the decking beneath.

Over on the other side—the side where Simply Eat was doing a brisk breakfast business—there was no evidence of a storm. The Pupcake had a sign on the door saying the owners were busy helping with cleanup efforts. Only the police tape across the antique store doors bore evidence of any damage there.

My eyes went to the second-floor windows. Nothing seemed out of place. I slid my gaze to Cassidy's home above Simply Eat, where I noticed that the patio furniture on her balcony hadn't even appeared to have moved.

And yet across the street the tornado had done its worst.

In that moment, I felt a profound sense of gratitude. And, as I looked at the line snaking out of the door of my restaurant, a need to do something.

Bypassing the men and women in the line, I pressed my way into the kitchen. Roz was calling out commands to a staff made up of my employees, my parents, and volunteers.

Mama was stirring pots of flavored oatmeal on the stove while Dad was filling plates with breakfast tacos and fruit and carrying them out to serve at the tables.

I went to Dad first for a hug that only my father could give. "Glad you're fine," he said with a twinkle in his eye.

When my mother spied me, her smile rose and then quickly froze. My hand went to my forehead. There was no hiding the butterfly bandages at my hairline.

"How many stitches?" she asked me, snaking her free hand around my back while holding the spoon.

"Two butterflies," I told her. "And I'll be fine."

"So you said." Mama frowned as she stepped back to give me an appraising look. "And you were here in the middle of the night with Lane."

A statement, not a question.

I decided the short version of the story was best. "He stayed with his father Tuesday night because of the storm. When he heard about the tornado, he called then brought me down here to look over the damage together. He knew I would come down here and didn't want me to be here alone."

She seemed to consider my words for a moment then nodded. "He's a good man, your Lane. Be patient with him."

So many responses came to mind, starting with reminding her that I had been waiting for a long time for a ring and yet was still with him. Didn't that constitute patience? But if I was honest, I hadn't been very patient most of that time.

Not until I took the ring out of my life plans and put the restaurant—and now the building next door—in its place.

"Thank you, Mama," I said instead.

Her smile returned. "Nora, I know this is your kitchen, but unless you want to take over for Roz, you need to do something useful or get out of the way."

I laughed. "I think I'll leave Roz to her work. She seems to be doing a good job of it."

Mama nodded. "I like her. You did well in hiring that woman."

Roz was in neon yellow today with lime green pants and tie-dyed high-top sneakers. She'd tied a colorful scarf around her hair and wore a slick of pink lipstick. And somehow it all worked to make her look like a runway model. If I tried that, I'd look like I dressed in the dark.

"She needs a man," Mama said, leaning close. "She told me she and her boyfriend broke up and that's why she's here in Brenham. I think we need to find someone for her."

"Mama," I said with a warning tone, "do not start matchmaking for my chef. I don't want to lose her."

"Oh honey, women don't quit work when they get married anymore. You won't lose her."

That wasn't what I meant, but I let her think so. "You're right, Mama. You know what? It looks like Daddy has everything under control with the front of house, so where am I needed?"

"I heard that," Roz called. "How about filling a couple of bowls with dog food and putting them out in the alley?"

At my confused look, she continued. "For the dogs that were displaced by the tornado. Or maybe there was just a lost one running around. I can't remember which. Anyway, Cassidy brought over a bag and some bowls this morning. They'd been getting calls on the rescue line, and they need dog food in the alley."

"Cassidy was here already and no one called me?"

Roz shook her head. "Nope. Lane told everyone to let you rest. So we haven't called or texted." She paused. "He's a good guy, Nora."

"Sounds like you've been talking to my mother," I quipped.

She shook her head. "Nope. I make up my own mind. And trust me, they're not all good."

I wanted to use that statement as the opening for a conversation about the boyfriend that my mother had told me about. However, Roz's eyes were already darting past me, a hazard of running a busy restaurant kitchen. Personal conversations could wait.

"So where's the dog food?"

After locating the bag, I filled as many dishes as I could carry and stepped out into the alley to place them against the wall. The mess I'd seen earlier had been cleaned up, and a pile of limbs sat waiting to be hauled away.

After glancing both directions and seeing no one—pet or person—I retrieved my phone from my pocket and called Cassidy. She picked up on the first ring.

"Nora! Are you okay?"

"I'm fine." I was also getting tired of telling people that. "Two butterflies and I'm all good. Next time I'll watch where I'm going. So everything is good at your place?"

"Everything is fine," she said. "The patio furniture didn't even move on the balcony, and yet right across the street the windows are boarded up and it's just a mess."

"I noticed," I said. "And what's this about calls on the rescue line?"

"As you know, Mari, Parker, and I went out on a rescue call Tuesday night. Someone had seen a big dog—maybe a German shepherd mix—running around in their neighborhood. We never did find the dog. Yesterday we had several calls about a dog matching the description, all from downtown or near to it. I figured it couldn't hurt to try and at least feed the animal and see if we can catch it. If it's still here."

I told her about the dog that had done a cameo in my FaceTime with Lane. "I couldn't see it well enough to know if it was the same one, but it was certainly the right size. Why put food out in the alley but nowhere else?"

"Suzy called from the Pupcake. She saw a German shepherd running behind the Ant Inn several times. They're closed, so Roz said to leave the food with her and she'd see that it got set out."

"I'm standing in the alley now," I told her. "There's no sign of the dog, but I'll try to watch for it." I paused, ready to talk about something that had been bothering me since I woke up. "So, have you talked to Jason today?"

"I spoke to him on the way to work this morning," she said. "He had Lane text me earlier to let me know he was busy and that everything was okay with my place and the restaurant. Then he had a break and we talked for a few minutes. Why?"

A trio of blackbirds landed on the pile of limbs and chirped noisily. "I assume you know about the fire next door."

"Yeah, weird, isn't it?"

"Beyond weird," I said. "How does a fire just randomly start in the middle of a tornado that's hitting the buildings across the street? It makes no sense."

Silence.

"Cassidy?" I paused, thinking of the yellow police tape fluttering in the breeze. "What did Jason tell you?"

"Not much," she finally admitted. "Just that someone was living there, and no one knew about it. That's so creepy. Our building is old, and it sometimes makes noises at night, but if there was someone in the building next door, wouldn't I have heard something at some point? I've been living here over a year."

"You would think so," I said. "Did he tell you anything else?"

"Just that it was odd and that the police were looking into it." She paused. "Why?"

"Because it's my building, and no one is telling me anything," I said on an exhale of breath. "Sorry, I'm just frustrated. I'm not supposed to go up there, and I can't go in the building. On top of that, something shady was happening up there, and I have no idea what it is."

"Well," Cassidy said, "I can be there in less than five minutes. Want to find out?"

I grinned. "Seriously?"

"Seriously. I was out running errands for the clinic. I'm literally around the corner right now. Can I get down the alley in my car, or is there still too much debris?"

"It's clear," I told her.

I hung up and stuffed the phone into my pocket just as I spied Cassidy's car turn into the alley. By the time she parked and joined me on the stairs, I was at the door.

When I turned to face her, she gasped. "Nora. I'm so sorry about your stitches. I was expecting something awful, but they don't actually look too bad."

"Just two butterfly bandages, and I'm fine."

How many times had I said that? I retrieved the keys from my pocket and sorted through them until I reached the building key.

"Are we just going to unlock the door and go in without permission from the police?" Cassidy whispered. "Do you think that's a good idea?"

"It's a terrible idea." I pointed the key toward the lock. "But it's the only idea I've got right now."

I tried again. The key wouldn't fit.

"That is not going to work," she said, stating the obvious as I tried for a third time. "The tenant probably has a different key, don't you think?"

"Okay," I said on an exhale of breath. "Except I don't have a tenant and neither did Mr. Lazlo. And this key does work to open the apartment door from inside the store. Dad, Tony, and I walked through the apartment when we inspected the place before I bought it. I watched Mr. Lazlo use the front door key to open the apartment."

When Cassidy said nothing, I continued. "We'll just have to go in the front. I know the key works on that lock."

"Except we can't," Cassidy said. "There's that whole police tape thing. And your restaurant is full of first responders."

"About that." I pocketed the key and turned to face her. "If there is police tape up on a building belonging to me, why hasn't anyone from the police department called to talk to me? The incident happened well before daylight on Wednesday, and now it's the middle of the day on Thursday."

"They're busy," Cassidy said. "Other things are a higher priority, I guess."

"Right." I retrieved my phone.

"What are you doing?"

"I've got Todd Dennison's cell number in my contacts from the time I organized a benefit for Mari's pet rescue. He was my security guy for the event. I'm going to call him. Maybe he can give me permission."

I tried the number, but it went to voice mail. I asked him to call me regarding the building. "I need to get inside as soon as possible. Please come get your tape. And call me back," I added before I hung up.

"Okay, now what?" Cassidy asked.

"Hold on," I said as a thought occurred. "There's an emergency exit downstairs. I saw it, but we never checked it out when we were walking the building before I bought it. There is definitely no police tape across it." I paused to grin. "Let's see if the key fits."

Obviously the door hadn't been opened in ages, because the lock was rusted and a jumble of trash cans were piled in front of it. Cassidy and I cleared a path, and then I tried the key.

It fit, but turning the thing was another matter. "It's rusty," I said, trying again. On the third attempt, the key turned and the lock slid open with a screech of metal against metal.

"That's great," Cassidy said. "So much for the surprise factor if anyone is in here."

I ignored the comment and stepped inside. A faint smell of smoke was in the air, but nothing as strong as I expected. Sunshine streamed through the front windows and filled the space with light. Outside on the sidewalk, someone was chattering on a cell phone.

Cassidy followed me in and wrinkled her nose. "Not terrible, but I get the definite scent of campfire in here."

"I'm thinking the books may be a total loss just because of the smell."

"That's sad," Cassidy said. "Maybe your insurance company will send someone in to remediate."

I added a call to my insurance company to the list of things I needed to do. We moved toward the stairs single file, making our way between shelves that looked exactly as I had left them.

The firemen must have come through to fight the fire, but they had been careful not to disturb anything. To my ever-growing list I added a reminder to send thank-you baskets of food to the Brenham Fire Department.

When I reached the back of the store, I paused to listen. If anyone was still up there, they were being very quiet.

"Let's do this," Cassidy said softly. "Do you want me to go first?"

I shook my head. Together we eased up the stairs. I hadn't noticed the squeaks before, but today they sounded like they echoed at high volume.

My hand shook as I tried to stab the key into the lock. "Oh, this is ridiculous."

I made another attempt. A moment later, the door swung open, and we both started coughing. I lifted the neck of my T-shirt up enough to cover my nose and mouth and then stepped inside.

The room bore no resemblance to the little furnished apartment we'd been shown by Mr. Lazlo. That space had been sparsely decorated, but the furnishings had obviously come from the antique store downstairs. In the living area was an old-fashioned blue-striped sofa, a pair of armchairs, and a black iron bistro set adjacent to the kitchen.

And the kitchen.

I gasped. The fire had obviously started in the sink because it and the walls around it were black with soot. Worse, the space had been stripped bare except for the bistro table and chairs and the striped settee—which now matched the table thanks to the black soot covering the upholstery.

"What in the world?" was all I could manage to say before the coughing took over again and my eyes began to sting. Despite my better judgment, I took a few more steps into the room and spied the remains of what appeared to be an exploded science lab on the countertop.

Understanding dawned.

"Nora," Cassidy said slowly, "this is a crime scene. That's why the police tape is still up. So don't touch anything."

I glanced over my shoulder at my friend. "I walked through here less than three weeks ago. It was fully furnished, and there was no chemistry lab in the kitchen."

Cassidy nodded toward the bedroom. "I'm guessing the bedroom wasn't furnished like that either."

There had been a carved wooden bed and matching dresser in the bedroom, along with an armoire that served as a closet. Mr. Lazlo had pointed out the braided rug beneath the bed and explained how he'd come to own it. Other than a dog crate that could have housed a small horse, the rug was the only thing left in the room.

"They took almost everything," I managed.

Cassidy touched my arm. "We need to leave now. We don't know what chemicals were in here. Even breathing in here could be dangerous."

I nodded. She was right.

Once we were back in the upstairs hall, I closed the door and locked it. Then we hurried outside.

Just as I finished locking the emergency door, my phone buzzed in my pocket, alerting me to a text. Cassidy's buzzed too. She retrieved her phone and glanced at the screen then looked up at me.

"It's from Dr. Kristin," Cassidy said. "She's letting us know there was no damage at the wedding venue and reminding us of the events coming up on wedding weekend."

"Wedding weekend. I'd almost forgotten," I said softly, finishing the statement with a cough.

"Bridal luncheon tomorrow at noon then rehearsal tomorrow night at five followed by rehearsal dinner at seven," she read aloud. "Then there's the day-of-the-event schedule. Do you want me to read that to you?"

"Thanks, but no," I said, pocketing the keys. "I'll look at it later."

"Okay, but suffice it to say we've got a long day on Saturday," Cassidy quipped.

I cringed thinking of all the events that would be taking place beginning on Friday morning and going on through the wedding on Saturday night. As soon as a complaint tried to form, I squelched it. The weekend wasn't about me. It was about Kristin and Tyler.

And no matter what was happening in my world, I would be a good friend and a good bridesmaid. I would try not to think about the exploded science lab in my newly purchased building, and I would do all I could to honor the happy couple over the next two days.

CHAPTER SIX

I said goodbye to Cassidy and stepped back into the kitchen of my restaurant in time to hear Roz berating a waiter in my office. She looked up when I stepped into view.

"Carry on," I said, moving away from the door with the intention of speaking with her later about using my office as her own.

Dad caught my attention, and I walked over to stand beside him. "What did he do?" I asked.

"I'm not sure, but I had a drill instructor at boot camp who scared me less than she does right now." He chuckled. "Glad I'm not on the receiving end of that lecture."

I braved another glance. From this angle, I could see the waiter's face. He was one of two hired by Roz in the past month. His name was Canon Ames, a student at Texas Tech University who was newly returned home for the summer. I wondered if the redhead was the waiter she'd been keeping her eye on. You never knew with college students whether they'd make good summer employees or not.

The other was Shane Newman, a young man who'd recently moved to Brenham from San Antonio to be closer to family. The lanky fellow with blond curls was currently bustling around the dining room like he'd been doing this for years.

I pitched in to help, moving from station to station as needed until I ended up in the dining room. I spied Trent Mendez, a detective with the Bureau of Alcohol, Tobacco, and Firearms, at a table with Todd Dennison and two other uniformed Brenham police officers. Unlike the other officers, Trent was not wearing anything that might identify him as a federal agent or even a first responder.

I met Trent a while back at a party given by Mari's aunt and her husband. He had been undercover on a case involving a bomb that Mari found near the former location for Second Chance Ranch. He and his team helped Mari, Parker, and the pet rescue team catch the culprit. I hadn't seen him in Brenham since then.

Given what I'd just seen in the building, I had a fairly good idea why he was here now. Not that I'd admit any of that just yet. At least not to an ATF detective.

But maybe to Todd. Yes, start with the friend I knew best and then maybe break the news to the detective that I'd walked through his crime scene.

Trent saw me heading toward him and waved. "Nora, right? You own this place."

"Yes, that's me," I said. "I opened it last year. I'm surprised you're here. You're not usually on tornado duty, are you?"

"Not usually," he said.

"I just saw you'd called," Todd said. "I'm guessing it's about the building."

"It is." I paused. "Have you been out here since the tornado hit?"

He shrugged. "All hands on deck in situations like this, although I'm headed home after this. And thank you for feeding us. You always put on a good spread here."

"This is the best, Nora," Trent added. "Truly. And it's much appreciated." The other officers voiced their thanks and approval.

Todd's expression sobered. "It'll be a while before we can release the building to you. I'm sorry."

I nodded, noticing that Trent was paying close attention to the conversation. "I figured." I lowered my voice. "Do you have a minute to speak privately?"

He nodded. "I was done here."

Then he said goodbye to his companions and followed me outside. Trent's eyes were still on us when I stepped into the sunshine. Once the door closed behind Todd, we walked a few paces away from the building and then stopped.

"I'm just going to admit it," I said, my attention on a pair of construction workers attaching plywood to the front window of the building across the street. "I used my key on the emergency door and went upstairs to check the damage."

I dared a look at Todd. He didn't seem surprised by my confession.

He nodded, and his expression remained stoic. "I have to ask, Nora. Did you have any idea what was going on up there?"

"None," I exclaimed. "After I closed on the building yesterday, I went in later in the day to do some cleaning on the first floor. I did go upstairs but only to grab supplies from the storage closet. I didn't go into the apartment at all. Frankly, I was too busy thinking about how I was going to get the downstairs in shape to even think about it."

"Did you see or hear anything while you were there cleaning?"

"I heard some noises," I said. "But I blamed them on the cat. There was an orange tabby downstairs. I guess it wandered in somehow. Anyway, I never thought it might be anyone upstairs. The place was empty except for the furniture when my family and I toured it before I went under contract for the building." I paused. "And now it's empty of most of the furniture."

He had his notepad out now and was making notes. "Can you give me a list what was in there?"

"I can do better than that. I've got video that my dad took. He said it was for insurance purposes."

"Smart man, your dad. Just email that to me." At my nod, he continued. "Did you touch anything while you were in there?"

"Only the doorknob," I admitted. "I walked in, crossed the room to get a little closer to the kitchen, then peeked into the bedroom before I left. I tried to be careful," I told him, leaving out the part that Cassidy was with me.

"Okay, your prints and probably Lazlo's would be on some of the surfaces anyway unless the perps wiped everything clean," he said.

"What do you think happened to the furniture?" I asked.

"Probably sold it or gave it to whoever wanted it." He looked up from his writing. "Whoever did this knew the apartment was empty. Any thoughts on how they would know this?"

I contemplated his question then shook my head. "None," I said. "The transaction happened fast. Mr. Lazlo came to me with an offer to purchase three weeks ago, but I don't know when he would have moved anything out. I can tell you he sold it to me with all the merchandise and fixtures in place. I never saw him again after that conversation. Everything was handled through Realtors."

"That will help us pin down who might have known," he said. "It's not like they would have seen Lazlo moving out."

"No," I said. "I'm not sure if he lived there or not. He never said. But I do know if he'd had a tenant, he would have told me. Whoever has that key did not get it lawfully."

"If indeed he or she has a key," Todd muttered as he went back to his writing. Finally, he stopped and looked up at me. "We don't know what they were making, although we have a good idea. If you have breathing issues from being around the fumes, call your doctor immediately, Nora. Even us cops aren't supposed to go in until the place has been cleared as okay to breathe in."

"Oh," I said softly. "I didn't know that might be an issue, so I just assumed everyone was busy."

"They are," Todd said, tucking his notebook back into his pocket. "That tornado wasn't as bad as expected, but it caused some damage. We're stretched thin handling that, so be patient with us."

"Absolutely," I told him. "Now that I know what we're dealing with, I'll help in any way I can. And I promise not to go back in until I have permission."

The door opened and Trent walked out with the two Brenham PD officers. The officers continued across the street, but Trent joined Todd and me on the sidewalk.

The ATF agent gave me a sideways look. "Has he warned you about contamination at the building site?"

I sighed. "I think we were just getting to that. How did you know I went in?"

Trent gave me an appraising look. "I didn't. You just confirmed it."

"If I'd known...," I began but stopped. "Who am I kidding? I wanted to see it for myself. But I might have at least worn a mask."

"What's done is done, but it shouldn't have happened, Nora." Todd gestured toward me. "You also might want to go home and wash the clothes you were wearing. Take a shower. Wash your hair. All of that. We don't know what was in the air, and I'd rather you not take a chance."

"I'll do that," I said with a smile. "And thank you for not arresting me." I met Trent's even gaze. "You too."

Todd laughed. "This time anyway," he said. "Just don't take chances like that anymore, Nora. Promise me."

"I didn't know what chance I was taking," I said. "But I promise."

Trent never cracked a smile. Nor did he comment.

We said goodbye, and I watched the two men walk away. Then I called Cassidy and relayed the information I'd just been given.

"Whoa," she said. "I guess I'm taking the rest of the day off."

"Me too."

I hung up with Cassidy, and then instead of going back inside and taking the chance of contaminating anyone or anything worse than I already had, I sent a text to let Roz know I wouldn't be back until the dinner shift and only if she needed me then.

I sent another text to Mama and Dad thanking them for the help but avoiding the details. They would call later—both of them separately—or text, but for now they were both busy. My parents had taught me the power of volunteer work in a person's life. They didn't just do it. They loved it.

I drove home and did as I was told. I had just stepped out of the shower and was drying my hair, carefully avoiding the bandage on my forehead and the cat weaving herself around my ankles, when my phone rang. It was Lane.

I placed the blow-dryer back in the cabinet and went into the bedroom to sit in the chair by the window. The sweet, nameless orange tabby trotted in a moment later but bypassed me to jump onto the windowsill.

"I hear you played detective today," he said.

"Word travels fast," I said. "I guess Todd or Trent Mendez told you."

There was a pause. "Actually, it was Jason," he said. "He must have talked to one of them."

"Really? Well, okay then." Once again, I elected not to rat on Cassidy. "So you'll be glad to know I did as Todd told me to do and came home to wash my clothes and take a shower. I told Roz I'd be back up there for the dinner shift if she needed me."

"Let's hope she doesn't need you. You need a night off."

I glanced up at the clock. It was already after five, and I hadn't had a call from her. We were still feeding first responders, so she must have had enough volunteers to manage that task without me.

"How's the bump on your head?" he asked. I could hear the sound of cars passing by on the other end of the line, and I realized he was outside and not in his office. "Does it hurt?"

"Not until you reminded me of it," I said. "Are you at home?"

"Just walking between buildings," he said. "I had to go out to the equine facility to consult with a colleague, and now I'm back. Why?"

I suppressed a sigh. "Just trying to imagine you at home at a reasonable hour," I said.

Silence fell between us. Then Lane spoke. "It'll be like that someday, Nora. I promise. It's what I'm working toward. I mean it."

"I hope so, because I would like that very much." I wasn't sure how to continue, so I decided to change the subject. "So, remember the dog that did a cameo in our FaceTime last night?"

"The big shepherd or Malinois? Sure. What about it?"

"Cassidy told me they had a report on the rescue tip line about a dog that matches its description. Then there was another report that the dog might have been seen behind the Ant Inn." I paused. "We put food and water bowls out behind the restaurant earlier in case he's hungry or thirsty."

"So, he was out in that weather and in the downtown area when the tornado hit?" Lane said.

"Yes to the weather, obviously, and possibly to the rest of it. At least it appears that way. They're going to keep looking." I paused. "So, Lane. About this weekend. You know it's Tyler and Kristin's wedding weekend, right?"

"Saturday evening at six. I've got it on my calendar, and I've sent two reminders, one for when I need to leave and the other for when I really need to leave. Genius, right?"

I suppressed a smile. "Definitely. And tomorrow night?"

Silence.

Of course. He'd forgotten about the rehearsal dinner. Now it was up to me to decide how—or whether—to remind him. I decided on the diplomatic route.

"So Lane, what about tomorrow? What are your plans?"

"Just the usual work stuff," he said casually. "Why?"

He'd definitely forgotten about the rehearsal dinner. I decided to make one more attempt at nudging his memory. "Do you have any dinner plans?"

"Whatever you want to do, Nora," he quipped. "I'll make it happen."

"Great," I said in my most cheerful tone. "Rehearsal for the wedding is at five with dinner after at seven. There is probably going to be some sort of gathering after that, but I'll likely bow out and go check on things at the restaurant since I'll be away from there all day Saturday." I paused only a beat then continued. "I'll text you the location."

"Right."

"I'm not hearing enthusiasm," I said. "Or, now that I think of it, any actual confirmation that you're going. Am I wrong?"

"Well, I mean, I'm always enthusiastic about seeing you. But. . ."

"But wedding stuff makes you uncomfortable?" I supplied, knowing that wasn't a fair question. I let out a long breath. This wasn't going well at all, and I was part of the problem.

Time to be the solution.

"You know what? You'd probably be miserable at this event. And late," I added as my irritation grew. "So let's forget I mentioned it. I don't have to have a plus-one. In fact, I'll be fine going on my own."

There I was once again telling someone I was fine. I should just put the words on a T-shirt and wear it everywhere I go.

"Nora, honey," Lane said. "I'm working on that late thing and all the hours I have to work. I really am. And if you want me to be at the rehearsal and the dinner after, I'll make it happen. I'll even stay up for whatever after event is happening. I'll do what I need to do to make you happy."

To make me happy. I noticed he didn't address the part where I said he'd be miserable.

"Look," I said on an exhale of breath, "I'll see you at the wedding on Saturday. How about that?"

"That would be great," he said, relief obvious in his tone. "I really could use the extra time to tie up some loose ends on this portion of the research I'm working on."

I tried—and failed—not to take it personally that my boyfriend was happy about a reprieve from spending an evening with me. And that he had other plans that he was obviously more excited about.

"Don't be late," I said instead of giving him a hint of what I was thinking.

"I love you, Nora," Lane said.

Yes, I loved him. I wouldn't put up with him if I didn't, and it was petty not to say so.

But taking the high road wasn't what I wanted to do right now.

"Prove it by showing up on time," I challenged as the orange tabby jumped up into my lap.

Lane's response was laughter. Actual side-splitting laughter.

I hung up, my temper instantly boiling. He said he loved me but spent time with me on his terms, and only when it was convenient. Once again that was absolutely clear.

I tossed my phone aside then scooped the cat into my arms and walked over to the window. "What am I going to do about that man?"

The cat meowed, and I looked down at her, grinning. "Now, if you could just translate that response to English, I might be able to understand."

She nuzzled against me, and my heart melted. How in the world was I going to ever manage to give this sweet kitty back to its owner?

My phone buzzed with a text from Lane. DID I SAY SOMETHING WRONG?

SEE YOU AT THE WEDDING, I responded as the cat batted at my fingers. BE ON TIME.

I PROMISE.

Of course he would say that. I let out a long breath. Back to the issue of this sweet girl.

Reluctantly, I called Mari. After we exchanged greetings, I got to the point.

"So I have this female orange tabby, approximately a year old, and I'm wondering if someone is missing her. She looks well cared for. I found her in the antique store when I did my first inspection after getting the keys, and I took her home with me. Has the clinic or the pet rescue had any calls about a missing cat?"

"I've heard nothing on a missing orange tabby that was lost downtown," Mari said. "Not before the tornado anyway. Do you want me to put out a notice?"

"No," I said, "but yes."

"She's captured your heart, hasn't she?" Mari asked gently.

I sighed. "She has, which is strange, because I've always been a dog person."

"And you've been thinking about getting another dog," Mari said. "We've had that conversation more than once."

"I have," I told her. "But maybe I've got a new cat instead. If she doesn't belong to someone else. Or a dog that likes cats, because this one is staying, I hope. Oh, Mari, I'm afraid to name her until I know she's mine for sure."

She chuckled softly. "Okay, well, I'll put up a photo in the lobby and have Cassidy add her to the social media posts, and then we'll cross our fingers. How's that?"

"Sure," I said, all the while thinking this was a terrible idea because the owner might find us. Ridiculous, I know.

"I'll email a picture of her," I said. "But only because, if she's missing, then her person must be really sad about losing her. I know I will be if she has to leave."

"Then we cross our fingers and hope to name her," Mari said.

That made me smile. "Yes, we do."

"Oh," Mari said. "Speaking of lost animals, I had an interesting conversation with Dr. Kristin this afternoon. She said that when she was out at the wedding venue with the planner going over the final details this morning, she thought she saw a big dog fitting the description of the one we were looking for before the storm."

"Really?" I said. "But that's quite a distance from downtown."

"I know. It's probably not the same dog. And to be fair, the dog was off in the distance. But she felt like it was possible."

"Interesting. We had food out in case the dog showed up in the alley again. Apparently there was a sighting behind the Ant Inn, but now that I think of it, I don't remember if Cassidy told me when that sighting was."

"And maybe there's more than one of them," Mari offered.

"I suppose." I paused. "Thank you again for posting about the cat. How long do these things usually take? I mean, before someone decides the pet is theirs."

"It differs," she said. "But usually people who want to find their lost pets look for them everywhere, and the ones who don't care, well, let's just say the pet is better with a new owner."

"Right. Well, okay, I guess I'll see you and the other bridesmaids bright and early at the rehearsal tomorrow then and early Saturday morning. It's going to be a long day."

She chuckled. "A very long day. But it's going to be a beautiful wedding."

CHAPTER SEVEN

NORA

Saturday evening
Thistledown Farms

The stars tonight were big and bright. But the real star of the evening was walking down the aisle. As Texas weddings go, this was a relatively small one. Just a few hundred friends and relatives were gathered under the dramatic glass ceiling of a stunning wedding chapel at Thistledown Farms outside of Brenham, Texas.

Dr. Kristin Keller was a vision in white as she clasped her father's arm. A colorful tangle of local wildflowers spilled from the bouquet in her other hand. Each of the bridesmaids wore a color taken from the bouquet. My dress was pale purple to match the lavender in my bouquet, while Cassidy, the maid of honor, had donned pale pink to match the evening primrose tucked into hers.

And true to our expectations, it was a long day. Between hair, makeup, and photos, my jaws were hurting from smiling, and I was absolutely certain I would never get the hairspray out of my hair. Or, as the hairstylist called it, my classic bridesmaid updo.

Somehow, she'd managed to hide my injured forehead, so I didn't care what she called it. She was a miracle worker.

After all the excitement with the tornado and the fire and the busy day of prewedding events yesterday, I was still reeling from the week. But there's just something about a wedding that makes me perk up.

And yes, I know that's kind of silly given the fact that I'd given up on getting Lane to the altar. I'm just a hopeless romantic, I guess, at least where other couples are concerned.

I moved my attention from the bride to the groom. Dr. Tyler Durham's smile was broad. Tyler and his groomsmen were decked out in matching suits and black cowboy boots, while the father of the bride sported a Stetson hat and a bolo tie.

Kristin and Mr. Keller reached the altar just as the mother of the bride dabbed at the tears glittering in her eyes with a blue handkerchief that matched her dress covered in sapphire-colored sequins fashioned to look like bluebonnets. During the prewedding photo session, Kristin's mom had declared that her matching bluebonnet earrings had come from her large collection of Lone Star–themed jewelry.

None of us who knew the happy couple were surprised that they'd become engaged. To be here at their wedding was the icing on the proverbial cake—or rather, the wedding cake.

I glanced around the chapel, hoping to see Lane. Of course he was late. I decided to deal with that later and not let my feelings ruin the happy occasion. Well, happy for the bride and groom anyway.

Lane's father smiled at me from his seat three rows behind the groom's family. It looked like he had brought a plus-one, although the sweet widower was popular enough to acquire one or two potential plus-ones after he arrived.

The casserole ladies, as Lane called the parade of potential wives for his father, were persistent but mostly unsuccessful. Dr. Bishop seemed oblivious to their attempts to snare him. And he certainly hadn't mentioned he was bringing a date.

After the I-dos were said and the photos were taken, attendees adjourned to the reception hall next door. Before the wedding, Kristin had gifted us with matching white cowgirl boots. We happily tossed off our fancy heels and donned the boots then followed the Drs. Durham to join their guests.

During the bride and groom's first dance, Lane slipped into the seat beside me. "You're late," I wanted to say. Instead, I merely listened as he launched into the current reason why he'd been unable to get to the chapel on time.

The band was playing "Waltz across Texas." Overhead, Lone Star–shaped chandeliers blazed light across the dance floor. When the deejay requested that guests join the happy couple, I let Lane lead me onto the floor then pressed my cheek against his shoulder as we danced.

Next to us on the dance floor was Isabel Fuentes, the groomer from Lone Star Vet Clinic, with her fiancé, Corey Wallis, a Houston Texans football player. The star quarterback had certainly gone all out on the sparkler she was wearing on her left hand.

Yes, this was definitely a Texas wedding.

And Lane was an amazing dancer. I told myself that was the only reason I allowed this indulgence. I would deal with him later on his tardiness.

"Nora Hernandez," Lane said against my ear, "I have a question to ask you, and it's important."

I did my best not to freeze.

What kind of important question could Lane ask while dancing on a dance floor at our friends' wedding? Perhaps a long-awaited proposal?

"Okay," I managed, trying my best to keep my tone casual.

Lane's palm pressed into the small of my back as he guided me through the crowd toward a less crowded part of the room. I braced myself for the big question even as I started plotting my own wedding.

"So, Nora," he began, "this may come as a surprise, but I would like to make a big change this fall."

I smiled sweetly, my ring finger itching to get that ring on it. I was beyond caring about how late he'd arrived. Not if this was the big moment.

Come on, Lane. Say the words.

"I'm always up for a big change," I said, hoping the statement would loosen the question that seemed lodged in his throat. "So go for it."

He leaned back just enough to show me his beautiful broad smile. "Yeah?"

"Yeah," I said as the waltz ended and the familiar opening of the "Aggie War Hymn"—played at any gathering of Aggie students and Former Students from sports events to weddings—began. Whoops sounded all around the room as all the graduates of Texas A&M hurried to form a circle in the center of the dance floor.

Lane planted a kiss on my lips then added his own whoop to the others. "I love how you just roll with things, Nora. You're the best."

He grasped my wrist and headed toward the circle. "Hold on," I said, stalling. "You lost me. What did I just roll with?"

Because it certainly wasn't a marriage proposal. At least not one that any normal human would recognize.

"Season tickets to the Aggie games," Lane said. "We've had the same seats every fall for years. I think it's time to explore more options."

I fixed him with an even look. "Lane, you have no idea how true that is. It is definitely time to explore more options."

Starting with my choice of boyfriend.

LANE

Saturday evening
Thistledown Farms wedding venue

I was the happiest man in boots. And at a Texas wedding, every man wore boots. At least at this one they did.

While George Strait sang about getting to Amarillo by morning, I gave thanks to the Lord that I had managed to get to Brenham in time for the reception. It was my fault I was late. It always was.

This time I got caught up in my research and lost track of time. Who was I kidding? I always got caught up in my research and lost track of time. And it seemed like Nora was the one I kept letting down.

I loved her more than anything and anyone on this planet. With Nora in my arms, I felt like I could conquer the world.

Even though the dance floor was crowded, my eyes were only on her. Her beautiful dark hair was swept up into some sort of bridesmaid do that matched the hair of the other ladies who'd stood at the altar with Kristin. They'd obviously brought in a makeup artist, and my girl looked drop-dead gorgeous.

But then I always thought of her as drop-dead gorgeous, even in a ponytail, jeans, and a T-shirt, mucking out a stall or standing beside me while we fished on the banks of the Brazos River. But my favorite image of her was captured in a photo that was framed on my desk and was also the wallpaper on my electronic devices.

In the photo, Nora is standing in the kitchen of her restaurant, Simply Eat. It was taken the day the place opened, and her expression is one of complete joy. Best of all, she's looking right at me.

I closed my eyes and swayed with her to one of our favorite songs, "At Last". Right then and there, I made a promise to myself and the Man Upstairs that I would never again be responsible for removing that expression from her face.

We danced until the song ended and the first strains of a Buddy Holly tune came on. Nora threw her head back and laughed as I grinned. Her family was famous for their fifties dance parties, usually held on their back porch after Sunday supper.

I hadn't known a thing about dancing the jitterbug until Nora's mother took pity on me and taught me the dance moves. Now I could toss Nora into the air and swing her around like a pro.

The dance floor cleared, leaving plenty of room for our style of dancing. I hadn't realized it was just the two of us until the song ended and a round of applause went up.

Apparently Nora hadn't noticed either. She looked up at me, her cheeks flushed. Then slowly she turned around and curtsied to the crowd.

I spied Pop staring in obvious surprise. It dawned on me that he had no idea I had that skill.

Maybe I should talk to Nora about inviting him to a Sunday dinner at her folks' place sometime. Maybe a dance lesson or two would be fun for him.

The next song—a Bob Wills waltz called "Faded Love"—began. The bride, who'd been chatting with some of the casserole ladies, hurried over to grasp Pop's arm and led him onto the dance floor.

"Let's dance, Dr. B," I heard her say as they hurried past.

My father grinned at me. "Yes, Dr. Durham," he said to her as they disappeared into the growing crowd of dancers.

I usually loved dancing a waltz with my girl, but after that last song, I needed a break. "Ready to sit?" I said in her ear.

When she nodded, I took her elbow and we made our way back to our seats. Nora settled in beside me and immediately started up a conversation with her friend Brianna Finch, the receptionist at Lone Star Vet Clinic. Brianna's plus-one for the evening was Dr. Cameron Saye, a veterinarian I knew well.

I glanced past the ladies to see that Cameron, in his suit and tie, looked as uncomfortable as I felt. We gave each other a commiserating look. Apparently attending weddings wasn't his favorite thing to do either.

After a few minutes of waiting for a break in Nora's conversation, I pushed back my chair and stood.

She glanced up at me, the remnant of a smile fading fast. "Are you leaving?"

"Just going to grab something to drink. Want something?"

When she shook her head, I made my escape. Cameron took the hint and followed.

"Are you in a hurry to get back to the table?" he said once we were nearly to the lengthy line to order beverages.

I looked back to see that Cassidy had joined the conversation with Nora and Brianna. "Not particularly," I told him.

We veered away from the line and moved toward the nearest exit. When the door shut behind us, the noise faded away.

"Much better," Cameron said. "I couldn't hear myself think in there." He paused to chuckle. "I'm sounding like my father now."

"Well, mine is in there having a grand time," I commented. "And yet I agree with you. I like it better out here too."

My father had opened the Lone Star Veterinary Clinic before I was born. I'd actually almost been born there because my mom went into labor while working on the bookkeeping. Pop was in surgery, and she'd just about decided she would have me there or try to walk to her doctor's office when he finally finished up and drove her to the hospital.

Come to think of it, I probably got my penchant for making women wait while I'm lost in my work from my father.

"I heard your dad's coming in to sub for Tyler and Kristin while they're on their honeymoon," Cameron said.

"He is, but frankly I'm worried about a retired veterinarian of his age trying to take care of a practice for two doctors. I think it's going to be too much for him." I paused. "Although he will have you there to rely on."

"I'm only part-time," Cameron said. "Maybe you should offer to help him. Maybe take a week off and go back to work at the old clinic where you got your start."

"Actually, I spoke to Tyler about it, but Pop got to him first." I paused. "I figured they would have talked you into full-time by now."

He grinned. "They've tried. But I just can't give up the work I do for the shelters. It's too rewarding to think of walking away."

I'd known Cameron since our undergrad days at Texas A&M and then at the vet school there. Although he had Hollywood-hero good looks, Cameron hadn't always been a good guy. There had been a time when he'd nearly lost it all thanks to a combination of bad attitude and bad choices.

I'd gone off to serve my time in the military after college. Cameron had been a different man when I returned. To see him work for free at the local animal shelters was to see a man who had completely changed.

As if he'd guessed my thoughts, Cameron chuckled. "I know. I'm a long way from the time when you had to bail me out of jail or warn me to stop flirting with everyone's girlfriends."

"That guy wasn't all bad," I told him. "Just maybe had something to prove."

"Oh, for sure," Cameron said. "Some of us have to learn the hard way."

I laughed. "That could be both of us."

"True, but there's just something about knowing your calling. I need to be helping those strays at the animal shelter, but more than that, they help me."

I let out a long breath. "I get it. But how did you figure out that was your calling?"

Cameron gave me a sideways look. "From the guy who has found his, that's an odd question."

I ran a hand through my hair as I thought about how to respond to Cameron. "I guess it is an odd question."

The expression on his face told me he wasn't going to back down. "But?"

I met Cameron's gaze. "But my job keeps me away from Nora too much. Since I'm crazy about her, I'm not sure that's the definition of a calling."

He lifted one shoulder in a shrug. "There's only two possible answers to that problem. Either change jobs or change girlfriends." Cameron paused. "Because knowing you, the option of continuing to disappoint Nora isn't going to work."

I frowned. "I didn't say I disappoint her."

Cameron's laughter didn't hold any humor. "Lane, you didn't have to. We all see it."

My spine straightened. I didn't like his tone or what he said. I felt my anger rising. "What is it you think you see?"

"Stand down, soldier." He shook his head. "Never mind."

"No," I said, my jaw tight and my fists clenched. "Say it, Cameron. It sounds like you know something about Nora and me that I don't, so go ahead and tell me about it."

The door burst open, and Brianna stumbled out. Cameron caught her, and they both laughed as he steadied her on her feet.

"Sorry," she said. "I didn't think the door would open so easily." She looked from me to Cameron. "Did I interrupt anything?"

Neither of us spoke for a moment. Finally, Cameron shrugged. "Just a debate on which of us should go back inside and ask you to dance. I won, so let's go."

The laughing pair disappeared inside, leaving me alone. I let out a long breath as my anger slowly cooled. After a few minutes, I put a smile on my face and returned to my seat beside Nora.

"Everything okay?" Nora asked. "I saw you and Cameron go outside."

I upped my smile and reached around the back of her chair to draw her close. "Everything is fine. I was just catching up with Cameron."

She seemed to be studying me for a moment, and then she turned her attention to the dance floor. "He seems happy with Brianna, and I know she likes him. Maybe he will finally settle down."

I pressed a kiss to her cheek. "Maybe so."

"It's what men want ultimately, isn't it?" She looked back at me. "To settle down."

Where was this going? I straightened. I wanted to tell her all the reasons that I wanted to settle down with her, but all the reasons that I couldn't came rushing toward me.

All I could manage was a swift, "Sure."

It didn't take a genius to know that response wasn't good enough. My watch buzzed with a text, and I checked it discreetly. While I couldn't read the entire message without drawing Nora's attention to the fact I was reading it, I could see enough to know where it was coming from and what it was about.

I glanced down at Nora and saw exactly what Cameron had said. Nora was disappointed. And I was the cause.

Worse, I was about to have to tell her I needed to get back to the research lab.

CHAPTER EIGHT

Nora

Saturday evening
Thistledown Farms

The rest of the evening passed in a blur of music, conversation, and well-wishes for the bride and groom. Of course Lane had to leave early to go back to work. He was right that I hadn't said he had to stay the whole time, but how dare he argue that point when he'd broken his promise to arrive on time?

I bid him a terse goodbye and made my way back to the dressing room to change into the clothes I had arrived in that morning. The room was done up in elegant cream colors with plush sofas filled with pillows, thick white rugs on the hardwood floor, and touches of rose gold everywhere, from the candlesticks to the lamps. It was like an expensive hotel room but better, and I secretly wished I could recreate this look in my own little home.

Even as I had the thought, I knew it would never work. I was too much of a pack rat to pull off such a minimalist look. Then there was the issue of my passion for horses and all the mess that accumulates from spending time at a paddock. White carpets and riding boots did not mix well. On top of that, I ran my own restaurant, which meant that I was frequently arriving home wearing clothing stained with something from the kitchen.

Then there was the cat I hoped I'd get to keep. Was this the decor of an animal lover?

Another glance around, and I decided I'd rather keep what I had at home. It might not feel like a villa in the south of France when I opened the door, but the fact that I walked in with who knows what on my clothes from the restaurant or the ranch didn't bother me nearly as much as it would if my place looked like this.

I thought of the dog I planned to get when my life slowed down. Ever since my last dog, Digger, had passed on, the place seemed too quiet. My dad had bought and trained another truffle-hunting dog since I no longer had the heart for it after losing Digger. Digger had been such a good boy, hardworking and so eager to please. His was a loss that had lingered.

So maybe I'd adopt a cat if the orange tabby didn't turn out to be mine. Someday.

I realized I'd put pet ownership on my list of things to do again once Lane and I settled down. I'd sell my cottage in town and we'd buy a ranch, maybe one near my family's property so I'd be close to them as they aged.

I could still buy that ranch someday. And I could still get that dog—or a dog that would get along with my cat. Or rather, the cat that was not currently my cat.

Someday.

My mind drifted toward the conversation with Lane and those stupid season tickets. "No," I said softly as I kicked off my boots, "I will not go there. I decided a year ago not to expect a marriage proposal, and I'm only upset now because I went back on that promise again."

As long as I had no expectations of him, I'd been happy. Letting go of the hope I'd soon be planning a wedding and a life together with Lane had been surprisingly freeing.

I had stopped putting everything on hold and had become happy and successful in the process. I stepped into the life I was meant to live. Maybe I would talk to Mari about that dog after all.

The moment the thought occurred, I knew that wasn't the change that must happen. Not yet anyway. Before I added anything to my life, I needed to get rid of something that wasn't meant to be.

I'd just finished dressing in my jeans and T-shirt and was slipping into my sneakers when Cassidy burst into the bridesmaids' dressing room. "There you are," she said, landing across from me on a plush chair covered in cream fabric. "If you keep hiding in here, you're going to miss the surprise fireworks show and the bride and groom's exit."

"That's okay," I said, trying to manage a smile.

Pillows scattered as she settled in. Then she frowned. "You've already changed out of your bridesmaid's dress. What's wrong?"

I gave up all pretense of trying to look like I was fine and sighed. "I broke up with Lane."

Cassidy leaned forward, concern etching her features. She didn't even look surprised. "How did he take it?"

"He doesn't know yet."

"Explain," she said. "And start from the beginning."

"How about I start from the part where we were out on the dance floor and he told me he had something important to talk about?"

I relayed the season ticket conversation in detail then sat back and waited for my friend's response. Predictably, Cassidy shook her head.

"You know," she said slowly, "I really like Lane. I do." She paused to reach behind herself and retrieve a small heart-shaped pillow covered in rose gold satin with white fringe then tossed it behind her. "But for a man who is so smart—I mean, Texas A&M research jobs are not easy to get—he is so stupid when it comes to keeping the romance alive, girl."

"Well," I said slowly, "I think his version of romance was to involve me in the season ticket choice. Sort of a couple's activity, I guess."

"No, Nora. A couple's activity is taking a cooking class like Jason and I have or choosing what movie you want to see. Season ticket seat choices are not couple's activities."

"I know," I said on an exhale of breath. "I was being sarcastic. Sort of." I paused. "Maybe I need a dog."

"Everyone needs a dog," she said. "But that's not going to fix the problem with Lane. Besides, you have a cat."

"Funny," I said as I reached for my purse and unzipped it to look for my keys. "I was thinking the same thing just a few minutes ago." I snatched up the keys, then looked over at her. "And I don't officially have a cat yet. Not until I know for sure that someone isn't going to claim her."

Cassidy sighed. "When are you going to tell him?"

I lifted one shoulder in the best shrug I could manage considering my level of exhaustion and sadness. "Soon."

"Soon?" Cassidy leaned forward. "If you really wanted to break up with Lane, you'd say now, not soon."

I stood and stuffed my bridesmaid dress into the overnight bag I'd left open beside me. Then I placed my boots on top and zipped it up.

"Nora?" Cassidy said.

"Yeah, I know," I told her, shouldering the bag. "I'll do it. The thing is, he's so busy, I need an appointment to talk to him. He's probably halfway back to College Station by now."

"Why would you think that? It's Saturday night, and the two of you just spent the evening together at a wedding."

"Because that's how things work with Lane. Research doesn't have office hours," I told her, imitating Lane's voice as I spoke the words he'd said to me more times than I could count. "Funny how research never seems to interfere with Aggie home games no matter what the sport." I paused. "When I fell in love with him, I thought I saw forever in his eyes. I just knew he was the one. The man I would marry and have babies with."

I stopped, knowing if I continued, the tears would come. And the last thing I wanted to do tonight was to cry over the man who was about to become my ex.

Cassidy kicked off her boots. "Have you ever talked to him about changing his career path? It sounds like that's the answer to everything."

"Yes. A few times, actually," I said. "I realized he wasn't interested in considering it beyond the talking phase, so I changed my career path instead."

"And opened Simply Eat," she supplied.

"That's right. And I also stopped expecting the ring I'd wanted so badly. It wasn't easy, but I love my new life. And truly I was able to just relax and enjoy seeing Lane whenever I could."

"But?" she said.

"But it really bugged me how late he would arrive for things. And sometimes he wouldn't arrive at all. The more he did that, the more it got to me."

"And then?" she supplied.

"Then tonight, out on that dance floor in that handsome man's arms, a whole year of not caring about the direction of our relationship disappeared. It happened just like that." I snapped my fingers. "And it scared me how badly I wanted him to propose."

"So, your response to that is to break up with him?" She shook her head. "Nora, that doesn't make sense."

"It makes perfect sense," I told her. "I cannot want something that Lane isn't willing to give. It's not healthy, Cassidy. I need to end this."

Cassidy seemed to be searching for a response. "I'm sorry," she finally said.

"Me too. I really thought he was the one. Did I mention that?" I hefted the bag onto my shoulder. "Anyway, I don't think Kristin and Tyler will notice I'm not there. If they do, tell them I had to leave early."

She gave me a sideways look. "Are you sure? You could always stay and hang out with me."

"You and Jason, you mean? No thanks. I know the offer is sincere, but I'm pretty sure your hunky game warden wants you all to himself." I paused. "Seriously, Cassidy, I know how much he works and how little time off he gets. Enjoy your man. I'm going to go check on things at the restaurant, and then I'm heading home for a hot bath and a good book."

Cassidy rose then stepped into her boots once more. "Okay, but I'm going to walk with you out to the car. It's dark out there."

I adored my friend, but her job managing veterinarians at the Lone Star Vet Clinic had her in the habit of also managing me on occasion. As always, I reminded myself that Cassidy's love language was taking care of people. That and pasta, but mostly taking care of people.

"Cass," I said firmly, "we're in the middle of nowhere at a wedding venue. I grew up on a ranch, also in the middle of nowhere. I'm perfectly safe walking to my car. Go find Jason and enjoy yourself. I do not need an escort."

Before Cassidy could protest, I walked to the door and opened it then stepped outside. The little cottage was tucked at the back of the venue behind the chapel and away from the lights and noise of the reception area. Here the stars twinkled overhead, and the scent of hay wafted toward me on a warm breeze. In the distance a horse nickered softly.

No more thinking about what I didn't have. I made myself that promise—again—and this time nothing would make me go back on it.

I inhaled deeply and let the moment settle in my spirit. God sure was showing off when he made this part of Texas.

On the way back to the parking lot, my phone buzzed. Since I had switched to silent mode before the service started, I couldn't tell whether I had received a text or a call.

Juggling my bag and purse, I retrieved my phone in time to see it was a call. From my father.

"Dad," I said as my heart lurched. "Is everything okay? It's late."

First came his familiar deep chuckle. Then my father's voice. "Everything is fine, sweetheart. And it's barely past nine. Your mother is still watching the news."

"Okay," I said on an exhale of breath. "I'm just not used to you calling this time of night."

"Well, it's like this," he said. "I was supposed to remind you yesterday about Sunday supper at the ranch, but I forgot. I realized that tonight when Mama was going over her list to make sure she had everything out for tomorrow's meal prep after church."

"I see," I said as I resumed my walk to the parking lot. "Okay, I'll be there. Do you need me to bring anything?"

"Speaking for myself, I would love it if you've got any of that jalapeño cheese sourdough bread that you sell at the restaurant left over. You know it's my favorite for sandwiches."

I smiled. "I'll bring some. Anything else?"

"Just your fellow," he said. "We haven't seen Lane in a while."

"He works a lot, Dad," I said, stopping myself from offering up

Lane's quote about research not keeping to office hours. "I doubt he'll be available."

My father paused a moment. "It'd mean a lot to your mother if he was here. She had her heart set on the whole family sitting around the table together, and for once it looks like everyone is in town and no one has practices, rehearsals, or sniffles. And she's making his favorite lasagna."

Lane's favorite double-meat triple-cheese lasagna. Of course.

"With all the children and grandchildren the two of you have, I doubt Mama will miss Lane if he's not there. We've already reached the point where we have to have two tables anyway."

"Nora," he said, his tone serious, "Lane is family. If even one member of the family isn't at a family gathering, that person is missed, okay? You know that."

Oh boy. Now was not the time to tell Dad that I was about to kick a member of the family to the curb because he refused to marry me. So I smiled though my heart was breaking. Because when I told Mama, hers would break too.

"I'll make sure Lane knows about the invitation for dinner tomorrow," I told my father. "Whether he can be there is not up to me, though."

Although it sort of was, I thought. I could wait until after the weekend to break up with him. That would fix the issue with tomorrow's meal.

But it would just be putting off the inevitable.

CHAPTER NINE

D ad's voice cut through my thoughts. "I'll tell your mother. She will be pleased." He paused. "Are you outside?"

"Yes, I was in a wedding tonight at Thistledown Farms. Tyler and Kristin, the veterinarians at the Lone Star Vet Clinic, got married, and I was a bridesmaid. I'm on my way to my car now."

"I remember your mother working on a purple dress for you," he said.

"Lavender, and yes, she was hemming it for tonight."

"Well, all I know is I guarantee you outshone everyone there, including the bride."

"Dad!" I exclaimed.

"Hey, you're my baby girl. I'm just telling you what I see."

"You might be a bit biased," I said with a chuckle.

"Say, I'm wondering now whether you've got any news on that building you just bought," he said.

"I spoke to Todd Dennison with Brenham PD yesterday. The fire was small and limited to the kitchen. I don't know when I'll get access, but we've determined that whoever set the fire wasn't supposed to be there. The police are considering the place a crime scene for the time being."

I left out the whole exploding drugs and stolen furniture part. Dad didn't need to know that. At least not until he heard it from someone else.

I was far too tired to delve into that tonight.

"I'm sorry, sweetheart. That's a shame."

"It is, but it can't be helped. And at least there was no storm damage. It's a sturdy building, and I'll be back in it soon enough."

My father launched into a discussion of the merits of the building's construction while I glanced around for my vehicle. Finally, I balanced the phone between my chin and shoulder and pointed my car keys at the lot.

The lighting wasn't the greatest out here, and there were several vehicles that looked exactly like mine. Plus it had been more than ten hours since I parked the thing, and there were only a few cars out here then.

When the taillights blinked and the alarm chirped, I headed in that direction. "Can I call you back when I get in the car?"

"No need," Dad said. "Just promise me you won't tell your mama that I waited so late to remind you."

"I promise."

"Okay, good. Oh, and you'll have a nice drive home. No chance of rain and no low cloud cover to hide the stars. I love you, sweetheart."

My father had been a rancher all his life, but he knew more about the weather than any television meteorologist. Keeping his children updated on the weather was one of his many love languages.

"Thanks, Dad. I love you too."

Pressing the button on my key fob, I watched the back hatch on my SUV begin to lift. Behind me, I heard a pop and crackle sound that signaled the beginning of the fireworks display. Then came the first loud boom and then another.

I tossed my things in then reached up to press the button to close the hatch. Brilliant red and gold streaks covered the sky as the fireworks went off. Out of the corner of my eye, I saw something heading my way at high speed.

A dog—and a big one—I realized as it raced past me, nearly clipping me at the back of my knees. It had to be the same dog I'd seen when Lane and I were on our FaceTime call. But what was it doing here?

Poor pup. It must be terrified of the fireworks.

Tucking my keys into the front pocket of my jeans and my phone into my back pocket, I set off in the direction the dog had gone. Each time the fireworks went up, the cars in the parking lot were cast in an eerie red and gold light.

As I wove through the parked cars, I whistled and called for the dog but got no answer. I had almost made my way to the back of the parking lot when I spied the dog wedged between two pick-up trucks.

One of those trucks looked just like Lane's.

With the next flash of light, I saw the dog was lying sprawled on the ground. "Oh no, he's hurt."

There were easily a dozen veterinarians and vet techs on the property, but none of them were here. I slowed my pace and edged toward the pup so as not to frighten it. I shouldn't have worried. By the time I reached the dog, I could see its focus was not on me but on a large lump of something slumped between the vehicles.

A flash lit up the sky, and I could see it was Lane. My heart lurched.

Still dressed in his trousers and pale blue dress shirt from the wedding but minus his tie and suit coat, my future ex was sprawled on the ground with his head and one shoulder leaning against the front tire of the vehicle next to his. The big dog—some sort of German shepherd or Belgian Malinois, I guessed—had his head pressed against Lane's midsection.

"Lane, are you all right?" I shouted over the popping sound of fireworks as I landed on my knees beside him.

The dog pressed his head harder against Lane's crumpled form, but its baleful brown eyes were now on me. However, Lane's eyes were not. His face was buried in the dog's rough brown fur, and he'd given no indication that he knew I was there.

"Lane?" I reached over to touch his arm.

He jerked and scrambled into a sitting position, releasing the dog then grasping it again. "Nora, I didn't hear you." He gestured skyward. "Too loud."

A riot of colors from the fireworks reflected on his face as the noise grew louder. The dog scooted closer, and Lane gripped him tight again.

"I'm glad you're here. Help me hold on to this dog until the fireworks stop."

I sat down beside Lane and assessed the dog. Up close I could see he—or she—was a beautiful Belgian Malinois. It wore a thick leather collar and some sort of dark vest like one a service dog would wear. Unlike others I had seen, this vest had no markings on it, although I thought there might be shadows and stitch marks where it once might have had them.

The animal's dark eyes studied me. I reached over and scratched behind the pup's ear. He snorted and snuggled closer to Lane.

"That dog looks content where it is. I don't think it's going to run." I looked up at Lane. "In fact, it looks like he's made a new friend. You always did have a way with dogs."

Lane gave me a wistful smile. "Better than people usually."

I nudged him with my shoulder but did not respond. We sat there without speaking until the fireworks culminated in a loud finale with multicolored explosions overhead. The dog stiffened and let out a yip just before silence fell.

"There," I said gently as I reached over to pat its rough coat. "It's all over, sweetheart." I shifted my attention to Lane. "It seems pretty calm now."

"Unlike when we first met." Lane shifted positions. "I never saw this dog coming until it was on top of me."

"I saw him streak past while I was loading my car." I paused. "I'm pretty sure this is the dog that everyone's been looking for. The one that made a cameo in our FaceTime call the other day. Should I go find Parker or Mari so they can take him to the rescue?"

Lane wrapped a protective arm around the dog. "No, don't do that. This animal has been well taken care of. My guess is it has run off from a home or training facility that's close by. Or maybe he belongs to someone who lives near Pop but somehow ended up out here."

"Wait. A training facility?" I asked. "Do you think that's why he's wearing a vest but it has no markings? I don't remember seeing it before, but then it all happened so fast and it was dark."

"Right. Same. Could be that someone is training this dog. There's no tattoo in its right ear, so he's probably not a military working dog." He nodded toward his truck. "Would you mind grabbing a leash from my truck? I don't want to stand until we get this guy leashed up."

"Right." I measured my moves as I opened the truck door and retrieved a leash.

"Just leave the door open," Lane said. "I'd rather not make any more unnecessary noise. And you might want to move slowly."

I found the leash and handed it to Lane, who quickly attached it to the dog's collar. "Okay, let's see if we can figure out where you came from and how you got here."

Lane inched away from the dog and climbed to his feet. A moment later, the Belgian Malinois was up and, it seemed, awaiting instructions from its new friend.

He handed me the leash then dusted off his trousers. Then he retrieved his phone from his shirt pocket and pressed the button to activate the phone's flashlight. Using the light, Lane inspected the dog's brown leather collar and black vest while I watched.

"Do you see any identifying information?" I asked.

"Well," he said slowly, "other than noting this is a male Belgian Malinois of average weight and size in good health, wearing a generic leather collar and unmarked service vest, and is approximately seven to ten years old, I do not."

"You sound like a veterinarian assessing a patient," I quipped.

Lane looked at me with the grin that had once made me fall in love with him. "Wonder why?" he said with a chuckle.

My heart did that stupid flip-flop that only this man could cause. I let out a long breath and reminded myself that this is the guy I was breaking up with, not the guy I was in love with.

"I thought you were on your way back to the lab in College Station," I said to redirect my thoughts.

His expression changed. The grin faltered. "About that. I was," he said. "But then I realized I—"

A cheer went up outside the reception building, and another round of fireworks split the night. The leash slipped through my hand, and in an instant, the dog was gone.

Lane

Saturday evening
Thistledown Farms wedding venue

I took off after the dog, but he was too fast for me. He darted between and around cars like a Porsche on a Houston freeway. Thanks to the running that Nora had convinced me to do with her, I was better at this than I should have been for a guy with a desk job.

Belgian Malinois were, as a breed, smart dogs. I watched this one dart in between cars as I tried to figure out where he might be going so that I could possibly outsmart him.

Then it occurred to me. The pup just might be going home.

With the wedding guests flooding toward the parking lot, I spied people jumping out of the way. "Sorry," I called. "He's not dangerous, but apparently he just doesn't like fireworks."

And I don't blame him, I left unsaid.

I spied Marigold and Parker Jenson walking toward me. Marigold was still dressed in her bridesmaid finery and carried an overnight bag in one hand and a purse in the other. Parker had his suit coat and tie draped over his arm. If anyone could catch a runaway stray, it was them.

"Grab that dog," I shouted, gesturing toward the dog.

As if by instinct, Parker stepped out into the Belgian Malinois' path at exactly the right time to cause the dog to swerve. He quickly tossed his suit coat and tie aside and snatched up the leash.

"Gotcha, boy," he said firmly, jogging along with the animal so as not to frighten him. "Sorry I don't have a cheeseburger."

"A cheeseburger?" I said when I caught up to them.

He shrugged. "Habit. I always have a cheeseburger when we're out on a report of a stray."

"Parker to the rescue," Marigold said when she reached us, her arms now filled with her husband's discarded wedding attire as well as her own things.

Nora caught up a moment later. "Parker to the rescue," she said, chuckling.

"That's what I said," Marigold told her, joining in the laughter.

"He's a nice-looking dog," Parker said, ignoring the ladies. "And he looks well-nourished and decently happy except for the fireworks situation. I'm pretty sure it's the dog we were looking for the night of the tornado. The vest tells me he's probably in training somewhere. Do you know where he belongs?"

"I don't," I told him, taking the leash back from Parker. "But I have a theory. The way he bolted away from us makes me wonder if he doesn't live nearby and was just trying to get home."

Parker nodded. "Maybe so."

"Oh, I bet he does," Nora said, bending down to scratch the dog behind his ears. "He really does look like someone's been taking good care of him. And why put a vest like that on a dog if you're not training him?"

"Agreed," I told her. "It might be a good idea to take this leash off him and see if he goes home."

Marigold exchanged a look with Parker. "It goes against everything we stand for at Second Chance Ranch to release a dog once it has been caught, but I think you may be right."

He handed the leash to me. I leaned down on one knee and scratched the dog behind the ear. Then I unclipped the leash and stood.

"Go home, boy," I said, then watched the massive canine bolt off to disappear between the cars.

Parker nodded. "How about I go find the facility manager first to see if anyone is familiar with him? That way if he shows back up here, at least someone on site will have seen him before and know he's lost."

"Great idea." I looked over at Nora. "I'll go with Parker since I got a better look at the dog than he did. Can we talk when I'm done? I'll meet you at your car."

She faltered only a moment, but it was enough for me to know she had to think about it before she responded with a nod. I jogged to catch up with Parker, who had already struck out for the management office.

We accomplished our mission quickly and returned to give the ladies the update. Marigold had apparently delivered the things she had been carrying before to their vehicle, for she was empty-handed now.

Marigold frowned. "So he's not familiar to the management, which means that he has always been well contained within a fence until now or he's new to the neighborhood. That worries me."

Parker patted his wife's shoulder. "I gave the manager a card with the contact information for the rescue. She'll call if she sees him again. And next time—if there is a next time—I will have a cheeseburger with me."

Marigold nodded then offered Nora and me a tired smile. "Okay then. I guess that's our cue to go home. It's been a long day."

I watched the couple walk away hand in hand. They had such a simple life—in a good way. They worked together, shared the cause of rescuing strays, and had found their happily ever after.

In comparison, my relationship with Nora was, to borrow a term from social media, complicated. Worse, I was the cause of the complication, and it had nothing to do with whether I loved her or not.

I absolutely did. And I was pretty sure she still loved me.

Even after I broke another promise to her tonight and showed up late.

Nora stifled a yawn. "Sorry. Like Mari said, it's been a long day. So what was it you wanted to talk about?"

Here it was. The moment I had been practicing for ever since I had the good sense to do a U-turn just before I reached the highway and return to Thistledown Farms to face the woman I loved and be honest with her.

"You're tired," I said instead as I brushed an ebony strand back from her face. "It can wait. What are your plans for tomorrow?"

"Dinner with the family like always," she told me. "It is Sunday."

"I know it's Sunday," I said, trying to keep irritation out of my voice. For all the years that Nora and I had been dating, the family dinners on Sunday had been a tradition.

It had been so long since I was free on a Sunday evening that I hadn't even thought about it. That certainly highlighted the issue that had become clear to me on the drive back to the venue.

Tomorrow evening I had more work than I knew how to accomplish. I had deadlines on action items and data to analyze. While I wouldn't miss Sunday morning worship, I really ought to skip Sunday night with the Hernandez clan once again.

"It's fine. I told my dad you'd be busy." Nora walked toward the driver's side door of her car then stopped to turn and face me. "He said my mother would be disappointed. I'm just passing on the information because I doubt anyone else there would be."

Ouch.

And there it was. The look of disappointment that Cameron had roasted me about. Once again, I'd put that look on her face.

"I'll be there," I said before I could stop myself.

Nora gave me a blank look. Then she shook her head. "Really, Lane, it's fine. You do not have to do this."

I gathered Nora into my arms and held her close. "I want to," I told her, and I realized that I really did.

I wanted to laugh at her father's corny dad jokes and weather reports again, to play flag football with her brothers until we were all exhausted—which wouldn't take long at our ages—and to dance with my girl under the stars until the old folks shut off the music and sent us all home.

Again.

I looked up at those stars and inhaled the soft floral scent of Nora's perfume. *Thank you, Lord, that she's still putting up with me.*

A few minutes later, we parted with a kiss, and I headed to my truck. As I rounded the back of the vehicle, I saw a light on inside and realized we'd never closed the door after the dog took off running.

I retrieved my keys from my pocket and climbed inside. Just as I was about to shut the door, I saw I wasn't alone. The missing mutt was sprawled out on the floor on the passenger floor mat like he owned the place.

I reached down and scratched the furry intruder behind his ear. "Hey there, boy. Looks like you weren't heading home after all."

At that point, I should have leashed up the big dog and walked him over to the manager's office. Or I should have called Marigold and Parker. They were the experts in finding homes for lost pets.

Either of those things would have been the right thing to do. But the pup gave me a look that said he was perfectly content right where he was. And after our experience with the fireworks, we were kind of buddies anyway.

"All right, pal," I said, starting the truck. "I guess you're going home with me tonight. But first we'll make a stop by my lab to see if you've been chipped."

A half hour later, I pulled into the parking lot of the Small Animal Teaching Hospital at Texas A&M University's School of Veterinary Science. The dog I'd decided I'd temporarily call Pal had been sleeping soundly—and snoring occasionally—until the engine stopped.

His head lifted, and a moment later, Pal had jumped onto the passenger seat and was staring out the window. It was almost like he knew where he was.

When I opened the door and slid out, Pal leaped over the center console to land on the driver's seat. I tightened my grip on the leash then scratched him behind the ear with my free hand.

"Okay, Pal. We're just going in to see if you're chipped, that's all."

Now, I am a reasonably intelligent person who knows that dogs cannot talk. I also suspect that most of them understand what is said when they're spoken to. This one certainly did.

Pal gave me what looked like a nod. He waited politely until I moved to the side, and then he jumped out to join me on the pavement.

I watched Pal's reaction as we entered the building to see if he might continue to act as if this was a familiar place to him. He seemed neither curious nor nervous as I led him along the corridors.

After a check for a microchip—there was none—Pal and I climbed back into the truck and headed for my place. With Parker's words on my mind, I made a pit stop at Whataburger—one for me and one for Pal.

It wasn't how I normally fed animals under my care, but tonight seemed like a good night for a treat. This guy was displaced and probably starving. And to be fair, much as I love a nice night out with my girl, the food they serve at weddings isn't always my favorite.

Nora and I had an ongoing disagreement about what we would serve at the reception when we said our vows. She wanted a beautifully catered affair with her restaurant in charge of the food. And while that did sound incredibly appetizing—my Nora was the best cook on the planet—I was determined to serve good Texas barbecue.

Since when doesn't a brisket and all the trimmings sound amazing?

I let out a long breath as I signaled to turn onto the road leading to my house. Deciding the meal at the reception was the least of the impediments to setting the date for a wedding.

And I was the greatest impediment of them all.

CHAPTER TEN

LANE

Saturday night
College Station, Texas

My house was set in the middle of an eleven-acre wooded tract a few miles outside of College Station. From my back porch, I could see the lights of Kyle Field, the college's massive football stadium, over the treetops. If not for that, I would have felt like I was a thousand miles from civilization out here.

I held tight to Pal's leash as we headed to the front door. If he got loose out here, I would never find him in these woods.

I was pretty sure it was the Whataburger bag and not the fact he liked me that had Pal shadowing me closely. I rummaged around in the pantry and retrieved a dog bowl big enough to accommodate Pal's meal. I filled a second one with water.

Pal waited patiently, unlike other dogs I'd owned that preferred to whine and bark until I had finished the task of preparing their meal. I put the bowls down in front of him, but Pal made no move to eat.

He was waiting for permission. I smiled. Definitely a well-trained dog. "Good boy." I nodded to the bowl. "Go ahead and eat. Enjoy that burger. From here on out, it's dog kibble for you and not people food. This is a special occasion treat."

While Pal devoured his feast, I grabbed a can of Dr Pepper from the fridge and settled down at the kitchen table to enjoy mine.

It had been a while since I had a dog or cat here. I'd always owned at least one of each, but over the years as members of my menagerie passed on, I hadn't replaced them. My excuse was that I had been too busy to properly care for them. That I was never at home. All of that had ended me up here in this place with no furry footsteps to break the quiet.

Until now.

Pal's loud slurping as he drank from the water bowl made me chuckle. When he'd had his fill, the big dog crossed the kitchen to sprawl next to my feet. Though I still had food in front of me, Pal didn't beg. He just got comfortable.

Another mark of a well-trained dog.

I finished my burger and sat back in my chair, the Dr Pepper in my hand. This dog was someone's pet—or someone's service dog—but I had already decided I liked him a lot.

After walking Pal one more time, I locked up and turned out the lights. The dog shadowed me down the hall and into the bedroom just as he had when I'd been carrying his dinner. I dug around in the linen closet and found a few fluffy blankets I could pile up to make a bed on the floor.

Pal watched my efforts closely. As soon as I was done, he messed up the neatly folded makeshift bed by sniffing and digging and turning himself around and around until he'd got things just like he liked them.

I shook my head and climbed into bed. Normally this would be the time when I sent Nora one last good-night text. However, I knew she was likely sound asleep by now, and I didn't want to wake her. I placed my phone on the charger and climbed into bed to the sound of Pal's snoring.

I woke up tangled in sweaty sheets with the sun blinding me. Dazed, I glanced over at the clock on the nightstand to check the time. Half past eleven. I'd already missed church.

I had been asleep almost twelve hours. I couldn't remember the last time I'd slept four hours straight, much less almost twelve.

I sat bolt upright—or rather, tried to. Apparently sometime during the night Pal had abandoned his nest of blankets and joined me. Currently his head was pressing down on my midsection and his watchful gaze was on my face.

I'd been around enough working dogs to recognize PTSD training in an animal. These big dogs used their heads pressed against a person in crisis to offer protection and distraction.

It wasn't the first time I'd seen Pal do this. He'd done the same thing back at the wedding venue when the fireworks laid both of us low. Now I wondered if his reaction was fear or training when he cornered me in that parking lot.

I thought back to last night. To falling in bed exhausted. It hadn't taken long to slip into the black oblivion of sleep. That was a miracle in itself.

But the dream? Had it invaded my slumber? I couldn't recall, although the condition of my sheets and pillows told me I'd fought against something while I slept.

It sure wasn't the somber dog that was watching me like I was his own personal assignment. In an instant, it all became clear.

I had slept because Pal did his job.

I reached down to scratch the dog behind his ear. "Thanks, Pal."

As if he understood that his assignment was complete, Pal stood up, stretched, and jumped off the bed. A moment later, he was remodeling his nest of blankets until he'd gotten them just right. By the time I swung my feet to the floor and reached for my phone, the big dog was watching me, his eyes half-closed.

I had missed a whole bunch of texts, most of them from Nora. She'd also called once.

I dialed her number but got voice mail before I realized she'd be in church with the phone on silent. I left a voice mail letting her know I'd overslept and I'd see her at her parents' place, then padded into the bathroom to shower and dress for the day.

I made scrambled eggs—plain for Pal and dressed up in an omelet for me—then we headed outside. Since I'd missed the main event down at the church, I took my Bible out to the back porch. Pal tolerated the leash but didn't seem to have any interest in taking off, so I decided to trust him.

"Stick close, Pal," I said, releasing the clasp on the leash. "There are a lot of woods around here to get lost in, and I don't want to have to go looking for you again."

The dog sniffed at the air and at several tree trunks then followed me back up to the porch. While I read, he snored.

I was beginning to realize this dog snored a lot. I didn't mind, but I wondered if it bothered his owner.

His owner.

I needed to do something about finding out who that was. Though the day was sunny and warm, a day where I'd rather be anywhere but indoors, I gathered up my things and went in to see what I could find online about local dog trainers.

It was Sunday, so the odds of catching anyone to ask questions was small. I decided to make a list of places to call. I was scheduled in meetings most of the day tomorrow, but I had an assistant and several interns who could divide the list and make the calls for me.

While I was online, I placed a curbside order from HEB for Blue Bell ice cream. Six gallons of six different flavors: one Chocolate Peanut Butter Overload, one Cookies and Cream, one Butter Crunch, one Pistachio Almond, and one Banana Pudding.

Of course, I had to add the perennial favorite Homemade Vanilla because it was almost certain that someone would bring a pie that needed to be à la mode. I might not be able to cook anything other than a decent omelet, but my mama did not raise me to arrive at someone's house for dinner empty-handed.

I glanced at the phone and thought about calling Nora again. Church should be over. Or was I remembering that it started at eleven and not eleven thirty? The fact that I didn't know the answer to that drove home the point that I'd neglected Nora.

We used to do everything together. Well, everything that we could manage given our busy schedules.

But there had always been time to spend Sundays together, first in worship and then just having fun. We'd fish or picnic, or sometimes we'd even go out to lunch. And most Sundays the day culminated with dinner at the Hernandez Ranch.

I didn't have to ask what had happened to change this. *I* had happened. The closer I got to asking Nora to marry me, the more I pulled away.

It was idiotic, and I knew it. I wanted to share everything with the woman I loved, and yet I couldn't share the most basic thing that troubled me: the nightmares.

I felt a nudge against my knee and spied Pal's head pressing down on my leg. His dark eyes looked up at me calmly.

"I'm an idiot, Pal," I told him. "A complete idiot. She probably has no idea how much I love her. Not anymore anyway."

The big dog continued to watch me, barely blinking. I reached down to scratch him behind his ears, turning my attention to the photograph of Nora and me on my desk. One of her brothers had taken it a few years ago while we were riding horses at the ranch during bluebonnet season.

The horses were trotting across a stream, and in the background was a field of bluebonnets. Nora's glossy black hair was flying in the wind, and I wore an expression of complete love and amazement as I looked at her instead of at the camera.

I still felt that way every time I saw her.

Cameron's words from last night came back to me. His casual statement that everyone seemed to know about Nora's disappointment with me stung.

Because it was very likely true.

I shifted positions and leaned forward to get a closer look at the photograph. The old wooden office chair that Nora had been nagging me to replace creaked loudly.

I remembered the wind that day and the sunshine and the ride we'd taken, but most of all I remembered Nora. It always came down to Nora, no matter what. Anything could be happening, but it would be Nora that I saw. Always Nora.

"I'm the only one who can fix the mess I made of my relationship with Nora." I sat back, my hand still resting on Pal's head. "It's up to me, isn't it? If she's the one—and I'm certain she is—then I need to take care of my business so we can have a life together."

Pal made a soft yipping sound. I looked down, and he hadn't moved. "I'll take that as a yes, then."

If only my business wasn't something I had no control over. A man couldn't decide whether to dream, could he?

I didn't know the answer to that question. And that was the problem.

I sent my therapist at the VA an email asking to schedule an appointment to talk about how to make some lasting changes. Hiding the fact that I struggled with PTSD wasn't going to cut it anymore. Who knew it would take a dog to teach me that?

CHAPTER ELEVEN

Nora

Sunday midday
Brenham, Texas

As soon as I stepped out of church and into the sunshine, I checked my phone. I had one missed call from Lane.

"Hey, Nora, I overslept. Can you believe it? I slept nearly twelve hours. It's crazy. Anyway, I just wanted to make sure you knew I love you and I'll see you at your parents' place later today."

I tucked the phone back into my purse. I wasn't going to hold my breath until I saw Lane's truck drive through the gates at the ranch. Anything could happen between now and then.

And it usually did.

Cassidy appeared at my side, smiling. "How about we go for salads for lunch? Your place is my favorite, but since it's not open on Sunday, there are a couple of other options."

A salad sounded wonderful, especially given the fact my mother's cooking, while absolutely incredible, generally contained a week's worth of calories in just a small serving.

Before I could answer, Mari and Parker joined us. "Lunch plans?" Cassidy asked.

"Nothing we can't change," Mari said. "What are you thinking?"

"Salads," I told them. "I've got dinner with the folks tonight."

"And Jason and I are double-dating with Cameron and Brianna tonight," Cassidy said.

Jason's job as a game warden often kept him busier than either of them liked. Now that they were dating seriously, he had committed to trying his best to keep Sunday evenings free for date night.

I knew this because I had pointed it out to Lane more than once after Cassidy told me. It hadn't worked on Lane, but it seemed to be a promise that Jason was keeping.

"Brianna and Cameron are getting serious, don't you think?" Mari asked, interrupting my thoughts.

"Mari," Parker said, his tone holding a warning. "It's probably not a good idea to pry into their business."

"It's not prying if you're just wanting to know if your prayers are working," Mari protested. "And we've been hoping that Cameron would find the right woman for a long time."

I nodded in agreement while Cassidy shrugged.

"I don't know how serious they are, but they seemed happy at the wedding," she added.

Everyone's phone but Cassidy's buzzed. I reached for mine and found a photo of a Belgian Malinois. The text was from Lane.

LONG STORY, BUT HE FOUND ME. NO CHIP AND NO EAR TATTOO. PRETTY SURE HE'S A RETIRED MILITARY WORKING DOG TRAINED TO HELP WITH PTSD. WE NEED TO FIND HIS OWNERS.

I pushed the icon to call Lane. He picked up with a laugh. "I figured you'd be the one to call first."

"We're all here together," I said. "Cassidy too."

"Okay, perfect. It sounds like you're outside. Is there a place you can all go that's quieter so we can talk about this?"

Parker nodded to the curb a few feet away. "Our car is just over there."

While we walked, Mari turned her phone around to show Cassidy the dog's photo. "The short version is that we saw this dog running around the wedding venue parking lot last night, presumably spooked by the fireworks. We lost him, but somehow Lane has found him."

"Hold on a second, Lane," I told him as we climbed inside. "Okay, we're all in Parker and Mari's car. Are you at home?"

"Yes, I'm still in College Station. I'm guessing that's not the only question you have."

"Lane," I told him, "stop stalling. How did you find the dog? That *is* the dog from last night, right?"

"Actually, he found me." Lane told us how he'd returned to his truck to find the dog waiting for him and then went on to provide the rest of the details.

"So no chip, nothing on his vest or collar, and no tattoo in his ear, but he behaves like a dog that's been trained as a MWD? You're certain?" This from Parker who looked as confused as I felt.

"Absolutely certain," Lane answered. "As you know, it's not out of the question for a chip to move or malfunction. The tech at A&M scanned the dog from nose to tail, and there was no sign of one."

"Is it possible that someone removed the tattoo?" I asked, thinking of an article I read about the recent popularity of tattoo removal.

"It's possible," he said slowly, "but to achieve removal, it takes multiple visits. Since we're talking about a dog and not a human, there's the added element of how you'd get him to sit still for the treatment."

"You'd have to administer a sedative," Mari said.

"Which means access to controlled prescription medications," Cassidy added. "Like in a vet office."

"The venue is out in the boonies," I said. "The closest vet office would be. . ."

I was still doing the calculations when Parker spoke up. "It would be ours, Nora. We're the closest office to the venue."

"I'm guessing you guys aren't in the business of removing tattoos, so I think we can strike you off the list," Lane said. "Anyway, we're getting ahead of ourselves. We don't know if this dog was trained out at Fort Cavazos at the MWD facility. This dog could have been trained by someone who had experience in training MWD and subsequently left the military for civilian life."

"True," I said. "So we're back to square one."

"Sort of," Lane said. "I've been compiling some lists of training facilities in the Brenham and College Station area. The reason I added College Station is when I got to the Small Animal Hospital parking lot last night, Pal perked up. He walked in like he owned the place or, rather, like he'd been there before."

"Pal?" I asked with a chuckle.

"Yeah," Lane said. "We kind of bonded over Whataburger, so I figured he needed a name, at least temporarily until we can get him home again."

Parker laughed. "So you tried the old cheeseburger trick. I'm flattered."

"Genius advice from a dog taming pro," Lane said. "We both enjoyed our cheeseburgers, but I drew the line at sharing my Dr Pepper. After that, he stuck pretty close to me. I guess he was hoping there was more Whataburger for breakfast. Although he didn't complain about the scrambled eggs."

"You've named him Pal and you cook for him," I said. "That's more commitment than I've had in five years of dating."

Everyone laughed, including me. However, the truth of that statement stung a bit.

"Unlike how I feel about you, I am not going to get attached to him," Lane said. "He has a home and family somewhere, and we need to help him find them. This dog is too well trained and healthy to have been a stray for longer than a night or two. I've been looking online to see where the nearest training facilities are to the wedding venue. I'll have my assistant call them tomorrow."

"That's a great idea," Mari said. "But what if the trainer isn't working at a facility? Can't we just send someone at Fort Cavazos a picture of our stray and see if anyone recognizes him?"

"No," Lane said. "Too many dogs like Pal have come through there. Belgian Malinois is a popular breed for training. Without any ID, his papers can't be located."

"Where would a dog go after training?" I asked.

"There are lots of places," Lane said. "It depends on what he's trained for. They have their assignments just like all the other soldiers who go through basic training. He'd have a handler, and they'd go where they were sent."

"For how long?" Mari asked.

Lane let out a long breath. "Pretty much until they're injured or retired due to age. And there's no set age. It all depends on the dog. Ours could be retired, or he could be AWOL, meaning he was stolen."

"Couldn't he have run away?" Cassidy asked.

"No," Lane said. "Not if he's a military working dog. These dogs are impeccably trained. Running away wouldn't occur to them."

"So stolen or retired then lost are our two options," I said. "That narrows it down a little."

"It does, actually," Parker said. "Lane, correct me if I'm wrong, but if an MWD is stolen, we can track that."

"Yes, military police would have a report of theft and also civilian police if the theft happened off base," he said.

"I could have Jason check," Cassidy offered. "He's state police. They would know, right?"

"It's worth a try," Lane said. "But again, we're only going to be able to narrow it down to Belgian Malinois males in his age group that were stolen or are missing."

"That would give us something to go on." I paused. "What if there's a third option? What if this dog was just someone's pet?" Before anyone could protest, I continued. "Hear me out. What if he was trained by someone who knew the technique? Say a handler or a trainer from Fort Cavazos. Wouldn't that be possible?"

"I don't see why not," Lane said slowly. "Fort Cavazos training couldn't be exactly replicated, but someone with the knowledge could come close, I guess."

Parker nodded. "I agree. However, we've now expanded our search to anyone who might have handler training or who has worked with an MWD."

"I guess we've got our work cut out for us," Mari said. "It's a mystery needing to be solved, and we have no real clues at this point. But since when has that stopped us?"

We shared a laugh. "Okay, I guess we need to divide and conquer on this one. Cassidy, you'll get with Jason to find out if there are any reports of missing dogs." At her nod, I continued. "Lane, you're going to have your people check on training facilities in the area to see if anyone is looking for their dog."

"I've already sent an email to my assistant and intern," Lane said. "I've categorized this as top priority. I asked that my assistant also put a call in to Fort Cavazos to speak to someone there. I'll be in meetings tomorrow, so I've given them your contact information if they find anything."

"Perfect." I turned my attention to Parker and Mari. "Could you use your contacts to find out if other shelters and rescues have heard of our dog? It's possible if he's an anomaly and does have a penchant to run, he's been picked up before. I know it's a long shot, but it just might pan out."

The couple nodded. Then Mari spoke. "Would you mind sending more photos of him, Lane? I could use full-length pictures of him from both sides and the front, as well as close-ups of any scars or identifying features."

"Will do," Lane said.

I thought of my brothers, all veterans and all residents of the area. All of them, including my father, were involved with local veterans groups in one way or another.

"Tonight I'll ask my dad and brothers about anyone they might know who would have been a trainer or handler or who might have the ability to train an MWD."

"Good idea," Mari said. "Sometimes it's who you know and not what you know that solves the case."

"Agreed. Okay, looks like we've all got jobs to do. I'm going home to get ready for dinner with my parents." I paused. "Lane, since you've got the dog, does this mean you're not coming tonight?"

"As long as Pal is invited, I'll be there. I'm not sure how he would react if I leave him alone. I'll keep him close."

My family gatherings were usually populated with people and pets. "Of course," I told him. "The more the merrier, to quote my mother."

"Great," Lane said. "I won't disappoint you, Nora."

But as we all said goodbye to Lane, I wondered whether that would be true. I didn't doubt that he meant it. He always seemed to be sincere. Lane's sincerity and his follow-through weren't always the same.

CHAPTER TWELVE

LANE

Sunday evening
Hernandez Ranch

N ora had three brothers, and none of them particularly liked me. They used to, but over the years I got the distinct impression that their sister's single status meant she was wasting her time with me.

They appreciated my military service, though I rarely figured into their conversation as to which branch was superior. Daniel Jr., known simply as Junior, was a marine through and through. Had he not been injured on his last deployment, he'd still be in the corps. Now he ran his father's ranch with an ease that made me forget he did it all with one good leg and one supplied by the VA hospital.

Junior's wife, Tamara, was a cookbook writer who'd been shadowing Mama Hernandez for years, trying to glean her secrets. The perpetual guessing game for ingredients had entertained the family for as long as I could remember.

Their son DJ's sole act of defiance had come in the form of earning a basketball scholarship to the University of Texas. For a family of Aggies, DJ's appearances at Sunday dinner were always peppered with teasing about the rivalry between the two colleges.

The middle brother, Miguel, was an army explosives expert who worked for a military contractor in Austin. He maintained a home on the ranch so his wife and children could live the country life they loved while he commuted. His two children—twin girls—were a delight when they weren't tormenting their father with requests for new phones, a car, and credit cards of their own.

While I didn't envy Miguel and his wife, Emma, their battle to keep two teenage girls in line, the girls looked so much like Nora that it made me wonder what our children would look like. And whether I'd be handing out cash and warnings about boys in equal measure.

Then there was Tony. Named for his maternal grandfather, Antonio, he was his mama's favorite. At least that's what his brothers claimed. Nora never involved herself in that discussion when it came up, because she knew she was Mama's favorite.

Her father's too.

I waited as the massive black iron gate that spanned the wide entrance to Hernandez Ranch swung open. Pal, who had been sleeping on the passenger side floor, climbed onto the seat to see what was happening.

A horn honked behind me, and I looked back to see Tony's battered green Range Rover. He was waving at me to stop, so I drove up just enough for both of us to get past the gate then pulled over.

Tony parked just ahead of me then jumped out to lope toward me. Unlike his more sedate brothers, Tony was always moving, always heading toward the next thing. We'd bonded early on over two things: the Air Force and our dislike of being told what to do with our lives.

After we'd done the time we promised when the Air Force agreed to pay for our Aggie educations, Tony chose to fly planes because he wanted to, while I'd left aviation entirely to go into veterinary research. I had to admit I did occasionally envy his set-your-own-hours lifestyle as a crop duster pilot when I was still at my desk well after everyone else had gone home.

Tony walked up to the open window of my truck with a grin that faded when he saw Pal. "That's quite a copilot you've got there, Lane."

"Meet Pal. He's a temporary guest at my place."

The dog was on alert but had shown no signs of aggression. However, I had no doubt if Tony made the slightest move to harm me, he'd come in close contact with an angry Belgian Malinois before he could blink.

"Stand down," I said to Pal, my voice even and controlled and my eyes on his. "Tony is one of the good ones."

"I try," Tony said with a chuckle.

Without blinking, the dog settled. "Good boy," I said, scratching behind his ear. Then I returned my attention to Nora's brother. "So, what's up?"

He had Nora's eyes and his father's way of pausing before he answered when the subject was important. The fact he hadn't answered immediately made me uneasy.

Finally, he swung his gaze back to me. "I just wanted to warn you, Lane. You're about to walk into an ambush. What you need to know is that Nora has no part in this. She doesn't know what they're planning."

A horse nickered in the field behind Tony. I looked past Nora's brother to see a pair of foals with their mothers. Pal sniffed at the air but otherwise sat very still.

"You've got me worried, Tony. What's going on?"

"Well, for starters Mama is making lasagna. Who is it in our family that loves her lasagna?" He shook his head. "That would be you, my friend. The rest of us don't care one way or the other. In fact, I love her dearly, but I'd take that frozen stuff from HEB over what my mother puts in front of us. But you? Oh yeah, that's your favorite."

"What's your point?"

"She's making lasagna for you, Lane. And our father? He's told us he's planning on taking you for a ride in his truck to see the new foals. We are absolutely not invited."

I gestured to the pasture, and Tony followed the direction I was pointing. "I can see the foals right there."

When he looked back at me, his expression was grave. "That is my point exactly."

I sat with that response for a second. Then I nodded. "I get it. Your mom is buttering me up with the lasagna that only I like, and then your father will take me for a ride to the far side of the ranch to have a talk with me about manning up and marrying his daughter."

"That's mostly correct," Tony said. "You missed the part where Junior's wife is making a key lime pie."

"Key lime pie?" While this was definitely my favorite, I'd only had one here once, and that was when Nora brought it for my birthday. In fact, I'd had all sorts of different types of pies, especially when Tamara was working on her pie cookbook, but not that one. Apparently the Hernandez clan weren't fans of key lime pie either.

Tony gave him a knowing look. "Now that you know what's waiting for you up there at the house, you've still got time to turn back."

With both hands gripping the wheel, I let out a long breath and looked up the road to the ranch house far off in the distance. "So they're all in on it?"

"Not everyone." He paused. "But I'd be lying if I said that Junior, Miguel, and I aren't wondering what's taking you so long."

"You're still single," I said. "And you're older than Nora. Why aren't they bothering you to get married?"

It was a dumb question and an obvious deflection, but it was all I had at the moment. In light of Cameron's comment last night, his parents weren't wrong to be concerned.

"The difference is, I'm happily single." He let the rest of the statement—the part where we both knew that Nora wasn't—hang in the silence between us before he spoke again. "Plus, Junior's got DJ to take over the ranch someday and the twins for Mama to pass on her recipes and wedding china to. I'm under no pressure here."

But I was. I got that loud and clear.

"Okay, well, thanks for the warning," I told him.

Tony gave me a curt nod. "So what's it going to be? Turn tail and run, or face the matchmaking?"

I grinned. "How long have you known me, Saint?"

Saint was Tony's call name in the Air Force. Pilots generally got their call names either by something related to their name or by something they'd done in pilot school. It had only been once, but Tony had lost his way back to the field when flying by instruments, and the flight instructor had to intervene.

To Catholics, Saint Anthony is the patron saint of lost things. Thus, Tony Hernandez heard himself called Saint every time the air traffic controllers spoke to him. On his last day of service, his military brothers gifted him with a silver compass engraved with the word *Saint*. It now hung from the rearview mirror of his Range Rover.

I stared at that compass for a moment longer then looked back at Tony. "Move out of my way. I'm going in."

"Brave man." He gave me a nod of approval then his expression went serious. "You do love her, don't you?"

"More than anything," I said without hesitation.

Another nod as he stepped away from the truck. "Carry on, then. Just go on ahead and don't wait for me. I'm just going to hang around out here and look at the foals for a while since I won't get to see them later."

True to his word, Tony strolled over to the fence. I rolled up the window and shifted the truck into DRIVE. After a few minutes of driving down the gravel road, I arrived at the ranch house.

The sprawling one-story home, clad in cream-colored stucco beneath a tile roof the color of burnished copper, was nestled into a grove of pecan trees. Owing to Mrs. Hernandez's love of extended family gatherings and entertaining, a circular drive out front accommodated a dozen or more vehicles and a driveway leading to a large garage that would hold at least that many more.

Nora was already here, as were Miguel and Emma. A white Volkswagen convertible with a flowered license plate holder and a pink fuzzy steering wheel likely meant that Miguel had given in and bought a car for his daughters.

I parked behind Junior's farm truck and turned off the engine. Pal's ears went up, but he looked to me for instructions.

Only then did I realize I hadn't thought about how I would get six gallons of ice cream and a Belgian Malinois inside and past the pack of pets that were yipping at us from inside the house.

This was going to take some finesse.

"Stay," I told Pal as I climbed out of the truck and went around to the back where the Blue Bell was stowed away in the Yeti cooler.

I rolled the Yeti around to the front door and then went back to the truck for Pal. Inside, the furry watch patrol were hitting the high notes. Surely someone inside the house would be heading this way soon.

I grasped the leash and held on while Pal easily jumped down from his perch on the passenger seat. If the noise on the other side of the door bothered him, he gave no indication. Instead, he remained where he landed, awaiting further instruction.

One of the twins—I could never tell which—opened the front door, and a posse of pups hurdled themselves toward us. I held firm to the leash, but Pal barely batted an eye. Instead, he sat very still, looking down at the quartet of pint-sized marauders as if they were of no interest to him at all.

This was one well-trained dog.

"Hush," I told the noisy animals.

Tony drove up just then. He spied me and shook his head.

"Why aren't you in the house yet? It was supposed to look like we didn't talk to each other beforehand."

"Five barking dogs, six gallons of Blue Bell ice cream, and a Belgian Malinois," I offered as proof.

"And a partridge in a pear tree," Tony said, climbing out of his vehicle and heading toward me. "I'll take the ice cream and you bring the MWD in. I can't help you with Mama's pack of hounds. Or Mama, for that matter."

CHAPTER THIRTEEN

Your mother's dogs are terriers, not hounds," I told Nora's brother. Tony shrugged. "They all look the same from an airplane."

"So, how did you know Pal is an MWD?"

I had removed the vest I'd found him in last night, so he only wore a collar.

"Look at him," Tony said, gesturing toward Pal with one hand and gripping the handle of the rolling cooler with the other. "He's the right breed, and he's got the training. No-brainer."

"But he doesn't have a chip or tattoo," I said. "And he found me in the parking lot of a wedding venue last night."

"Which venue?"

I told him, and he frowned. "That's the new one. I remember watching it being built from my plane. I wonder if someone around there has an MWD that's gone missing. I'd have to go up and look again, but all I remember around there are farms and ranches."

Just then Nora stepped out into the afternoon sunshine, and my heart did that stupid teenage boy thing that rendered me temporarily unable to speak. She wore a pale blue button-down shirt over faded jeans with her hair pulled up off her neck in a messy bun, showing off the strand of seed pearls that I'd given her on our first anniversary.

Tony leaned toward me. "When you look at my sister like that, all my questions about how you feel about her are answered. Just make it happen soon, okay?" he said softly.

"I heard that," Nora said.

Tony grinned then wheeled past Nora, stopping only for a moment to give her a hug. When he opened the front door, the pack of dogs followed him in.

Nora walked toward me, and I embraced her then kissed her. It had only been last night that I'd held her like this, but I missed her all the same.

I was on the far side of thirty but acting like a lovestruck kid. I mustered a smile.

"So this is Pal." Nora knelt in front of the dog, keeping a respectful distance. Pal sniffed in her direction. "He's beautiful."

It took all I had not to say, "So are you." I know, but that's what I was thinking.

"And well trained," I told her. "He barely noticed your mother's pack of dogs when they came out to investigate."

Nora chuckled. "Are you sure he's not deaf? I heard them all the way back in the kitchen."

"Oh, he heard them just fine. I suspect he was waiting on me to give him permission to chase them off."

"Hey there, Pal," Nora said to the dog as she held out her hand for him to sniff. "Do you mind if I pet you?"

Pal looked up at me as if asking for permission. When I nodded, he moved closer to Nora. A moment later, he was cozying up to Nora and getting his belly rubbed.

"So much for his military training," I quipped.

Nora looked up at me and smiled sweetly. "I guess I have a way with soldiers."

I knelt beside her and gave her a kiss on the cheek. "You have a way with this one." Pal nudged me with his nose.

"I think he's jealous."

I matched her grin. "Too bad. If I want to kiss my girl, I will."

Pal scrambled to his feet just as Nora's father walked around the corner of the house. "I just might have something to say about that," Daniel Hernandez Sr. said.

I stood and reached out to shake with him, holding the leash tight with the other hand. He gave me an appraising look then turned his attention to Nora and the dog.

"Good of you to show up," Daniel said, his tone neutral. "The missus made your favorite lasagna." He paused. "See you got yourself a dog. Good to know you can commit to something."

"He's not mine," I said, ignoring the dig.

"He found us at the wedding venue last night," Nora added. "We're trying to find his owner."

Daniel knelt down in front of Pal. The dog tensed and looked up at me.

"Stay, Pal." I kept my tone even but firm.

"He's an MWD." Daniel leaned in to inspect Pal's right ear then climbed to his feet. "There's no tattoo. What gives?"

"We know, Dad," Nora said. "That's what we're trying to figure out."

Daniel offered the back of his hand to Pal, who sniffed at it approvingly. Then he allowed Nora's father to scratch him behind the ear. All the while he sat very still.

"He's a good one," Daniel finally said, climbing to his feet.

One of the twins appeared in the door again. "Nana says we're eating on the patio. Go around or come inside."

The door slammed shut again.

"Well, all right, then," Nora said. "Something tells me she quoted Mama word for word."

Daniel shook his head. "Those girls are sounding more and more like my wife every day. Good thing the weather's going to be nice tonight. No clouds and a low in the upper sixties. Good old Texas spring weather."

Nora laughed. "That's our cue. Come on, Lane. He's already met Dad, Tony, and Mama's menagerie. Let's introduce Pal to the rest of the family."

The ranch house's flagstone patio spanned half the length of the building, stretching out to stop at the edge of the pecan grove. Pal and I followed Nora over to the massive copper firepit, surrounded by a dozen Adirondack chairs.

Miguel stoked the fire while Junior sat nearby telling him what he was doing wrong. The air was thick with the scent of woodsmoke and whatever was cooking on the grill that was located just outside the kitchen door.

"I thought we were having lasagna," I whispered to Nora.

She smiled. "You're having lasagna. The men in my family think it's not Sunday supper if steaks aren't on the table."

"Steaks and lasagna," I said with a smile. "I'm not mad about this."

"Or the key lime pie, I'm sure." She slowed her steps. "Between the two of us, I think something's up. I get my mom wanting to entice you here with your favorite of her dishes but when your favorite pie—one that none of us are particularly keen on—is also on the menu?"

I exhaled slowly and tried to decide if I ought to pass on her brother's warning. I decided I'd handle that without involving her.

"I am her favorite." I upped my grin. "And I brought six gallons of Blue Bell for the rest of you."

"And a dog," Miguel said, stepping back from the firepit. "Is he yours, Lane?"

As Miguel drew closer, Pal went on alert. He sat bolt upright and nudged me then strained forward as if awaiting the command to bolt.

"What's up, Pal?" I stood and moved closer to Miguel. "You want to meet Mikey?"

That was Nora's nickname for her brother. I used it sparingly and only when I wanted to stay on good terms.

The dog inched closer, circling Miguel, who stood stock-still. "He's not going to bite me, is he?"

"He's too well trained for that," Nora said. "Watch how he looks up at Lane for permission before he makes a move."

Pal sniffed at Miguel's pants legs then zeroed in on his boots. He went into a seated position and looked up at me then let out a soft yip.

"He's alerting," Miguel said.

"To your boots," Nora said. "What's on them that would attract his attention?"

"These are my work boots. Emma won't let me wear them in the house because she's afraid I'll track in something from the jobsite," he said.

"Explosives," I said. "This dog alerts on explosives and PTSD."

Miguel gave me an even look. "How do you know he alerts at PTSD?"

"The fireworks," Nora said. "I found him cowering in between two vehicles at the wedding site when the fireworks were going off. I thought he'd smother Lane before he got the dog off him."

Miguel's expression changed only slightly, but it was enough to let me know he understood. I reached down to scratch Pal behind the ear as Miguel walked over to check the steaks. The dog stiffened then once again strained at the leash. I gave in and let Pal lead me to Miguel.

"He's persistent," Miguel said.

I shrugged. "I guess so."

He lifted the lid to inspect the food cooking there. Without looking away, Miguel spoke softly. "Does Nora know?"

I shook my head.

Miguel closed the lid and turned to me. "That's why there's no ring on her finger yet."

"Yeah," I said, meeting his gaze. "I love her too much to make her deal with my issues."

He seemed to be considering what I said. "Then fix it."

"I am," I said on an exhale of breath.

Miguel gave me an appraising look then a curt nod. "See that you do."

While we were talking, Nora had settled onto the chair next to Junior and filled her brothers in on how Pal came to be with me. By the time she was done, Daniel had wandered out to take over the tending of the steaks. Pal's nose lifted when the elder Hernandez walked up, but otherwise he remained at my side. His attention, however, rarely wavered from Miguel.

This dog was definitely trained in some sort of explosive detection. He had to be. Either that, or he really liked Miguel.

"Got some new foals," Daniel said as he walked toward us. "Thought you and I would go take a look at them after we eat our supper, Lane."

"I'll go too," Nora said. "I would love to see the foals up close."

Daniel reached our circle of chairs just in time to look down at me with a serious expression. "Just Lane and me."

NORA

Sunday evening
Hernandez Ranch

Before I could make an argument for going to see the foals with Dad and Lane, Tony burst out of the house with Miguel's wife following a step behind. "Tell him what you told me, Emma. About the trainer."

My ears perked up, as did Pal's.

"Dog trainer?" Lane asked before I could.

"No," Emma said, crossing the patio in a swirl of skirts. My sister-in-law loved the boho look, and today's outfit was no exception. She'd somehow managed to make a black T-shirt, a multicolored skirt, and a messy bun look like they belonged on a runway model.

Maybe because that's what she used to be.

She perched on the armrest of her husband's chair, and Miguel wrapped his arm around her. "So Tony said you were wondering if there was anyone in town who might be connected to military dogs." She glanced down and noticed Pal for the first time. "Oh my goodness, who is that?"

I introduced her to our furry guest and gave her the short version of how he came to be here with Lane. "So you can imagine that someone is missing him terribly," I said, finishing the story.

"Of course. He's beautiful. And so well trained." Emma looked down at Miguel. "Why can't we get our dog to sit like that?"

Miguel chuckled. "Because our dog is twelve pounds of fur and not much else. I'm pretty sure the doll clothes the twins put on her have hurt her little brain."

Emma gave him a playful nudge. "Be nice. Pup Tart might not be the smartest dog on the block, but she's loyal and loving. And those doll clothes, as you call them? Let's just say that Peach Nelson's doggie attire is sought after and expensive." She shrugged. "She's practically the Vera Wang of Brenham."

I suppressed the laughter that tried to erupt. Peach Nelson, or

Grandma Peach, as Marigold called her, was the wife of Reverend Nelson. She designed dog clothes and, until her recent retirement, baked pies professionally.

She was also a hoot. And most of the time it was intentional.

"Emma," Tony said, "could we get to the part where you tell everyone about the trainer, please? I don't want a discussion with my brother about the price of your dog's clothes to derail the conversation."

Miguel gave her a we'll-talk-about-this-later look. Emma ignored her husband to smile at me. Then she turned her attention to Lane. "I go to that new ladies-only gym downtown—the one that's in the same block with Nora's restaurant. Just the other side of the Pupcake."

"Pupcake?" Miguel said.

"They make treats for dogs," Daniel supplied. "I've been known to buy a thing or two for my hounds and your mama's pack of house dogs on occasion. Just going in to see what's there after eating at Nora's place, of course."

"Back to the gym?" I suggested gently.

"Anyway," Emma continued, "the best part about the gym, other than the heavenly whirlpool, is the classes they offer. There are all kinds, so I love to switch them up."

"The trainer, Em?" Miguel said gently.

"Yes, right. Well, a couple of weeks ago, a new class started up called Babes Boot Camp that meets three times a week. Monday, Wednesday, and Friday at nine. It's fun but not fun, you know?"

Her gaze swept the chairs containing the Hernandez brothers, their father, and Lane. All five shook their heads.

"I know what you mean," I said. "So is this class taught by a trainer who's in the military?"

"Was in the military," she corrected. "Her name is Leigh Fraser. She told our class that she left for medical reasons, though I cannot imagine what those might be. That class is hard."

"Does Leigh train dogs?" I asked, wondering what the connection might be.

"I don't know, but she owns a dog that looks just like that one."

She nodded toward Pal. "Same breed and size, so maybe that's where he belongs?"

"How do you know this?" Miguel asked his wife.

"Oh, that's the best part. She always brings the dog, Sarge. He's well trained, so he just sits in the corner and keeps an eye on us." Emma paused. "He wasn't there on Friday."

Lane spoke up. "You wouldn't happen to know if Leigh lives out near Thistledown Farms, would you?"

"No idea," she said with a lift of her shoulder.

"Thanks, Emma," I told her. "After I open the kitchen in the morning, I'll walk down to the gym and see what I can find out."

"Speaking of finding things out," Dad said, settling on the chair next to Lane, "I would love to find out when I'm going to need to pay for a wedding. Nora's not getting any younger."

"Dad," I exclaimed in unison with my brothers.

My father had the nerve to look like he had no idea what the problem was. "You're over thirty, Nora. Your mama had three kids by your age, and they were already in elementary school."

"Come on," Tony said. "I'm not married either, and I'm older than her. Leave Nora alone."

"It's not Nora I'm talking to," Dad said, shifting positions to look at Lane. "Son, I have had arthritic hound dogs that move faster than you."

CHAPTER FOURTEEN

LANE

Sunday evening
Hernandez Ranch and Brenham, Texas

The worst part about what Daniel Hernandez Sr. had just said was that he wasn't wrong. However, all four Hernandez children and one Hernandez daughter-in-law were telling him just the opposite.

Loudly.

Miguel gave me an "I can't help you" look. As a fellow serviceman, he knew my story was mine to tell. I appreciated that.

The dinner bell—actually a giant triangle hung by the back door—clanged, interrupting the noise. Mama stood surveying the group. "I changed my mind. We're eating inside. So come on in before it gets cold."

I rose and met Daniel's gaze, intent on saying something but not sure what that something was. Pal nudged my leg as if reminding me of his presence.

I reached down to scratch the dog behind his ear. He hadn't liked what had just transpired, and I wouldn't doubt he'd have taken a bite out of Nora's father's leg if he'd been given permission.

Then Miguel walked by and he sat, alerting. Nora's brother shook his head and kept going.

"Come on now, Lane," Mama called. "And bring that dog in, long as he won't bother mine."

"He won't, Mama," I promised. "He's well trained and does what he's told."

She grinned, and I saw Nora's smile in hers. "Well, that's better than all of my dogs then. And for that matter, better than most of the menfolk who sit around this table."

I grinned and followed Nora inside to settle around the massive dining room table. Pal curled under the table at my feet, oblivious to the other dogs' curious sniffs.

With the energy of a woman more than half her age, Nora's mother buzzed around the table delivering dishes of food and chattering about recipes, ingredients, and just about anything else she could think of. When Mama Hernandez finally took her seat at Daniel's right, silence fell.

Anyone who had been at this table more than once knew it was time for the blessing over the food. Just as Daniel began the prayer, my phone rang. I quickly reached to silence it without looking at the screen.

Daniel gave me a look then resumed. He'd just reached the part where he was calling down blessings on the food and the hands that made it when my phone rang again.

This time I checked for the caller before I hit silence. It was Pop.

I waited until the prayer ended in a chorus of amens then retrieved my phone again. "I'm so sorry," I said to the group. "It's my father, and he's called twice. That's not like him."

"Call him back," Nora's mother urged while Nora gave a worried nod. "I know Elvin, and he wouldn't call twice if it wasn't something important."

"Okay. Sure. This won't take long."

Pal and I went out to the back deck and then I hit redial on Pop's last call. He answered on the second ring.

"What's wrong, Pop?" I asked.

"Hey, Lane," he said, his voice tight. "Are you by any chance in Brenham tonight?"

"Close to it," I told him. "I'm out at Nora's folks' place having dinner. What's up?"

"Oh goodness. I certainly don't want to interrupt your dinner. Tell Maria I'm so sorry to be a bother."

"You're not a bother," I paused. "But I can tell something is wrong. Spill it, Pop." Then I added, "Please."

"Well, all right." He paused. "I'm over at the clinic. Since I'm taking over for Tyler and Kristin starting tomorrow, I thought I'd come in and familiarize myself with the place just in case they've changed anything since I worked there."

"That makes sense," I said, trying my best to refrain from telling him to get to the point.

"It would have," Pop said, "except that there were a few things that I needed to grab off the top shelf in the storeroom. I never did put anything up there because it requires a ladder to reach it."

"Pop," I said. "What happened?"

"Well, the good news is I now know where everything is in the clinic." Another pause. "The bad news is I fell off that ladder, and I'm pretty sure I've broken something."

I groaned as my heart lodged in my throat. Pal nudged my free hand.

"Pop, we just talked about you not climbing ladders, remember? If anything happened to you. . ."

"Lane," he said testily, "I landed on my rear, not my head. I remember. But that doesn't fix the current situation. So should I go ahead and call for a ride to the hospital? I'd normally think just a trip to my doctor would be in order, but I've managed to do this on a Sunday."

Nora stepped outside and gave me a questioning look. I held up my hand to indicate for her to wait a moment and then I'd fill her in.

"Are you in any pain right now?"

"I'm all right. I'd just prefer to have two working legs. I'm guessing this is going to be a fracture of the tibia, not compound, so I'm sure I'll heal just fine." He paused "Anyway, I think I can get to my feet."

"Don't you dare," I said sharply. "You stay right where you are, and I'll be there in ten minutes. Got it?"

"If you're sure," he said, and I heard the gratitude in his words.

"Pop, I'm absolutely sure."

"The back door at the employee entrance is unlocked. I won't be hard to find once you're inside."

We said goodbye, and I tucked the phone into my pocket. The wind rustled the leaves of the pecan trees, and off in the distance a horse whinnied. Nora closed the distance between us to take my hand.

"You look worried."

"I am. Pop fell at the vet clinic," I told Nora. "He thinks he's broken his leg. I need to get him to the ER."

"Yes, absolutely." Nora nodded. "Go. Now." Then she looked down at Pal. "Do you think he's okay to stay with me?"

"He likes you," I said. "So I think so. If there's an issue, he can always be crated until I can come back for him."

"I don't think that will be necessary. I'll take him home with me after dinner, and you can call me with an update later, okay?"

I walked over to Nora and embraced her, kissing the top of her head. "Pray he's okay," I said. "I can't lose him too."

"Oh, Lane," she whispered.

This was the first time since Mom died that I thought about what it would be like without both of them. Sure, it was just a broken leg, or so Pop thought. But it was too close to losing him for my taste. What if he'd hit his head instead?

And worse, what if it had happened at a time when I wasn't available to take the call? I'd ignored so many of his calls because I was busy or, worse, just wasn't in the mood to talk to him at that moment.

I'd neglected him and Nora. Who else had I neglected?

"Lane," Nora said softly. "Are you okay?"

I felt Pal leaning hard against my leg. "Yeah," I said, my voice rough as I held her at arm's length. "I will be okay."

She smiled then reached up on tiptoe to kiss me softly. "And so will your father. How about I walk you out? I'll explain to the family where you've gone. That'll be much faster than being quizzed by everyone before you can get going."

We walked around the house to the spot where my truck was parked. Pal's ears twitched when I opened the door.

"Stay," I told him firmly.

Nora scratched him behind the ear. "We're going to hang out at my place for a while," she told him in a gentle voice. "And to make sure you don't eat my cat, I'm going to feed you plenty of steak before we go home."

"He's not going to eat your cat," I said. "But lots of steak is probably a good idea. Or rather, a moderate amount so he'll have a full belly and feel sleepy. It's not what I would normally do, but—"

"This from the guy who fed him a Whataburger last night?" she said with a grin. "Go see about your dad. I've got this." She paused. "And Lane? I'm sorry about the pressure my father put on you tonight. It was embarrassing."

"He's not wrong, Nora." I paused. "But that's a conversation for another time."

"It is," she agreed.

I gave Pal the command to stay one more time before I climbed into my truck and closed the door. I needn't have bothered because he was lying on his back getting a belly rub from Nora before I left the driveway.

I might have exceeded the posted speed limit a time or two on my drive into town, but I figured if I got stopped, that would likely mean an escort to the clinic. As it was, I made it there in record time with no speeding tickets.

Now to get Pop to the hospital.

I found him sitting on the floor, his back against the wall and the ladder nowhere in sight. His eyes were closed, which gave me a moment of panic before he opened them.

"Pop," I said on a rush of breath, "where's the ladder?"

"In the storeroom. I told you that."

"But you're out here."

"Someone had to open the door. It's bad enough I'm in this fix. I sure didn't want to have to tell Tyler and Kristin that their back door got busted out so I could be rescued."

"Pop, you told me the door was unlocked."

He shrugged. "After I hung up with you I figured I'd better check. Sure enough, I was wrong. I had locked it."

The distance from the storeroom to where he currently sat was about twenty yards. He would have had to crawl that far with a broken leg in order to reach the door.

I thought of reprimanding him but shook my head instead. "Let me take a look at that leg, tough guy."

"Not feeling so tough right now," he admitted.

I lifted his pants leg to assess the damage then sat back on my heels. "I'm going to call for a paramedic, Pop. If I try to get you into my truck to transport you to the ER, I may make things worse."

I made the call then put my phone away. "They'll be here in a few minutes." I thought of offering to get him something to eat or drink then decided not to do that. If surgery was necessary to repair the break, it'd be better if he hadn't recently had something.

"Thank you again," Pop said smiling. "You're a good son."

"And you're an even better father," I told him. "Except for that penchant for climbing ladders, that is. You really need to stop doing that."

"I've learned my lesson," he said. "Believe it or not, while I was waiting for you to get here, I did a little online shopping."

"You're joking."

"Nope, I'm serious." He reached for his phone then navigated to a website. A moment later he showed me the screen. "It's one of those grabber things that lets you reach high shelves. Reminds me of that cartoon you used to watch. *Inspector Grab It*, I think it was called."

"It was *Inspector Gadget*," I said, thinking of the cartoon sleuth who used a plethora of gadgets to solve crimes. "And yeah, it does a little."

The reminder of the cartoon sent my father down a rabbit trail of conversation that involved his favorite memories from my childhood. Pop was just beginning a story about the year I decided I wanted to be Carrot Star Man—a carrot-eating superhero I made up—when the wail of the ambulance sounded in the distance. I had to insist that I wasn't the real Carrot Star Man until the greenery was added.

"I'm going to go to the parking lot to make sure they know which door to stop in front of." I stood but my father grasped my hand. "I'll be right back."

"I know you will," he said. "It's just that I've missed you so much. I know you're busy, and I'm so proud of you. Your mother was too. First college, then the military, and now a researcher at a prestigious university? Once the ambulance arrives, I may not get a chance to tell you that. And I sure didn't want to miss that chance."

His words took me by surprise and made me a little wobbly on my feet. I always knew my parents were proud of me. But hearing it now? With Pop waiting for an ambulance?

But the part that really pierced my heart was him admitting how much he'd missed me. "I missed you too, Pop," I said as the scream of the siren grew louder.

First Nora and now Pop. What job was worth being away from the people I loved the most?

The ambulance lights reflected in the room as I stepped outside to wave the driver toward the door. The back door opened and a familiar face looked over in my direction.

I couldn't remember his name, but I did remember the conversation we'd had before he stitched Nora's forehead. "Army medical corps," I called.

"USAF DVM," he said with a chuckle as his partner removed the stretcher. "Twice in one week? Are you looking for a quantity discount?"

I closed the distance between us to shake his hand. Then I spied his name tag. Ewing.

"Different patient this time," I said. "Good work on Nora, by the way. She's doing great."

"Glad to hear it," he said then nodded toward the open door. "Dispatch says we've got a seventy-two-year-old male with a possible broken leg."

"Yes, that's right. My father was here alone and fell off a ladder. He's just inside the door. He's lucid and answering questions, and he claims he hasn't hit his head."

"Sounds like you did a decent triage on him. Not bad for an expert in animal medicine." Ewing grinned as he wrote down what I'd said then tucked away his notepad. "Thank you."

I stepped out of the way and let the experts in human medicine take over. Once Pop was loaded, I let Ewing know I'd meet them at the ER.

Then I climbed into my truck and retrieved my phone. I had a call to make.

CHAPTER FIFTEEN

Nora

Monday
Brenham, Texas

I was sitting in my car in the alley behind Simply Eat when the call came in from Lane. With papers scattered over the front seat and Pal napping in the back, it took me a moment to find my phone.

He'd texted at some point during the night to let me know that his father's leg had been reset and he'd be staying overnight with him at the hospital. I was hoping he had good news.

"How's your dad?" I asked. "Mom sent me home with a whole pan of lasagna for the two of you, so I hope he still has his appetite."

"Tell your mom thank you from both of us. Pop is doing fine." The moment Lane's voice came through the car speakers, Pal's ears perked up. "No surgery required, which is great. He'll stay in the hospital until tomorrow at the earliest. He's not happy about that, but since when does my father like sitting still?"

"True. Does he need a place to stay once he's been released? When I told the family what had happened, Mama insisted your dad be brought out to the ranch to recuperate."

"That's nice of them," he said. "I'll let Pop know."

I wanted to say that Dr. Bishop was family. He was like a second dad to me. But just yesterday I'd been planning to break up with Lane, and I wasn't certain I felt any different today.

"How did Pal do at your place? I guess he didn't eat the cat, or I would have heard about it by now."

I reached over to the passenger seat to pat Pal. "He did great, and no, he did not eat the cat. In fact, when I woke up this morning the two of them were curled up sound asleep together on the blanket I had put down for the dog."

"Sounds like he likes you," Lane said with a chuckle, "and your cat."

"I think so too," I told him as I spied the trash truck coming up the alley. "Although she's not my cat yet. We're still looking for her owner. I've got Mari and her team putting the word out. Hang on a sec. It's about to get noisy."

The big truck barreled past, leaving a cloud of dust and trash-truck aroma in its wake. I rolled up my window and then rolled down the passenger side so the car wouldn't get stuffy.

"Okay. All clear."

"So, where are you?" he asked.

"In the alley. I had to come up and do payroll for the staff. And since it's Monday, we also had to place a grocery order. That needs to happen early, and I'm supervising the details today, not Roz, so I've been here"—I checked my watch and saw it was now half past seven—"for about thirty minutes."

"You brought Pal to the restaurant? Is that allowed?"

"Not in the kitchen," I said. "The health department would shut me down if they found out. And a dog that size is a little hard to hide under my desk. Which is why I'm in the alley. Mari is going to come by and pick him up—if Pal will let her—and take him to the clinic. She's there now, so I'm waiting until she gets a minute to swing by here. If he's fussy about it then I'll take him home and let Roz run the place today."

"Actually," Lane said, and then a dog barked in the background.

Pal's ears went up again, and he looked at me as if I'd been hiding a canine somewhere in my car. Then he sniffed the air.

"Lane, you don't have a dog other than the one that's in my car right now. Where are you?"

"It's kind of a long story."

The dog barked again, this time louder. Pal leaped over the front seat and into the back in search of the phantom pup.

"I've got time," I said.

"So if you have time, do you mind dropping Pal off at the clinic yourself?" He paused. "It'd be less traumatic for him, don't you think?"

"Sure, I can do that."

The background barking got louder. Pal growled softly under his breath as he jumped back into the front seat.

"It's okay, pup," I said as I scratched him behind his ear. "It's just us here. No other dogs."

Pal stuck his head out the open window and sniffed as the barking continued.

"I should hang up. That barking is making Pal a little crazy."

Just as I got the words out of my mouth, Pal gave the air one more sniff then bolted out the window. "Oh great," I said. "Gotta go."

I ended the call and stuffed the phone into my pocket, then climbed out of my car, and went in pursuit. I didn't have to go far.

I stood at the bottom of the staircase leading to the apartment of my new building. The apartment that was off-limits to man and beast.

However, Pal hadn't received that memo.

My phone rang. It was Lane.

"Did you lose him?" he asked, the barking in the background now gone.

"No, I'm looking at him. Your dog has broken through police tape and is currently trying to figure out how to get inside the apartment."

"The one next door?"

I called the dog, but he ignored me. "That would be the one. I'm going to get the leash."

"Before you do that, do you have any dog treats in your car?"

"Fresh out, Lane," I said with more than a little sarcasm.

"Then grab something from inside the restaurant and bring it out. Tell him he did a good job and you have a treat for him. See what he does."

I did as he said. Pal sniffed the air, remaining in a seated position. When I said, "Good dog. Here's your treat," he came running.

"It worked."

"Then I've got good news and bad news." He paused. "First the good news. Pal is a well-trained dog, which we guessed at but weren't completely certain."

"And the bad news?" I supplied.

"The bad news is I'm about 99.9 percent certain that he's trained to sniff explosives. Miguel and I thought he was alerting to Miguel's boots at your folks' place. Now I'm sure he was."

I looked up at the apartment then down at the dog who was happily munching on a buttered dinner roll. "Then that means that it wasn't drugs that caused the fire." I let out a long breath.

It also explained why an ATF agent was on site yesterday.

Pal finished his treat and looked up at me as if asking for another. "That's enough for now." I opened the passenger door and patted the seat. "In the car, big guy."

Obedient as ever, Pal did as he was told. I closed the door and hurried around to get in the driver's seat. Then I sent a text to Mari to let her know I'd be delivering the dog to her at the clinic.

Great. I'll be in the back. Tell Cassidy to let me know when you arrive.

"Bomb-sniffing dog," I said, looking at Pal in the rearview mirror. "Well, all right then. Good boy, Pal. I wish I'd had you with me in the building on Friday."

Pal's tail wagged. Then he gave me that adorable doggy grin again.

"Lane, are you still there?"

"I am."

"Okay, doggy transport is in motion," I told him as I buckled my seat belt and shifted the vehicle into Drive. "We'll be at the clinic in a few minutes."

Not long after, I walked into Lone Star Vet Clinic with Pal on his leash. As we exchanged greetings, Brianna jumped up to greet us with papers in her hand. "I was just about to put these on the bulletin board. We'll find the owners for this guy and the tabby cat, Nora. Don't you worry."

I mustered a smile. "Is Mari here? I'm supposed to be delivering Pal to her."

Brianna placed the flyers on the counter between us. I kept my attention on her rather than looking at the lost pet photos. "I'm supposed to send you back to Exam Room 1," she said, matching my grin. "Someone will be with you in a few minutes."

"Thank you."

I headed down the hall. The room held the familiar veterinary office smell of antiseptic and cleaning solution. I hadn't been in one of the exam rooms since I gave up my job with the pet food company, but the same posters from my old company were still on the wall.

I glanced down at Pal, who looked surprisingly at ease here. Then the door opened and Lane stepped inside.

Wearing scrubs with the Lone Star Veterinary Clinic logo on the shirt pocket.

He ran a hand through his hair, his smile a little crooked and his eyes tired. "I was going to buy flowers to surprise you, but there was this emergency call with a Chihuahua who thought he could take on the neighbor's cat, so I ended up going straight from Pop's hospital room to the clinic."

"Well," I said slowly as Pal nudged Lane. "You definitely surprised me. Are you helping out today?"

Those tired eyes twinkled. "I'm taking over for Pop until the newlyweds return. Cameron is helping as his schedule allows, but I'll be the only full-time vet for the next two weeks."

"Who are you?" blurted out of my mouth before I could stop myself.

Instead of taking offense, Lane laughed. "I know, right? I had already spoken to my supervisor about doing this, but when Pop got the gig instead of me, I called it off. It was just a matter of making another call to let him know what happened." His expression sobered as he reached out to grasp my hand. "I told you I was working on fixing what I've broken, Nora."

A flood of emotions washed over me. I stared at his hand in mine.

Pal wove his way between us to lean hard against the back of my knees, sending me lurching forward into Lane's arms.

"Good work, Pal," Lane said with a chuckle, "but you're an explosives dog, not a matchmaker. And I could have managed this without your help."

I looked up at Lane. "Oh, I don't know. He has a talent for putting people together."

"We were already together, Nora. Never forget that, because I haven't, even when it may have looked or felt like I had."

So many responses came to mind. I said none of them. Nor did I tell him that on Saturday night we most certainly were at the edge of not being together.

Ever.

Instead, I pressed my cheek against his shoulder and listened to the steady, even beat of his heart.

"Nora," Lane whispered, his voice rough. "Look at me."

I did, and he leaned down to kiss me. Then the door flew open.

"Oops, sorry." Mari stood in the doorway, one hand covering her mouth and the other grasping the door frame. "I didn't know this room was occupied."

Pal padded over and pushed against the door with his nose in an obvious attempt at closing it. I couldn't help but laugh, and neither could Mari and Lane.

"You've got him trained, Dr. Lane," Mari said.

"I think he picked up that move on his own," Lane said.

Mari looked down at the dog. "Well, okay then, sir. I will leave."

"Actually, I was just going," I said. "I've got work to do at the restaurant and a call scheduled with the insurance company about the building. I'm sure you guys will be keeping Lane busy today."

Mari nodded. "We had already cut back on our usual number of appointments in anticipation of Dr. Lane's dad being here, so there's that. But we're still busy, which means Lane will be busy."

He shrugged. "I don't mind. Except that I'm probably going straight from here to the hospital to see about Pop. If I don't fall asleep there, I'll be dragging myself to his place for a few hours of shut-eye."

Mari shook her head. "Brianna has already talked to Dr. Cameron about being the overnight on-call doc, at least until your dad is home and settled. He agreed." She paused to nod at Pal. "Anyway, I thought I might take this guy with me to the back and let him run around in the outside area."

"Thank you," he said, his tone grateful. "Let me know if he gives you any trouble. Remember, he responds to rewards."

Mari leaned down to scratch the dog behind his ear. "I think we'll do fine. But I will." Then she looked at me. "Do you have a minute to chat before you get going?"

"Sure," I said.

"Great. Just come see me when you're done here." With that she took Pal's leash and walked out. The dog gave Lane a brief look then followed the vet tech to disappear down the hall.

Lane watched them go. Then he turned to me. "I'd better get back to work. What are your plans today? After you talk to Mari, that is."

"I have that insurance call at ten, and then I'll help with the lunch rush. After, I thought I would follow up on that lead that Emma gave us yesterday and see if I can talk to the trainer at the ladies' gym down the street." I paused. "And I'm considering calling Trent Mendez. He's the ATF agent I met while he was working a case involving Mari's aunt and the rescue. Her husband, Wyatt, helped them catch a guy who was doing some shady things with bombs."

"That sounds dangerous," he said. "I don't remember any of that."

I shrugged. "It could have been, but it all turned out okay. And I'm pretty sure it was all kept quiet. That kind of publicity isn't good for Brenham. No one wants to live in a place where people are randomly planting bombs. Anyway, I thought it might be a good idea to let him know what happened with Pal this morning."

Lane seemed to think a moment, then he nodded. "Good idea. Has anyone in law enforcement talked to you about what happened in the apartment?"

"Other than a quick conversation with Todd Dennison, no. I sent him a copy of the video that Dad made when we were looking at the place. I'm hoping that will at least establish what the apartment looked like before the creeps who almost blew it up broke in."

Lane gave me a tired smile. "I wish I could be of more help with that."

I touched his arm. "I'm just glad you're here. In Brenham, I mean."

I gave Lane an appraising look. The jury was out on whether he'd continue this behavior, but if this was the new Dr. Lane Bishop, then I would definitely be sticking around to see what he did next.

He traced my jawbone with his finger. "You just went deep in thought there, Nora. Care to share?"

I met his gaze and matched his grin. "No, I absolutely do not."

"Figures," came out on a long breath. "I'll call you later."

I nodded, kissed him soundly, and then watched him walk away. Then I went in search of Mari. I found her in the outdoor pet run watching two small mutts who were running in circles around Pal. Meanwhile, the big dog seemed content to sleep in the sunshine.

She smiled when she spied me. "It's good to have him here, isn't it? Lane, I mean."

"It is." I closed the distance between us. "You said you have something you want to talk about?"

"I do, but first how's your head? The cut, I mean."

"Healing," I told her. "Other than keeping the bandages dry while I shampoo, I haven't had any issues."

Mari nodded. "Good. So, about the search for Pal's home. After church on Sunday, Parker and I went home and started looking into the question of whether any of our contacts had heard of specialized training facilities for dogs like Pal in the Brenham area. So far we haven't come up with much."

"That's too bad," I said. "I was hoping there would be some simple solution like Pal had run off or been stolen from a place that trains military dogs and advertises locally."

"Not so simple," she told me. "Most of them don't say what they do other than use cute names like Train-R Dogs and Bad Dog B Gone. Their ads tell you very little, and so far on the calls that Parker and I have made, we aren't getting much information as to the types of training offered."

"You'd think that a trainer doing this kind of training would advertise that," I said. "Speaking of trainers, that reminds me. My sister-in-law told me about a personal trainer named Leigh Fraser who teaches a class at the ladies' gym called Babe Boot Camp or something like that. Apparently she has a dog that looks like Pal. I plan to go over after the lunch rush and talk to her."

"About what?" Mari asked.

Her question took me by surprise. "Well, first to see if her dog is missing. And if it's not, then I guess I figured I could ask her if she knows of anyone in the area who breeds dogs like hers. Oh, and I'll also find out if she took her dog to a trainer or if she knows of one." I shrugged. "It all sounds silly, doesn't it? But that's the best I can think of at this point."

"No, it sounds like you're following every lead," Mari said. "And she may be plugged into a community of dog owners with information that will help us."

"That's what I'm hoping."

"I can tell you that if there's a Belgian Malinois or German shepherd missing, no one has reported this to any of the shelters or rescues that I've spoken with," Mari said. "Dr. Cameron confirmed that he hasn't heard of any inquiries either."

"That's good news, I guess." I paused. "I really think Lane wants to keep him."

Mari grinned. "And from what I saw in the exam room, Pal wants to keep Lane."

"He's a good dog," I said. "So well trained. And that makes me a little nervous as to what Lane's assistant and his intern are going to find out when they make their calls."

"Oh, that's right," Mari said. "He was going to assign his assistant and intern a list of calls to make based on some research he'd done."

"Including calling Fort Cavazos to see if anyone is missing a trainee dog. Is it too much to pray that they don't find anything either?"

"Not too much at all." Mari smiled. "I'll agree with you on that prayer."

"But, Mari, I've got a bad feeling about the Fort Cavazos call." I glanced over at Pal. "He's just so well trained. Oh, and I don't think I told you this, but Lane believes he is trained in detecting explosives."

Her eyes widened. "Really? What makes him think that?" I told her what happened in the alley. "Oh no. So someone tried to blow up the apartment? That's terrible."

"I don't know if they tried, but they almost did." My phone buzzed with a text from Roz. I read it and frowned. "Looks like I'm headed to the restaurant instead. There's a mix-up with the grocery order again, and this time the whole thing has been canceled. I knew I should have stuck around to follow through after I placed the order this morning." I leaned down to scratch Pal behind his ear. "Be a good boy, Pal."

Then I glanced up at Mari. "Start praying. I'm off to see if I can get some answers. After I figure out the grocery situation."

I swore that dog grinned at me.

CHAPTER SIXTEEN

I was still smiling a few minutes later as I arrived at Simply Eat and let myself in the back door with the key. The kitchen was empty, but the sound of voices in the dining area told me that prep was underway.

By the looks of the food on the counter, the grocery issue appeared to be settled. The order must not have been canceled after all.

I spied Roz and Shane rolling silverware into napkins at a table in the dining room. It was nice to see the two of them chatting and acting friendly. Although Shane appeared to be well able to do all the tasks he was assigned, I got the distinct impression that he and Roz did not get along. I was glad to be wrong about that.

Turning away, I went to my office and closed the door. The little room I claimed for my office had literally been carved out of a former storage closet, so there was no window and only just enough space for my desk, a file cabinet, and a bookshelf. A poster of van Gogh's *Sunflowers* on the wall in front of me provided the only spot of color in the cramped space.

I'd promised myself I would do something creative in here—bright paint or cheerful wallpaper—when I had time. A year later, I still hadn't found the time.

"Speaking of time," I said under my breath as I checked my watch, "time to do something productive."

With a little over an hour before I was due on the phone with the insurance adjuster, I decided to make a call to my friendly neighborhood ATF agent to see if I could get some information out of him. It didn't take long to find a number for Trent Mendez.

Brenham might be a big town, but when it comes to its citizens, it can be a very small town. It turned out that Miguel knew him from work and had his office number. The only problem with going that route was it took me far too long to get off the phone with my brother. Finally, after I promised I'd give him a report if I discovered anything new, we ended the call.

Trent answered on the second ring.

After we exchanged greetings, I got right to the point. "My apartment caught fire because of explosives, not drugs."

Silence.

"Trent? That was a statement, not a question. Did you hear me?"

"Loud and clear," he said.

"And?"

I heard what sounded like the squeak of an office chair on the other side of the call. "And I'm wondering how you have come to this conclusion."

"The dog told me."

Silence.

"Nora," he said slowly, "you're going to have to elaborate."

I told him all about what happened with Pal this morning. "Lane—my boyfriend, Dr. Lane Bishop—saw Pal alerting to Miguel's boots yesterday at my folks' house. He was wearing his work boots, so he and Miguel think that Pal was alerting based on something Miguel was exposed to at a jobsite."

"Pal is the dog?"

"Yes, a Belgian Malinois."

More silence and another squeak of a chair. "Nora, how did you come to own a Belgian Malinois that detects explosives?"

I told him the story of Pal and his run through downtown and eventually the parking lot at Thistledown Farms. "So basically he found Lane, but we were all looking for him first. If that makes sense. He doesn't like bad weather or fireworks."

"It does, and neither do I, if I'm being honest," Trent said. "And you don't know anything about him other than he alerts to explosives?"

"I know he's smart and he's protective of Lane already. But no, we don't. He had no chip or tattoo, or if he did it had been removed. Between Lone Star Vet Clinic staff, the Second Chance Ranch team, and Lane's assistant and intern at A&M, we're hoping we can find out who he belongs to."

"It's odd that he doesn't have a chip or tattoo," Trent said. "That's standard procedure for the MWDs and bomb dogs."

"Right," I said. "It's possible it has been removed, but that's a long shot as far as proving this. You'd think there would be a scar, though."

"Not necessarily, although I can't imagine how that could be accomplished. The procedure is painful on a human—this I know from personal experience—so I cannot imagine how anyone could get a dog that big and strong to sit still long enough to accomplish it."

"Right," I told him. "It just doesn't make sense."

"Would you like me to do some checking?" Trent said. "It's possible the agency is missing a dog somewhere. It'd likely be a dog from elsewhere. We don't have a local canine."

"Well, if he doesn't go home to someone else, maybe Lane will let you borrow Pal when you need one."

Trent chuckled. "You know, we've deputized citizens, but that would be the first time I deputized a dog. I'll let the brass know about your offer." He paused. "Now back to your building. Dennison took your statement in the restaurant on Saturday, but has anyone formally interviewed you?"

"No," I said. "But I didn't expect them to. Todd said someone would call me if they needed anything else. Other than having a video of the apartment as it looked when I viewed it before I bought the building, I really don't know anything."

"Yes, he shared that video with ATF. It appears we've got theft charges pending as well as the explosives issue."

"So how does this proceed?" I asked. "I have a call at ten with my insurance adjuster. I'm sure the insurance company will want access to assess the damages soon. What do I say?"

"You have my number," he said. "Tell the adjuster to call me, and I'll set up an appointment. It's going to remain a crime scene for a while longer, but I don't see the harm in letting your insurance folks start working on a claim."

"Thank you, Trent. I really appreciate this." I told him the name of my insurance company. "I might not be able to use the building I just purchased, but at least I can start the process of getting the apartment back to how it was before the fire."

"What are you going to do with that building?" he asked. "Just curious."

"Actually, I hadn't made up my mind. Before the store and fire, I thought I might just hire someone to run the place just as Mr. Lazlo had. At least temporarily. But I think there's too much work to be done organizing and cleaning for that to be feasible now."

"It's not for everyone."

I let out a long breath. "Someday I hope to either break through the first-floor wall and have a larger dining room or maybe open another type of restaurant in the downstairs. There had been some discussion among some of my family members about turning the apartment into a short-term rental, but I wasn't comfortable with that." I glanced around then chuckled. "I could use a bigger office, so there's that."

"You serve good food, Nora. I can see how a bigger dining room would be an asset."

"Thank you, Trent."

"And short-term rentals can be profitable but bring their own unique headaches. You're wise not to rush into that kind of thing." He paused. "Do you mind if I ask a few more questions?"

I sat back in my chair. "Of course not. Fire away. No pun intended."

He chuckled. "Okay, so you said you were in the building a few hours before the storm and the fire. You told Dennison that you heard a few thumps but thought it was coming from either next door at the pet bakery or from the cat you found hiding downstairs."

"That's right. At one point, I went upstairs to get cleaning supplies from the closet, but as far as I can recall, the apartment was dark and silent." I paused, remembering. "I didn't approach the door, but it seems like I would have heard if anyone was inside."

"Possibly," he said. "Unless they were taking great pains not to be heard."

"It's creepy to think of what was going on up there while I was downstairs dusting books." I shuddered. "I was alone down there. . ."

"And nothing happened until you left," Trent supplied. "That tells me that the explosion was probably accidental and you or the building were not the target."

"Okay, well, I hope that's the case. So, Trent, I'm trying to decide whether you were surprised when you were called to an explosion in my building or whether you already knew there was a threat there." I paused. "Which is it?"

"I can't tell you that, Nora."

Outside my door, I heard a crash and then someone grumbling. A second later, I heard Roz commanding that a mess be cleaned immediately. Rather than go out and investigate, I concentrated on my conversation with Trent.

"So you can't tell me because the ATF doesn't comment on ongoing investigations?"

He chuckled. "No comment."

"Not funny."

"It wasn't meant to be." Trent paused. "I'm going to send Dennison an email to remind him to follow up with you regarding the stolen items. These idiots are in a lot of trouble with ATF, but they are also thieves. I saw the video you sent us. You had some nice pieces in that apartment, so I'm sure Brenham PD will be filing charges on them for theft too."

"Well, Mr. Lazlo did. I hadn't even had time to go see them once the place was mine. But I'll cooperate any way I can." I paused. "Just so we're clear, you do understand that I had no idea what was happening over there, right? And as far as I can tell, neither did anyone in my restaurant." Then a thought occurred. "My employees hang out in the alley. They should have seen something, shouldn't they?"

I heard his chair squeak again. "How do you know they didn't?"

His question took me aback. "Well," I finally said, "I guess I don't know for certain. But I can certainly ask."

"Don't do that, Nora," Trent hastened to say. "If you ask the wrong question of the wrong person, that could put you back into the center of the target. Is that what you want?"

I touched the bandage on my forehead. "No," I said softly.

"Okay, then let my people and the Brenham PD do our jobs. We want you safe, okay?"

"Right, okay," I said. "So do you think one of my employees is—"

"I didn't say that." Trent paused. "I'm just saying you have to be careful who you talk to about this. Your casual question may get you in big trouble. And I know you don't want someone with a grudge against you and a talent for explosives showing up at your home, do you?"

"Who would?" I sighed. "Okay, I get your point. So the next question is whether Cassidy is safe upstairs. I don't want her in danger."

"She's fine," he said. "The explosives were removed, and there was no exposure beyond the apartment itself. Besides, have you met her boyfriend? He's been hounding me about this topic ever since it happened. I had to go up there myself and check the place out just to get him off my back."

I chuckled. "That sounds like Jason."

"Your brother has been after me too," Trent added. "Have you asked him if he's been up there to look at the damage?"

"No, why?"

"Because he admitted to me that the minute he heard the fire call, he was up there." He paused.

" 'Up there' as in at the scene or 'up there' as in actually going into the burning apartment?"

"He didn't clarify," Trent said. "Does it matter?"

"No, I guess not. Miguel's a volunteer fireman," I said. "That would explain him being there. But he didn't mention it to me, and I just saw him at the ranch yesterday. I certainly didn't see him on the day it happened."

"That's because the volunteer fire department wasn't called in for that fire," he said. "It was small and under control almost immediately after Brenham FD was on the scene. There was really only smoke damage other than what little burn pattern ended up on the wall behind that sink. As for your brother, I'm not going to bust him for it. I'd do the same if it was my sister."

I let out a long breath. "Right. Guy code or something."

"Well, it's what a brother would do," he said.

"So where do we go from here, Trent? What comes next? And when do I get my building back?"

"Local authorities will complete their investigation in conjunction with us and possibly other agencies. That's really all I can tell you other than I wouldn't be planning a grand opening of anything on the first floor of that building for a while."

"Thanks," I told him.

"I wish I had better news," he said. "But I will ask around about that dog. I'm intrigued now."

After I hung up with Trent, I checked my phone. There were no messages from Lane. Not surprising since he was probably up to his eyeballs in work at the clinic. Plus I had no idea what time his assistant and intern reported for work. It was early yet.

I smiled. I loved the idea of him working here in Brenham, even if only for two weeks.

After placing a call to the elder Dr. Bishop to check on him, I tucked the phone into my pocket and stood. I hadn't heard any more noises outside my door, but I was curious what had happened.

I slowly opened the door and peered out. Shane was stirring something in a massive soup pot. I'd have to make a note to commend Roz on having Shane wear gloves to work at the stove. Roz had pushed back on that suggestion when I made it recently, so it was nice to win a battle so easily. That wasn't always the case with my headstrong but extremely capable chef.

I stepped out and walked past them to look into the dining room where I expected Canon would be setting up for lunch. The room was empty.

"Where's Canon?" I asked when I returned to the kitchen.

"He called in sick," Roz said.

"Okay, well, do you need any help with setup?" This I asked of Roz, who was concentrating on a menu covered in notes she'd made.

"All good," she said without lifting her head. "I'll put Shane on it in a sec."

With everything here under control, I decided now was a good time to walk down to the gym to see if I could speak with Leigh Fraser, or at least get her contact information. I had just walked out the front door and onto the street when my phone rang. It was Dad.

"Honey, what's the name of that place where the two vets got married? It isn't Thistledown Farms, is it?"

"Yes," I said. "That's the one. Why?"

"Well, it looks like someone blew up a building there."

CHAPTER SEVENTEEN

I pulled out a chair at the nearest bistro table and sat down. Across the street, a glass shop truck pulled up in front of the building with plywood on the windows.

"When? And what happened? And which building?"

"Overnight," Dad said. "And no one knows yet. I think it's one of those little houses on the property."

"Where the bride and bridesmaids get ready?" I said, remembering that beautifully decorated oasis I'd fallen in love with on Saturday.

"Could be nothing, but the boys and I just wondered because of what happened at the building if the two were related. I know this one wasn't weather related any more than the situation in the apartment."

Dad had a regular Monday morning coffee with his buddies down at the Dairy Queen closest to the ranch. Nothing that happened in Brenham passed the notice of this group. It helped that more than one of the half dozen men who usually attended were first responders, and all were military veterans.

"It's not like we have many explosions in Brenham," I said, "so it is suspicious that two happened so close together. What is law enforcement saying?"

"They're keeping tight-lipped as far as I can tell. Just like they've been doing with your building." He paused. "I blame the ATF. Local law enforcement pretty much just stands down when they come to town."

This was not the time to tell my father that I had just had a call with Trent. I wished I'd known about this new development before I spoke to him.

"But anyway," my father continued, "I worry about you, honey. I know you won't close the restaurant until whoever is blowing things up gets caught, but I sure hope you're watching out for yourself downtown."

I resisted the urge to tell him I was fine. He was my dad. He'd worry anyway. And it didn't help that I'd had a tornado across the street, a bomb next door in a building I owned, and a visit with a paramedic all in less than four days.

I smiled, knowing it would show in the sound of my voice if I didn't. "We always take precautions at Simply Eat," I told him. "You know. You practically wrote the training I give the staff on security. And it helps that the police station is practically around the corner."

"It also helps to know that my daughter is smart, tough, and a woman who is making me proud."

"Thank you, Daddy," I said softly.

After a few minutes of chatting about other things, we hung up. The glass shop employees were now busy unloading glass for the windows. City employees had already picked up the downed tree limbs, and roofers were busy with their repairs as well. By the end of the week, it would look as if the tornado had never happened.

I rose. The police tape was still tied around the brass handles of the building's double front doors, the ends dancing in the breeze. I bypassed the doors and kept walking past the Pupcake Bakery until I reached the gym.

This time last year, the place had been a cell phone repair business. The lime-green exterior had been toned down to a subdued sky blue. I stepped inside, and rather than being greeted by a basic white lobby, the space was now open all the way to the back of the building.

The same sky blue was painted on the walls and ceiling, while the floor beneath the workout equipment gleamed bright white. A Pilates class was going on in the back of the space, with a dozen or more ladies bending and twisting at the command of their instructor, a pretty fortysomething blond in a dusty rose tank top and matching leggings.

She turned toward me and grinned. "Nora!"

I searched my brain to try and remember how I knew her and what her name was. Then it hit me. This was Bitsy Sumner, formerly Decker. Or maybe it was Bonnano. I kind of lost track.

Bitsy had been a local Realtor until she married a well-to-do accountant from Houston whom she'd met while showing him the most expensive ranch in three counties. Witt Sumner had bought the ranch, taken Bitsy for his bride, and whisked her away to the big city.

At least that's the story I remember.

I was stunned to see her back in Brenham. I was even more stunned at her transition from her previous image—let's just say that Marilyn Monroe and Dolly Parton were her fashion icons—to the slender pony-tailed Pilates instructor who was dabbing her forehead with a towel that matched her outfit.

Bitsy instructed her class to begin their cool down stretches then hurried toward me. We embraced, her arms wiry and strong and mine showing evidence of the fact that I owned a restaurant instead of a gym.

Up close she was even prettier in this current version than she ever had been in full makeup with peroxided hair and bright pink clothing. Her outfit, like everything else about Bitsy, had been toned down considerably.

"You look fabulous, Bitsy. Is this your gym?" I asked.

"Oh no, I just work here." She gave me an appraising look. "Are you interested in taking a class? We give a discount to downtown business owners. Ten percent isn't setting the world on fire, but it's something." Her face fell. "Oh, I'm so sorry. I didn't mean to joke about fire. Not after what happened to you. Well, not you, but your building. . ."

"It's fine." I checked out her wedding ring finger and spied a massive sparkler. "Why are you working here?" The question came out before I could stop myself.

She grinned. "I get asked that a lot. So, to save us some time, here are the answers: I love Pilates and my husband, not in that order, but since he's retired and we moved out of Houston, I get bored. I'm not much of an outdoors girl. Working here gives me something to do."

"That makes sense."

Bitsy leaned closer. "Just between us, my husband owns the place. I don't like for anyone to know that. I like being one of the girls with the staff and our guests. Plus if something goes wrong, I just tell them I'll have to inform management. Then I let Witt handle it. And just so I'm telling the truth, I pay myself a dollar every Friday whether I've earned it or not."

"Genius." I matched her smile. "You really look happy, Bitsy."

"I am. Being Mrs. Sumner suits me." She paused. "So if you're not here to sign up for a class, what can I help you with?"

"I'm looking for Leigh Fraser," I said.

Bitsy glanced over at the cloud-shaped clock on the wall and then looked back at me. "You're in luck. She'll be here in a few minutes. You're welcome to wait." She nodded to the pair of pale blue velvet wing chairs centered under a massive painting of billowy clouds on a pale blue sky.

"I'll do that," I said.

"If there's time, we can catch up later. However, right now I need to get my ladies in hand or they'll fall asleep during stretch time. Pilates is more tiring than you'd think."

She hurried off, and I settled onto a chair to wait. I had barely had time to check my emails when the door opened and a woman who could only be described as the opposite of Bitsy stepped inside.

In contrast to her coworker, Leigh Fraser had dark hair piled on her head in a tight bun and the solemn expression of a person who was always watching out for danger. She had a lean physique and a tan that appeared to come from the outdoors and not Sweeties Beauty Shop and Tanning Salon down the street.

I recognized her immediately as some sort of first responder. Lane and every male in my family wore that same expression out in public.

"Leigh?" I said, standing.

The woman, dressed in navy-blue yoga pants and a tie-dyed Toby Mac T-shirt jerked her attention toward me. It took a moment before she responded.

"Who's asking?" she said slowly.

"Sorry. I'm Nora Hernandez. I own Simply Eat, the restaurant down the street."

Her expression changed from wary to warm. "I've eaten there. Great food. How can I help you?"

"Thank you," I said. "I wonder if you might have a few minutes to talk."

Leigh's eyes narrowed. There was that wary look again. "About what? Are you looking to join the gym? Because that's Bitsy's department, not mine. She's the manager."

"Nothing like that," I said. "It's kind of complicated, but the short version is my boyfriend found a dog, and we were wondering if you'd lost yours. My sister-in-law Emma Hernandez is in one of your classes, and she said you sometimes bring the dog here while you're teaching. It's a German shepherd or a Belgian Malinois—she wasn't sure which—but she said it looked a lot like the one we're trying to place."

"Mine is a shepherd," Leigh said.

I nodded. "Right. Well, Emma wasn't sure, but she said it's a beautiful dog and really well trained."

Leigh actually smiled. "She is."

Now what? It wasn't the same dog. I considered stopping the conversation now, but I decided to see if I might find out anything else that would be helpful, especially in regard to training facilities.

"So the missing dog is obviously not yours." I paused. "We think the Malinois is an MWD."

Her eyebrows went up, but she said nothing. I had no doubt she knew what the abbreviation meant.

"Anyway, I was wondering if you know of any places around here that train working dogs." I spoke casually and tried to convey the idea that I'd just come up with the thought.

Leigh shrugged. "I'm not from here, so I wouldn't know."

"Okay, well, thank you, Leigh." I took a few steps toward the door then paused to look at her. "Do you know any other owners of dogs like yours? Or ours, for that matter? Maybe one of them has a dog that's missing."

She shook her head. "Like I said, I'm not from here. I really don't know too many people."

"Okay, well, if you hear of anyone looking for a Belgian Malinois, please let me know. You can find me down at the restaurant. If I'm not there, just leave a message and I'll contact you. Or call Lone Star Vet Clinic. They're helping us. We all really want to see this dog reunited with his owner."

Bitsy's class began streaming out, causing the lobby to be crowded. I stepped closer to the wall, but Leigh didn't move. However, her expression softened.

"There are probably some online forums for the breed," she said as ladies with yoga mats strolled between us. "If it were me looking for my dog, I'd start there."

"Where is your dog today?" I asked casually.

"At home with my husband." She shook her head. "Remind me again how you knew I had a dog."

"My sister-in-law Emma Hernandez told me," I said.

"Right." Then she nodded. "Okay, yes, I remember Emma. She's got a little ankle biter dog, right? Dogs are welcome in my class, but sometimes she brings him in his kennel—or did until we had to ask her to stop. The thing is cute but wouldn't stop barking in time to the music. Nothing would make it stop. We try to be pet friendly, but there's a limit. She said they'd tried obedience class but it hadn't worked."

I grinned. "Yes. Cute but not so smart. The dog, not my sister-in-law," I hastened to add. "Although Emma is cute, but she's smart. Except for the part about marrying my brother. Well, you know what I mean."

Leigh joined in with my laughter. "I understood what you meant."

"I guess that's what you get when you name your dog Pup Tart."

"Oh, but it does fit, don't you think?"

"True," I admitted. "She is sweet."

"Sweet. Right." Leigh sobered as the last of the class left the building. "Look, about that Bel Mal. I'll ask around. I don't have contacts here in Brenham. I've only been here a few months. But maybe someone I know from my online groups will have a local connection for you. I'd hate to see a dog go missing."

"Thank you, Leigh," I said. "And to be clear, the only answer we're looking for is where the dog belongs. We don't care how he ended up here, only that he gets home."

Bitsy joined us, swiping at her forehead. "Oh good. You two have met. I've been meaning to introduce you." She turned to me. "Did you know that Leigh and her husband are practically neighbors with your future father-in-law?"

Leigh immediately looked uncomfortable.

"They live in that darling white cottage with the climbing roses in front."

I knew the house. It was just around the corner from Lane's father's place and used to belong to good friends of Dr. and Mrs. Bishop. The original owners had passed on, and the home had been sold.

"That's a great neighborhood," I said. "Dr. Bishop has lived there for decades. I don't think he'll ever move. He loves it there."

"Yes, so do we." Leigh nodded toward the interior of the gym. "I need to get going. It was nice to meet you, Nora."

"Same," I said then watched as Leigh hurried away to disappear into a room I decided was either the ladies' room or a dressing room.

That left me here with Bitsy. "Okay, well, I guess I'll get going then," I told her. "Congratulations on your new. . ." I paused. "Your new job."

Her smile broadened. "Thank you. I'm so happy now, Nora. Truly happy. Much as I loved being a Realtor, this is so much more fun."

I gave her a sweeping glance. "It shows."

"Pilates and a good man changed me," she said. "Okay, and Jesus. First Jesus then the other two." She paused to let out a long breath. "After that close call with a bomb in my purse, I had a reality check about what I was doing with my life."

Bitsy had been in the middle of a divorce when she managed to end up with a bomb in her pink Kate Spade tote. A long story—I could write a whole book about it—but let's just say her ex had some unsavory friends and she hadn't realized what the explosive was when she tossed it into her bag.

"When I realized I was still around for a reason, I went looking for what that reason was." She beamed. "And I found it."

"Speaking of bombs," I said, an idea dawning, "your ex hasn't been released from prison, has he?"

"Oh no, Joey has eons of time to spend behind bars before he's up for release. My lawyer says I'll be informed when the time comes so I can testify at the parole board hearing if I want." She shook her head. "Why?"

"I was just wondering," I said, determined not to say more than I had to.

"Because that upstairs apartment fire was caused by a bomb?" She looked at me as if what she'd said wasn't surprising.

"Where did you hear that?"

My dad and Miguel were the only members of my family who knew what Pal had alerted to. And Miguel only knew about his boots, not the apartment. I sure didn't expect tight-lipped Agent Mendez to be spreading the word about the cause of the fire.

Bitsy shrugged. "Leigh's husband told me. Well, he said it was an explosion, so I just guessed it was a bomb. Wasn't it?"

"Oh," was the best I could manage in my surprised state. "And how did he know this?"

"He's a first responder," she said. "He was one of the first on the scene. At least that's what I was told." She shrugged. "I slept through the whole tornado thing. Once I get my earplugs in and my sleeping mask on, I'm dead to the world. I guess it's a good thing it didn't happen here."

"True," I told her. Then I had a thought. "You and Witt don't live above the shop, do you?"

Bitsy laughed. "Oh gracious no. It's all I can do to drag my husband off the ranch. He'd never live in town."

"So, what is on the second floor here?" At her confused look, I continued. "I'm just curious."

"Oh, right. Honestly I don't know."

"You've never looked?" I said, lifting my eyes to the ceiling. "I'd be curious if it was me."

Bitsy grinned. "Well, I am now. I never thought about it before." She walked over to the registration desk and snatched a bouquet of daisies out of a silver vase then turned it over. One gold key landed on the desk, and Bitsy snapped it up. "Let's go see."

I followed her through the gym and then into a back office decorated in a glam style that meant it had to belong to Bitsy. Rather than the computer, printer, and other office things you'd expect at the desk of someone who managed a business, there was a massive lighted mirror and enough makeup products to stock a small store.

I had to hand it to her, though. She had it all beautifully organized on clear acrylic shelves with the labels facing out.

I had a bit of organization envy. Maybe I'd ask Bitsy for some help getting my act together when I had the time to think about it.

Trudging across a thick white fur rug, I noted there was a window behind the desk that looked out into the alley. Or rather, it would look into the alley if you pulled back the glittery curtains, moved the opalescent beads aside then lifted the white lacquered shutters. Difficult but doable, I decided.

Bitsy opened a door, which I assumed led to a closet, only to flip the switch on a light that revealed a stair landing. I followed her up the steps.

She jabbed the key in the lock and then twisted it. The key refused to turn.

"Oh well," she said, looking at me over her shoulder. "I guess we won't be finding out today."

"I guess not, but that's okay." We retraced our steps then stopped in the reception area so Bitsy could return the key to the vase.

"Maybe another day?" she said. "I'll see if I can get a locksmith here. You've got me curious."

"Sure. Anyway, I really need to go. It was great to see you, Bitsy. Really great."

With that, I made my way out of the gym and back down the street to the restaurant. In the corner of the kitchen, Shane was standing over the sometimes-fussy printer we used to print the daily menus. With his gloved hand, he opened a package of pale yellow paper, the color I always used for the menu on Mondays, while the machine churned out the printed pages.

Shane grinned when I walked toward him.

"It's working today."

"Don't jinx it," he exclaimed. "Roz got the menu done just in time. She made the delivery guy come back with something he forgot, so we had to wait to make sure we weren't going to have to make any more changes."

I frowned at Roz as she stepped into sight. "We've been having a lot of trouble with the grocery orders, don't you think? Do we need to find another grocer?"

"I've already told this one he's done a tap dance on my last nerve for the final time. One more wrong order and I'm finished with him."

A thought niggled at my brain. "How long has this been going on?" I asked.

She shrugged. "I'd have to look at my records."

"Please do that when you get a chance, and let me know. I'm not in a hurry, but I'm curious." I headed toward my office, pausing just as I passed Roz. "And good job on getting Shane to wear gloves while he's working with the food."

Roz gave me a blank stare then looked past me to Shane. "Oh, yes, right. You're welcome. I did notice he's been wearing them for a few days. If I could just get the other one to comply. Canon's just not into gloves. That's his take on it anyway."

I continued on to my office to grab my keys then stepped back into the kitchen. Roz only had Shane working today, so I really should stick around and help out through the lunch rush. Retracing my steps, I tossed my keys and cell phone into my desk drawer and went to work alongside my team.

CHAPTER EIGHTEEN

LANE

Monday afternoon
Brenham, Texas

Nora wasn't answering her phone. I tucked mine into my pocket and leaned against the counter in the clinic's minuscule employee kitchen.

It was an interesting feeling being back here and in charge of the place. This had always been Pop's domain. And then it wasn't once he sold the practice. But it had never been mine.

While the coffee brewed, I called Pop. As I expected, he was antsy to get out of the hospital and go home. I understood, but the problem with that scenario was I wasn't sure he could be left alone all day.

And I sure couldn't be there. Not when I was so busy here.

I needed to hire someone to look in on him for a few days, maybe a week, after he got home. I made a note on my reminder app on my phone then tucked it back into my pocket.

There was always the idea of having Pop bunk at Hernandez Ranch until he was well enough to get around safely on his own. The trick there was convincing my father of this.

Nora would know what to do. She always did. And she could probably find someone to take care of Pop, although it wasn't fair to put that responsibility solely on her.

We'd figure it out together. If she was willing to help, that is.

I was just dumping my usual three packets of sugar into my coffee when Cassidy burst in.

"Have you heard the news about the wedding venue?" Before I could answer, she continued. "Someone blew up the little cottage where the bride and bridesmaids get ready. Can you believe that?"

I stirred my coffee then took a sip. "You're joking, right?"

Cassidy frowned. "That wouldn't be a funny joke, Dr. Lane. I'm totally serious. I was just talking to Jason, and he let it slip. Apparently the ATF has the site locked down, so the news hasn't spread yet."

"Any idea who did it?" I asked, feeling like the issue was more likely an issue with a faulty gas line than someone actually bothering to blow up a building at a wedding venue. That made no sense.

"No clue," she said. "With the feds in charge, local law enforcement is staying outside their perimeter. That's a direct quote. He wasn't too happy about that."

"I guess not," I told her, taking another sip. The coffee here wasn't the best I'd ever had, but considering the amount of sleep I'd had was roughly a quarter of the time I'd spent awake today, it was much needed.

"He thinks that whoever is behind this may also be the one responsible for the fire in Nora's building." She paused. "Since it's next door to my place, he's pretty upset that he can't get in there to see what kind of explosives were used and whether the bad guys left any clues. He thinks they may strike again."

I placed the coffee cup on the counter. "I get it, but don't you think it's odd that of all the targets in Brenham, some crazies would pick Nora's apartment and a random building at a wedding venue in the middle of nowhere?"

"Of course it's odd, Dr. Lane." Cassidy shook her head. "It's odd that anything is blowing up anywhere. This is Brenham. Things like that don't happen here."

"They do now."

My phone buzzed with a text from my assistant at A&M. SENDING YOU AN EMAIL WITH THE INFORMATION YOU REQUESTED.

"Sorry," I told Cassidy. "I need to go check my emails. My assistant may have found something in regard to Pal." I paused. "Speaking of Pal, how's he doing in the back?"

"Oh, he hasn't been in the back since early this morning. I've had him in my office and so has Mari. Right now he's up front with Brianna. He's such a sweetheart."

"Okay then. As long as he's behaving and not making a pest of himself, I guess it's okay."

I walked into Tyler's office—now mine for the next two weeks—and opened my laptop. While my emails loaded, I called my father.

"Good news, son," he said.

"Well, hello to you too, Pop. You're in a good mood."

He chuckled. "You bet I'm in a good mood. I'm getting sprung from here."

I suppressed a groan. That left me no time to get a plan in place to take care of him. With the afternoon packed with appointments, I'd never get this accomplished.

And yet I had to somehow.

Maybe I would speak with Nora's parents. Pop would hate not getting to go to his home to begin his recuperation, but he did like Daniel and Maria. And he would be well cared for—and well fed—there.

"Lane? Did you hear me?" Pop said.

"Yes, sorry. That's great news. I was just trying to figure out how we're going to make that timeline work. With my schedule full at the clinic, I won't have the ability to get you settled in and check on you like you need."

"Don't worry. I've already handled everything. I won't be released until this evening. Just show up when you're done at work, and that'll be fine."

"That does solve the first problem," I said, "but what about tomorrow when I have to leave for work? No way are you going to stay by yourself all day. Not the first day after surgery."

"No problem, son. I hired help for tomorrow and Wednesday. I won't be alone."

This time I couldn't hide the groan that escaped. "Pop. No. You're still under the influence of anesthesia. And you need professional care, not just some nice person who is willing to sit with you."

"You're right on both counts," he said.

"So you've hired a professional." I relaxed a notch. "Where did you find this person? I assume he or she is a nurse."

"He's not a nurse," Pop corrected. "He's a paramedic. And considering I haven't had much chance to be social, you can imagine I met him here in the hospital."

"Okay, Pop. I admit I'm impressed that you could hire a paramedic to help for the next two days, but—"

"How did I manage it?" He chuckled. "He came in here looking for a buddy of his while he was on his break. The guy had been discharged, and I was given his room. I told him since he was already here to visit someone, he could visit me if he wanted to."

"That sounds like you. You never met a stranger."

Another chuckle. "That is true, son. Apparently I'm not the only fan of *Murder She Wrote* mysteries. Kirby and I watched two episodes together this morning. I say we watched, but actually I mostly slept through them."

"I thought you said he was on his break."

"Did I? Well, it was a long break, I guess. He just left."

I wanted to press him for more information. However, I decided to keep it simple. He had, after all, only been out of surgery less than a day.

"You said his first name was Kirby," I said. "What's his last name?"

"Ewing," Pop said.

"I know that name." I described the paramedic who'd fixed up Nora's wound the morning of the tornado. "Does he look anything like that?"

"He looks exactly like that. Oh, and he's an army veteran."

Definitely the same person. I'd be checking into this guy ASAP, but for now I wouldn't be mentioning that part to my father. There would be no need unless I discovered a problem.

"I said he's a veteran," my father repeated. "Like you and me. That ought to count for something."

"That's great, Pop. And of course it does." I paused. "So, what kind of arrangements did you make with him?"

"He is off tomorrow and Wednesday, so he'll make a point of being at the house before you leave for the clinic. That's around seven, right?"

"Closer to eight, but seven will do," I said.

"He'll stick around and help out as needed until you get home."

"Are you paying him for this?"

"I wouldn't think of *not* paying," he said, his tone indignant. "I know I'm a genuine pleasure to be around, but nobody needs to be doing aftercare post-surgery with me for free."

"Okay," I told him. "Fair enough. Are you going to tell me how much you're paying him?"

"Nope."

"I figured that was going to be your answer. Then will you at least give me his phone number so I can talk to him before he shows up tomorrow?"

Silence.

"Come on, Pop. You recognize that you're post-surgery. I don't want you to forget to tell him something just because you were still dealing with the effects of anesthesia."

I congratulated myself for thinking of an excuse that actually sounded valid. The real reason I wanted his contact information was to have a conversation with him.

Not only did Kirby Ewing need to know that I'd be watching his every move with my father via the nanny cam I'd be buying on my way to the hospital this evening, but he also should realize that there were a lot of people who loved Dr. Elvin Bishop, and they'd be watching too.

Okay, not everyone, but I wasn't above having a few handpicked friends stop by during the course of those two days to see what was going on. And maybe I wouldn't mention that nanny cam. But my father did need skilled nursing care for at least the first forty-eight hours, maybe longer. I knew I might be overcautious, but I'd rather have a degreed professional looking after him instead of one of the casserole ladies.

"All right," Pop finally said, "but only because I'd be giving him your number anyway so you two can converse during the time he's with me. I'm sure you'll be wanting to do that."

"Yes, I do, but honestly, Pop, I just want to talk to him. He needs to know you're not someone who is alone in the world."

Pop laughed. "Oh goodness, I can't imagine that. The pastor came by to visit just now, and he told me the ladies' society women have put me on a meal train. Have you ever heard of that?"

"I have."

"Well, I hadn't. Pastor wanted to know if I had any allergies because the ladies would be bringing me two meals a day for a while until I could cook on my own." He paused. "I told him I wasn't allergic to a single thing except cooking, and it didn't sound like I was going to have to worry about that for the foreseeable future. So by that standard alone, I will not be alone. Unless my caregiver takes a shine to one of the casserole ladies. Then I might find myself alone in the house."

"You're being silly, Pop. But I get the point."

We conversed for a few minutes—by that, I mean he talked and I listened—then I heard another voice in the background.

"Sorry, Lane. Must go. These nurses just can't get enough of me. The doctors either. They keep coming in to visit."

I could hear a woman's laughter on the other end of the phone.

"Do what the doctor and nurses tell you, Pop," I said. "But give me that phone number before you hang up."

"I'm going to have this nice nurse read it to you, okay? I don't have my reading glasses on right now."

A moment later, a woman came on the phone and asked if I was ready to take down the number. I said that I was.

The nurse read out the phone number. "Did I go too fast?"

"No, I think I've got it." I read the number back to her, and she agreed that was what she saw on the paper. "Can I ask you a question? What do you know about Kirby Ewing, the EMT who spent some time with my father this morning?"

"Not much really," she said. "I haven't seen him around before, but then I don't work in Emergency Services, so I wouldn't have anyway."

"But does he seem like an okay guy? My father has hired him to do a side job taking care of him, and I'm just making sure he's not letting someone dangerous into his home."

"Well, I certainly didn't get that impression, but then anyone can be nice for a few minutes, can't they? Here, let me give you back to your father." Then she handed the phone back to Pop.

"All right, son," my father said. "Now that you're done with the cross-examination of my nurse, I'll be waiting for you outside at the curb with my suitcase."

"Hardly, Pop. You'll be right where you are now. I'll come in and check you out, okay?"

"You're no fun," he said in a teasing tone.

"Neither were you when you were telling me I couldn't do something," I countered. "See you this evening. I'll call to let you know when I'm on the way."

"Okay, son." We hung up, and then I placed a call to the number I'd just been given.

"Kirby Ewing," the man on the other side of the call said.

I introduced myself and told him why I was calling. "Oh, I know all about you, Lane." He chuckled. "Your dad sure is proud of you. It's obvious how much he cares for you."

"Yeah, I feel the same about him. That's why I'm calling."

"Sure, of course." He paused. "Hey, how's your girlfriend? Any problem with that laceration I treated?"

"She's good," I told him. "No problem at all. You did fine work."

"I treated her as I do all my patients, by giving the best care I can. That's what you were calling to find out, wasn't it? Whether I was going to take care of your father?"

"Actually," I said slowly, "I was calling to find out why you were willing to spend your days off with an old man who you barely know. A wealthy old man, if I'm being honest."

"Valid question," he said without pausing. "He probably told you that we met by chance. I'd come to see someone else, but that person had already been discharged. We got to talking—"

"You mean Pops got to talking?" I offered.

"Yeah," Kirby said with a chuckle. "E.B. likes to talk."

E.B.? No one called my father E.B.

"Anyway, he mentioned that he didn't want to take you away from your responsibilities at the vet clinic while he was recuperating. He feels bad that he's let the clinic down."

So now he's telling me how my father feels? I let out a long breath.

"Right," I said. "So he'll go home under doctor's orders. Whoever I choose to be on site with him during the day will be asked to follow whatever orders his discharging physician gives. This isn't a babysitting position."

"I understand." Was it me or did the humor disappear quickly from his voice? "I take my job seriously. And to be clear, I do pick up extra jobs on my days off as they come along."

"How do you usually get these jobs?"

The fact he wandered into Pop's hospital room on the same day I was tasked with hiring help seemed awfully coincidental. And I do not, as a rule, believe in coincidence.

"I'm on call with a home health agency." Kirby gave me the number of an agency I recognized from when my mom was sick. "I figured I'd hear from you, so I've given permission for them to speak to you. Just identify yourself as Dr. Bishop's son, and they'll answer your questions. That's the usual way I find work outside of the day job. The other one is to wander into a room by accident and hit it off with a patient."

"So that's happened to you before?" I asked.

"A time or two." He paused. "Look, I get it. You're concerned. Check me out, and you'll find that I'm on the up and up."

"What's Pop paying you?"

He immediately answered with an amount that I considered fair.

"Okay, well, I'll be in touch."

A few minutes later, I dialed the agency. The owner remembered Mom and asked about Pop. Then she verified that Kirby worked for them as a freelance caregiver.

I hung up satisfied that my problem of having someone take care of Pop for two days was solved. Even better, if my father needed care beyond the two days that Kirby offered, the agency would send someone else.

Lifting my gaze heavenward, I whispered, "Thank You, Lord, for Your provision."

I sent an email to my assistant with Kirby's number and asked for her to call and let him know to arrive at my father's home tomorrow morning at seven o'clock. Then I went back to my laptop and navigated to the email program I used for work. I spied several from my assistant, but the one that interested me most had a subject line that just said Dog.

I scanned the email and then read the attached documents. "Bingo," I said. "Pal, it looks like we're one step closer to finding your home."

Typing a response as best I could manage with my hunt and peck method, I instructed my assistant to forward this and all other emails on this topic from my team to Nora. My finger hovered over the Send button when Parker Jenson appeared in the open door and knocked twice.

I sat back, the email still in front of me. "What's up?"

"Sorry, Doc. We've got an emergency in Exam Room Three. I put a call in to Dr. Cameron, but he's completely booked up today, so I'm afraid you're going to have to handle it."

"How bad is it?"

"It's bad," he said and then began to give me the details.

I jumped up and headed down the hall toward the exam rooms, my mind already going over the potential issues the patient might be facing. Much as I loved research, saving a life really was my calling. And this animal needed exactly that.

CHAPTER NINETEEN

LANE

Brenham, Texas
Tuesday morning

The doorbell rang at 7:25. I'd been just about to call Nora to explain to her why I had fallen asleep last night without calling to tell her good night. It was something we usually did, and here I was messing up so soon after promising I wouldn't.

I opened the door to see Kirby Ewing. He wore jeans, a pair of navy Adidas running shoes, and a red-and-white-striped polo shirt. In his hand was a bag that looked like some sort of medical kit.

"If you're on time, you're late," Kirby said with a shrug. "At least that's what my commanding officer used to say."

"Mine too," I admitted. "Come on in."

I ushered the former Army medic inside and showed him to the den where Pop was already settled into his recliner watching a news program. After the two of them exchanged a greeting, I nodded toward the breakfast table. "Let's chat a minute before I go to the clinic. Can I get you a cup of coffee?"

"Thanks, but I'm good." Kirby seated himself at the chair across from me, and I handed him the instructions I'd received last night before Pop left the hospital with me. I briefed him on Pop's discharge orders then told him where he could find the medicine he would be administering later in the morning and again this afternoon.

"I'll check in as I'm able, but I'm always reachable by phone. Other than bathroom trips and the occasional short walk inside the house, he needs to remain off his feet today. We'll see how he does today, and that will determine whether he can be more mobile tomorrow." I nodded toward the television. "Pop loves watching the news, but if he gets too riled up and starts talking back to the hosts, change the channel," I told Kirby. "There are times when he loves nothing better than educating the folks on the other side of the TV screen on whatever topic they're discussing. I'd rather we avoid that scenario while he's recovering from surgery."

Kirby cast a sideways glance at Pop then returned his attention to me. "Got it. I know he's always down for a few episodes of *Murder She Wrote*. I'd prefer that any day over those talking heads."

I nodded. "Look, I'm trusting you today. Do not give me a reason to regret that," I said, keeping a level gaze as I enunciated each word with care.

"I've got this, flyboy," he said with a tilt of his head. "I'll treat your father just like I would treat my own. I promise."

"Long as you loved your father, then we're good."

Kirby's smile was swift and broad. "I would do anything for my father. Absolutely anything."

"Glad to hear it." I pushed back from the table and stood. "I need to get going."

The EMT climbed to his feet then looked around. "Where's the dog?"

"Pal is outside, but he'll be going with me. Why?"

I might have been mistaken, but I could have sworn that Kirby looked disappointed. "I don't mind keeping an eye on him too. Your father says he's a good dog."

"He is," I said, "but let's take it one day at a time. Just focus on Pop today."

I walked over to the door and whistled for Pal to come inside. He did as I commanded but stopped short when he spied Kirby.

Neither dog nor man moved, although Pal did sniff in the general direction of the EMT. I was about to say something when my phone buzzed with a text from the clinic. Cameron was stuck in surgery, and an emergency was coming in.

"Come on," I told the dog. "We've got to get going. Pop, you're going to behave for Kirby, right?"

"I'm not seven, Lane," my father said good-naturedly. "Of course I won't."

"See what you're dealing with," I told Kirby. "Good luck."

I laughed then headed for the door, expecting Pal to follow. He didn't. Instead, he continued to sniff in the general direction of Kirby Ewing.

"He must smell the breakfast tacos I had this morning."

Not likely, I knew from watching this highly trained dog for the past few days. But maybe civilian life had made this MWD forget some of the discipline he had learned while on active duty. I know it had worked that way for me.

"Let's go," I said to him firmly. "In the truck."

At that command, Pal did as he was told and shadowed me outside. And although he climbed inside when the door was opened, the dog didn't stop staring in the direction of the front door until we'd turned the corner and my father's home was no longer in view.

"What's up, buddy?" I said, reaching across the distance between us to scratch him behind his ear. "I'm sorry I didn't have time to introduce you to Pop's friend. I promise I'll do that when we come home tonight. And between us, I like a good breakfast taco too."

Pal sniffed at the air one more time, let out a soft whimper, and then climbed down onto the carpeted floor of my truck to assume his favorite napping position. After the dog was settled, I buckled up and called Nora.

Once again I owed her an apology.

NORA
Brenham, Texas
Tuesday morning

"I meant to call you," Lane was saying into the speakers of my car as I navigated the country roads outside of Brenham. "I really did. But there was an emergency in the middle of the afternoon, and Cameron isn't available on Mondays, so I had to handle it. Once that situation was taken care of, I was running late on clinic appointments, which made me late leaving to pick up Pop at the hospital."

"Sounds like the day was crazy," I offered as my GPS indicated a left turn up ahead.

"Then I got Pop home and went to work getting him settled. Before I realized it, I'd fallen asleep on the sofa with my phone in my hand. I remember getting it out to call you, but the rest is hazy. Anyway, Pal woke me up around midnight. I guess he was missing his bed and thought I ought to go to mine. I almost slept through the alarm. I can credit Pal for that too."

"Lane, I get it," I said in an attempt to stem the tide of apologies. "You're here in Brenham, but you have lots of responsibilities, and some of them were unexpected."

I paused, considering what he said. Lane had struggled to get more than five or six hours a night for most of the time I'd known him. "And you're suddenly sleeping well."

"I am," Lane said, and I could hear the smile in his voice. "It's nice."

"Oh, I'm so sorry." I made the turn onto a narrow gravel road. "I never asked about your father."

He caught me up on his father's release from the hospital and subsequent hiring of the EMT who cared for me at the scene of the tornado. "So that was my day. Anyway, I'm surprised you didn't at least text me when you got the emails from my staff."

"What emails?"

There was a long pause. "I instructed my staff to send you emails with the results of their research. You didn't get them?"

"No." I rounded a curve in the road and spied a slow-moving tractor up ahead. "Nothing."

"Check your spam filter," he said.

"I'm in the car using my hands-free. What did the emails say?"

"The main takeaway is that a Belgian Malinois was reported missing by Fort Cavazos. Kidnapping is suspected, although they haven't ruled out the dog just running off."

"Running off from Fort Cavazos? I doubt it. Pal isn't the one."

"The dog wasn't missing from Fort Cavazos," Lane finally said, "but he did go through their program until he was determined not to be suitable. Those dogs are placed elsewhere, either in private homes or with a foster in training for other duties. That's where the dog went missing."

"So, Pal may have failed MWD school?" I asked. "He sure seemed skilled at alerting on explosives. That would also explain why he seemed comfortable wearing a vest. And if he flunked out, that may be why the patches were removed. But he seems like such a good dog. I can't imagine that he would fail at anything."

"I only scanned the information, but apparently the dog that left the program was too nice."

I thought of the morning I found the big dog and the little orange tabby cat curled up together. Then there was the way he loved attention from me. "Okay, I can see that."

"Me too. I had the staff send over the labs that were done on Pal when I took him in to be checked for a chip, and I emailed a photograph of the vest. I didn't mention it before, but I went ahead and ordered a routine set of labs on him just to make sure he didn't have any health issues that needed to be addressed."

I felt an unexpected pang of disappointment. "So, Pal's owners will be found if the labs match with the missing dog."

"It's possible, yes," Lane said on an exhale. "I hate to say goodbye to him, but if he belongs to someone else, then that's what will have to happen."

"So if Pal is the missing dog, then does that mean the military will come and claim him?"

"Probably. Until he is officially adopted by his new owners, he belongs to the government. That means they can come and claim their asset at any time."

"Pal isn't a government asset, Lane. He's a sweet dog who loves you and tolerates my cat. He can't go anywhere but home with you."

I was aware that I sounded like a seven-year-old having a minor hissy fit, but I didn't care. The thought of that sweet dog going back to an institution instead of a loving home broke my heart.

"Honey, we have to do whatever is required of us. It's not like we can hide him, and we certainly aren't going to break the law and keep him from going back where he belongs." He paused, and I could hear someone speaking to him. "Sorry, I've got to go. We can talk more about this later if that's okay with you."

"Just one more thing. Do you have a second to send me the emails again or text me the contact information? If they're local, I can do some digging while I'm out."

"Sure." He paused. "Thanks for your help, babe."

I grinned. "I like that dog, Lane. He's brought out something in you that I haven't seen in a long time. I really want to prove he's not someone else's."

We said our goodbyes and hung up. With a continual stream of trucks and cars coming from the opposite direction, there was no way of getting around the rolling roadblock in front of me.

I continued following the tractor at a snail's pace until my GPS alerted me to the turnoff for my destination. I drove under the arch that spelled out WELCOME TO THISTLEDOWN FARMS and veered past the chapel and reception hall, almost hidden in a carefully planted forest of trees and shrubs. Up ahead on the left was the parking lot where Pal had made his appearance. To the right was the beautiful cottage we ladies had used for dressing.

Only, the cottage wasn't so beautiful anymore. Instead of the stone building with thatched roof and climbing roses, there was a burned-out shell with blackened stones. The thatched roof was gone, and yellow police tape fluttered in the breeze and snagged in the charred branches of the rosebush.

Unlike what I imagined, there was no sign of any ATF agents, Brenham first responders, or anyone in law enforcement. There weren't even any twirls of yellow tape caught in what remained of the building.

There was just a pile of ashes and a remnant of the building that once stood there. It all looked desolate and sad, especially with the early morning mist still blanketing the fields in the distance.

I should have just driven past here on my way to the training facility that Roz texted me about last night. She'd heard from a fellow dog owner about an establishment that advertised MWD training and thought I might want to know about it. I'd figured I'd get out here early and check it out. Since Canon had texted last night to say he was sick and wouldn't be in, it was unlikely that I would have another chance to do this today.

When I saw the training facility was less than a mile away from Thistledown Farms, I had to stop and see the damage for myself. But I wished I hadn't.

I was heading back to my car when I spied a golf cart heading my way. I didn't recognize the driver—a man in his late forties wearing jeans and a purple polo shirt—but the wedding venue logo emblazoned on the front of the cart was unmistakable.

"Can I help you?" he called as he parked the vehicle between me and my car.

Up close I could see the man had close-cropped red hair with strands of gray around his clean-shaven face. The pocket of his shirt proclaimed him as a fan of the Texas Christian University Horned Frogs.

He climbed out of the cart but didn't move any closer. I hurried to introduce myself, both by name and as the owner of Simply Eat in Brenham.

"We don't usually get caterers out here on a Tuesday morning, especially this early," he said in a low, slow drawl.

"Oh no, I'm not here for that." I glanced over my shoulder then back at him. "I was just in a wedding in the chapel on Saturday. When I heard that this had happened and I was already heading out here to talk to a dog trainer, I wanted to come see it for myself. I'm just so sad about it."

I was babbling a bit, but something about the man's steely gaze made me nervous. I offered a smile to punctuate my words then resolved not to say so many the next time I spoke.

The man nodded. "I'd go you one further and say I'm downright mad. Sorry, I didn't introduce myself. I'm the property manager out here. The wife runs the wedding operation, and I handle everything else. Name's Pat. Pat Ames."

I took note of the similarities in hair color and build between this man and my newly hired waiter. "Are you any relation to Canon Ames? He's a member of my staff at Simply Eat."

No reaction other than a curt nod. "Yes, Canon is my son."

"I hope he's feeling better. My chef told me that he called in sick for his shift this morning."

Pat's face went stony for half a second, then he nodded again. "He'll be fine in time for his next shift. Don't you worry about that."

"No, I wasn't worried. I just mentioned it because. . ." My words trailed off. I tried not to frown at the intensity of his response. "Okay, well I guess I should be leaving. I'm sorry if I've trespassed."

He shrugged. "I don't think your visit constitutes trespassing. More like curiosity. We've had a few people here to look, but the cops have pretty much kept this incident quiet. I suspect once the word is out, we'll get more. I'll probably hire security then, so be advised that if you come back it likely won't be as easy to get through the entrance undetected."

"Right, okay. I hadn't planned a return trip," I told him. "Just the once is enough for me."

"That dog trainer you're looking for wouldn't be the one just down the road, would it?"

The change of subject took me off guard. "Yes, that's the one. I'm seeking information that might lead me to the owner of a dog that was found here on your property last Saturday. A Belgian Malinois. I thought they might be able to help."

"The wife asked me about that dog," he said. "Said someone had told her one had been found on Saturday. Personally, I hadn't seen it, nor have I noticed any dogs running through here lately."

"Yes, that was my boyfriend and a member of the Second Chance

Ranch rescue team who spoke to her." I cast another glance behind me at the pile of ashes then returned my attention to Canon's father. "Do you know what happened here?"

"It blew up," he said as if I was asking the dumbest question ever. Then he shook his head. "Sorry. My wife is always telling me I'm too blunt. There wasn't anything in that building that should have blown up, yet it did. But there was plenty of fluff and finery that would burn, that's for sure. I'm sure you saw it if you were in a wedding."

"I did, and it was beautifully decorated, but I agree there were lots of pillows and soft furnishings."

"I'll take your word for it. I try to stick to the plumbing and repairs and let the wife do all the fancying up of the buildings." He paused to look past me, presumably at the remains of the building. "So either someone came out here and caused it to blow, or something dropped out of the sky and exploded on it. That's the long and short of it as far as I'm concerned. Doesn't matter to me which."

"Why is that?"

"It'll be rebuilt either way. Insurance folks have already come and gone, so I guess they'll coordinate with those ATF fellows who were here up until a little while ago."

That explained why the place was now empty. Whatever Trent and his team had wanted to find out here had already been found. Or perhaps there was nothing to find.

Sometimes things just blew up. That had been Miguel's take on the incident. It wasn't a comforting thought considering my brother was an explosives expert who worked around these kinds of substances every day.

Mr. Ames swiped at his forehead with his sleeve, and a glint of diamonds on his gold wedding band caught the light. "Like I said, all I care about is getting it rebuilt. Doesn't matter to me how it went down. Long as we don't have a place for the ladies to get ready, we're in danger of losing bookings to other venues. This needs to be fixed, and fast. And for the record, the wife and I do not profit from the loss of this building. In fact, we'll go in the hole to get it all redone. But it can't be helped."

"Right." I paused to consider my question carefully. "Is Canon around?

I'd like to speak to him."

Mr. Ames' eyes narrowed. "What for?" He gave me a sideways look. "I'm thinking you either believe he ditched work and wasn't sick, or maybe you want to ask him if he knows what happened with this big blowup here. Maybe that's why you came here in the first place?"

"Not at all. Actually, I was going to ask him if he knew anything about dogs in the area," I said, not letting on that I would indeed ask about the other two things as well if I got the chance. "He may know where the dog we found belongs, or perhaps he's heard about someone who is missing a dog. Those are the questions I really would love to ask him if I can."

"Of course you can." He paused. "Next time he comes to work."

My first instinct was to keep quiet. Then I decided to continue. "Mr. Ames, the building next to the restaurant where your son works belongs to me. During the tornado, there was a fire upstairs that was caused by explosives. Then last night your building was destroyed by an explosive device."

"I noticed," he said, sarcasm dripping from those two words. "As I said before, the cops and the ATF are working on it. So, what's your point?"

"My point is two explosions in a week in a town as small as Brenham is suspicious. The fact that my property is involved makes it personal. I know that law enforcement is working on this, but I want to help if I can. And on top of that, I'm looking for Pal's home."

"Who is Pal?"

"The Belgian Malinois I told you about. The one that was found running around in your parking lot."

Mr. Ames seemed to think about it a moment. Then he nodded. "Fair enough. If you want to find that dog's owner, I think it's time you went on to look for that dog trainer." With that pronouncement, he climbed back into his golf cart and reversed out of the spot where he was parked.

"If I can't talk to Canon, maybe I could speak with your wife?" I called as he drove away without responding. "Okay then. I guess not."

I retraced my steps to get into my car and drive away. As I glanced in the rearview mirror, I took one last look at the beautiful cottage that was now reduced to rubble.

Two explosions in one small town was just too coincidental. But what could this wedding venue and my building have in common? There had to be something I was missing because I couldn't think of a thing.

Or maybe it really was just a coincidence.

CHAPTER TWENTY

I slowed down as I passed the main building. Mr. Ames' golf cart was parked outside the main entrance, but he was nowhere to be seen, so I drove on. I paused for a moment under the arch and debated whether to go back and try to locate Mrs. Ames or Canon. However, the idea of meeting Mr. Ames again while searching for his family held no appeal.

Instead, I pressed the icon on my car's screen to activate the GPS once more. Then I followed the directions to the location Leigh had told me about. As it turned out, the training facility—a former roadside souvenir shop located a quarter of a mile from the entrance to Thistledown Farms—was no longer open.

The small parking lot was empty and so was the interior of the building. A walk around the building proved useless as there was no indication that anyone had been there recently.

A sign on the door indicated the property was for sale by owner. I snapped a picture of the sign then returned to my car to place a call to the number listed on the sign.

"Hi, I'm looking for the owner of this property because I've got a dog that I'm trying to place with his owners," I said when the voice mail picked up.

A few minutes later, while I was searching my spam folder for the emails that Lane had mentioned earlier, my phone rang. "Nora?" came through the speakers of my car in a familiar voice.

"Bitsy? Hi! What's up?"

"I should ask you that," she said. "You called me. Something about finding a home for a dog?"

"Thank you. So, I called the owner of. . ." I realized what had happened. "You own the dog training building?"

She laughed. "I must if you're calling me. Honestly, I have no idea what my husband buys. I guess Witt must have bought that place thinking either he or I could use it for something, then changed his mind. Would you like to see it?"

"Actually, I'm more interested in who owned it before you," I said. "Would you happen to know that?"

"Since I didn't know we owned it, I'll have to ask. But let me do some checking and I'll see what I can find out."

"Thanks, Bitsy."

"So, do you mind if I ask why you want to know the previous owners of that building? I mean, I heard your message, but do you think your missing dog might belong to the former owners?"

I let out a long breath as I braked for a stop sign. "Honestly, I don't know," I said. "But if there was a dog training business there before it was sold to you, then maybe the owner might recognize the dog and point us toward his owner. There has to be a reason why Pal was running around the parking lot of the wedding venue that night. I know it's a stretch, but I figure it can't hurt to try."

"Of course. It sounds like your pup is lonely for his former home if you're trying so hard to find it for him."

"Actually," I told her, "I'm not sure that's true. But I need to find out if there's someone out there missing him." I paused. "See, there's a dog missing from Fort Cavazos, and I don't want it to be Pal. If I can find an owner here, then maybe we can convince that owner to give him to Lane. He loves Lane, Bitsy. He really does."

I had become emotional. This surprised me. And yet over the days since Pal had been in Lane's life—and in mine—the changes in my boyfriend were answers to prayer.

Lane was sleeping at night, he'd vowed to change and was actually doing something about it, and he'd even taken a job here in Brenham. The job was temporary, but I'd be happy if the other changes were permanent.

"I would love it if Pal stayed in our lives," I added. "But to do that, I have to make sure he doesn't belong to someone else."

"That makes perfect sense, Nora. I'll do what I can." She paused. "So do you mind if I ask you about something?"

"Go for it," I told her.

"Has anyone talked to you about the fire in your building since it happened?"

I sighed. "Other than a brief conversation with law enforcement, no. Why?"

"This may be nothing, but after you left I called a locksmith to make an appointment to have him open that door and change out the key. Once I finished doing that, I decided to take a look at the security camera footage from the night of the storm. See, I don't use my desk very much, at least not for work things, and I certainly don't bother with security footage. I mean, nothing happens in Brenham, right?"

I recalled the elaborate beauty setup I'd seen and smiled. "Right. What did you find?"

"Lots of wind and rain for one thing," she said. "I kept seeing garbage cans rolling past and rain blowing sideways. It was crazy out there. I'm really glad I slept through it."

"So did I, but then neither of us lives near where the tornado hit."

"True," Bitsy said. "But anyway, at one point while the wind was swirling the rain around and there was just chaos out in the alley, I saw a flash of light."

"Lightning?" I asked.

"Maybe," she said slowly. "Or it could have been the moment the fire started."

"Oh," I said. "What time was that?"

"I'd have to go back and look to give you an exact time," she told me. "But if I had to guess, I'd say it was while the tornado was hitting the buildings across the street. Things were flying past, and it looked like even the rain was sideways. There was a lot of noise too. From what I've been hearing, that was sometime around three in the morning, I think."

"That sounds right," I said. "Have you called the police to let them know what you saw?"

"Not yet," Bitsy said. "I spoke to Witt, and he suggested I call you before I turn this over to the authorities." She paused. "See, that flash isn't all that was on the video."

"Oh?"

"I don't know how to tell you this, but I'm pretty sure I saw one of your employees running by."

"One of my employees?" I only had three right now, and none of them seemed capable of something like that.

"Yes, actually, I'm certain it was."

"Okay, but that was well past the time when they would have a reason to be in the alley."

"Nora, this was definitely a male and absolutely one of your waiters." She described the uniform of black pants and shirt with the Simply Eat logo that my waiters were required to wear. "And it gets worse. I'm almost positive I recognized him."

A few minutes later, I hung up and called Cassidy. Before she could say more than just a quick greeting, I told her everything I'd just heard from Bitsy.

Silence fell between us as I reached for my water bottle and took one sip and then another. All that talking had made me thirsty.

"Whoa," Cassidy finally said.

"Yeah, whoa," I repeated, replacing the water bottle in my cup holder. "I'm sorry. I should have asked if you have time to talk before I blasted you with this news."

"It's fine. Things are somewhat quiet right now. We don't see patients until nine on Tuesdays. But back to Bitsy—she really believes she saw Canon Ames in the alley at the time of the explosion," Cassidy finally said. "The clean-cut, red-haired college kid? Like, she saw him for herself on her security camera?"

"Yes," I said. "I'm kicking myself all over again for not having ours on the back of the restaurant repaired when Dad warned me last week that it was broken. And I hadn't had time to get one for the new building, so there's that."

"That would have been helpful," Cassidy said.

"Exactly what my insurance adjuster told me," I lamented.

"But back to this bombshell news—pardon the pun. Do you think it's possible that Canon Ames was behind the explosion?"

I thought a moment. "It's possible. Theoretically, anyone who worked in that block had knowledge about the comings and goings in the alley. That's where many of them took breaks or parked their bicycles or whatever. None of them would have looked out of place or raised suspicion."

"Unless it was the middle of the night and there was a tornado touching down across the street," Cassidy supplied.

"True." A thought occurred. "Oh, Cassidy, what if the explosion happened because someone—possibly Canon—was in the kitchen at the building doing whatever it was he was doing and he was spooked by the tornado? That might explain the explosion. That's Bitsy's theory, and I have to admit it makes sense."

"I'm with Bitsy. I think it does explain it," Cassidy said. "If I was working with something flammable and I had no advance knowledge that the buildings across the street were about to be damaged, I'd be pretty surprised when it happened. And I'd likely drop whatever I was holding."

"Which would make a spark, cause a fire, or do something else that ended with the explosion in my apartment sink," I said. "Also, Canon called in sick the day after the tornado, and he's out again today. Up to then, he'd never missed a shift."

"That's not exactly following a pattern since he was at work yesterday, right? The explosion happened on Sunday night, not Monday."

"Exactly." I paused. "Which is why I'm not so keen to convict him just yet. It could be random and he's innocent, or it could prove his guilt. I'm totally confused as to which. And even if we place Canon at the scene, what was he doing there?"

"Nora, there are a lot of things he could have been doing there, starting with stealing the furniture."

"Well, true, but that doesn't cause an explosion or the residue on the stairs that Pal alerted to."

"Right, so what do we do now?"

I exhaled slowly. "I'm waiting on Bitsy to send me the video. She said that's Witt's department, but she'd make sure she got it to me by the end of the day. We really can't do anything about this until then. I'm certainly not going to confront Canon."

"Okay, so there's no proof yet that it's Canon, and I'm kind of hoping it's not. He's so nice."

"Sometimes bad guys are nice," I said. "But I agree. He seems like the least likely person I would ever imagine to get involved in something like that. If I had to pick an employee who would be involved in this, he wouldn't be my first choice."

"I agree, but who would be?"

"Shane is the only other waiter right now, so if pressed to choose, it would be him, not Roz. Besides, she doesn't wear the same uniform, although if I'm looking at all the factors, she does have a key to the closet where we keep them. And speaking of clothing, I've had a few employees come and go over the past year, but I always make them turn in their uniforms before they get their final paycheck. Also, none of them were fired, so I can't even say that I know of anyone out there who would have a grudge against me or the restaurant."

"Right. You've been extraordinarily lucky—blessed, truly—with staff at Simply Eat."

"I have." I rested my head against the headrest and watched a cattle truck rumble past. "And I've been there every day the restaurant has been open, except for the day I did a tumble in the street after the tornado. I've been hands-on all the time."

"You have," she said. "I thought you'd never hire a chef so you could have a break. I know that Lane is awful with keeping long hours, but this isn't the first time that I've told you that you are too. Or was until Roz came along."

"Roz has been a godsend," I said. "Maybe I need to share Bitsy's information with her. She's running the kitchen now, so she should know if an employee is up to no good. I'm sure she's seen things that I haven't. Practically said as much not so long ago. She told me she was watching one of the employees, so she may not be as surprised as we are about Canon."

"Agreed. But back to the camera image for a second. Bitsy was absolutely certain the logo on the shirt she saw was yours? I'm still trying to figure out how that's possible given the fact it was dark and stormy."

"It was a dark and stormy night, all right." I said with a humorless chuckle as I drummed my fingers on the steering wheel. "And yes, she was certain. And she swears she recognized Canon by his hair color."

"How is that possible? I have one of those doorbell cameras, and it gives me grainy black and white footage at best. She couldn't know that the man had red hair."

"Her husband says nothing but the best for Bitsy," I said, smiling. "Apparently one of the companies that Witt Sumner invested in does a high-resolution security camera for home and small business use. She's got the prototype installed at the gym, one in the front and one out back facing the alley. Did I mention she—or rather, her husband—also owns the building where the dog training facility that Roz told me about was located? I'm in the parking lot now."

"No, you left that part out. Any luck there?"

I glanced at the building that was visible in my rearview mirror. "No, the place is closed, and it's empty inside. The sign is still there, but the facility is gone. I called the number on the For Sale sign and ended up with Bitsy."

"Cassidy, could you get Nora on the phone for me?" I heard Lane say in the background. "I would normally ask Brianna, but she's deep in conversation with Cameron, and I hate to bother her. I'm pretty sure those two are making plans for date night."

"Actually, I've got her on the phone right now. Nora, I've got Lane here. I'm going to put him on speaker then make myself scarce so the two of you can talk."

"No need," I heard Lane say. "This is about Pal, so you'll probably want to hear it too." There was a pause, and then he continued. "Nora,

I've heard back on the lab results."

My heart thudded. *Please, Lord, don't let Pal be a match.*

"They refused to compare the tests without a tattoo number or information from his chip. Since Pal has neither and there are no visible markings on the vest I sent the photo of, the determination is that isn't their dog."

I let out a breath I didn't realize I had been holding. "Well, okay then. That's good news."

"I hope so," he said. "It's not definitive proof, though. We already know that identifying marks and the chip could have been removed."

"Or Pal never had them," Cassidy countered. "You can tell there were patches removed from the vest. Why not consider that the chip and tattoo were removed from the dog?"

"Also possible," Lane agreed. "But again, we are just guessing. I won't feel comfortable until there's definitive proof."

"Always the scientist," I said. "Truly, Lane, can't we just let that go now and pretend that there was never an option that the government owned Pal?"

"Nora," he said in that tone he always used when he didn't agree but also didn't want to argue with me.

"So," Cassidy said brightly, "this means we can move forward with our search for a private owner. If evidence comes up that shows Pal was associated with a chip or had a tattoo, then we'll cross that bridge when we come to it. How's that?"

"You sound like my mother," I said, smiling at one of Mama's favorite sayings.

"Hey, there's nothing wrong with thinking positive and worrying about bad stuff only if it actually happens."

"I can't disagree," Lane said. "But I'm not ruling anything out without proof."

"So you said." A sleek red sports car whizzed past on the road, kicking up a storm of dust that rolled into the parking lot.

"Oh, Nora, tell Lane about the video," Cassidy said.

"I don't want this to sound bad, but can I have the short version? I've got a few more things to do before I'm ready to see patients, and they'll start arriving soon."

"Sure," I said. "There's a security camera video taken behind the gym of someone running down the alley immediately after a flash of light, and the timing places it at roughly the moment the explosion happened in my building. It's possible the person is wearing the same shirt my waiters wear. It's also possible that person has red hair. And before you ask, the footage was recorded by some fancy HD camera that captures sound and color. I'll have the file to view sometime today."

"Have the authorities been told?" he asked.

"Not yet, but Bitsy is going to give them a copy after I see it," I said.

"Why?"

"No clue, Lane. That's just what I was told."

"Okay," he said on an exhale of breath. "Well, that's interesting."

"Especially since only one of her waiters has red hair," Cassidy commented. "And that waiter called in sick the morning after the tornado and then again today."

"There's more," I said. "That waiter's parents own Thistledown Farms wedding venue."

"Where the second explosion happened," Cassidy said triumphantly. "So while we haven't solved the mystery of where Pal came from just yet, we have figured out who blew up Nora's kitchen and made the connection between the two events. Oh! And I almost forgot, thanks to all the excitement. I found out how the orange tabby cat ended up in your building, Nora."

CHAPTER TWENTY-ONE

Nora

Brenham, Texas
Tuesday afternoon

I had been waiting all afternoon for Bitsy's video to arrive, and I was still waiting. Simply Eat was closed for the dinner service thanks to a catering event off-site, so I had the place to myself until the crew returned.

Dad had surprised me by volunteering to step in and fill the vacancy left by Canon's absence. Not to be outdone, Mama insisted on coming along to help. Thus, I was absolutely not needed at this event unless Roz called out a distress signal.

Knowing that my parents were involved and that my mother had a bit of trouble being in a kitchen where she was not in charge, that absolutely could happen. I had to admit she'd behaved herself on the day the tornado hit. According to Roz, she was helpful without being the least bit bossy.

While I was happy to hear it, I decided to stick around the restaurant and get some work done in my office just in case. You never knew what would happen with Mama when cooking was involved.

My phone buzzed with a text from Lane. Busy?

When I answered that I wasn't, the phone rang. "Hey, handsome," I said, leaning back in my chair to stretch. "Are you finished at the clinic?"

"Thanks to Cameron volunteering to take the rest of my shift—likely so he can spend more time with our receptionist—I was able to leave an hour ago. I'm home with Pop now. We're deciding which casserole we'll be having for dinner," he said with a chuckle. "Apparently my father is popular with the church ladies. If they keep delivering food at the rate it arrived today, I'm going to have to buy him another fridge to hold what this one won't."

"Of course he is," I said. "How did he do today with his new caregiver?"

"From what I can tell, it went great. I'm glad he and Pop found one another. I would have been in a bind otherwise." He paused. "Kirby wants me to leave Pal with them tomorrow. I'm considering it, but I want to know that Pop gets all of his attention."

"That's reasonable," I said.

"And then there's this weird way Pal acts around him. Not like he's alerting to something but just like. . ." His words trailed off. "I don't know. I can't explain it. This morning Kirby laughed it off and attributed it to the breakfast tacos he'd just eaten, but Pal did the same thing when I got home."

"What did he do?"

"Sniffed at him," Lane said. "I know. Not exactly something to worry about."

"It's what dogs do," I said. "Maybe he likes Kirby's smell. Like his aftershave or detergent smells familiar to him."

"I wouldn't know. I didn't get that close to him, and it's probably perfectly normal. Anyway, did that video ever come through? I'm anxious to see it."

"Nothing yet," I said. "But to be fair, Bitsy's husband's IT guy may have more important things to do."

"Okay, let me know when you get it," he said. "I'm interested in seeing for myself whether this is one of your waiters on that film. So, anyway, what are you up to for the rest of the day?"

"Just finishing up some paperwork while I wait for the crew to come back from a catering job. I'm considering cleaning out my office. I haven't done that in a while."

Since I'd moved in, would be the truthful statement. I had dusted, mopped, and done all the things to keep the space tidy, but as to actually sorting through what was there and getting rid of the things I didn't need? Yeah, that hadn't happened. Ever.

I glanced up at the shelves. Proof of my lack of sorting through the unnecessary items sat right there on the shelf, wedged between a stack of cookbooks and a paperweight that my niece had made for me when I opened the restaurant.

I rose to retrieve the dog toy that I had grabbed from the building's back stairs last week. It looked clean enough, but I should take it home and wash the thing before I offered it to Second Chance Ranch.

"So about the cat," Lane said. "Are you going to keep her?"

Cassidy's news that the tabby cat had been dumped at the building by a contractor named Rhett Burns who had been hired by Mr. Lazlo to make some minor repairs before closing had been the bright spot in the day. Apparently he had seen Cassidy's posts on social media and come forward as the guilty party. He claimed his daughter had been diagnosed as allergic to cats, and he'd been desperate.

Knowing Mr. Lazlo, he felt like the cat would be taken care of. He hadn't bargained on the cat being so good at hiding that Mr. Lazlo had never realized she was there.

"Of course I'm going to keep her," I said. "But now I need a name for her."

Lane offered a few options, none of which appealed to me. "I guess I'll have to wait until I solve these mysteries before I can think clearly enough to name that sweet girl."

"Oh, Nora. Mysteries." He paused. "I've got it. Agatha Kitty."

"Actually," I said slowly as I considered his suggestion, "I like it."

My computer dinged with an email. I glanced at the subject line.

"It's here, Lane. The video, I mean."

"Okay, well, download it, but wait for me. I'll be there in a few minutes."

I clicked on the icon to begin the download. "Is it safe to leave your father?"

"My father is currently visiting with the pastor, his wife, and three women who have insisted on bringing more casseroles even though we've got plenty. Have I mentioned that I'm considering buying another refrigerator to hold the excess?"

I grinned. "You might have said something about that."

"Well, there is this one nice widow lady who brought cakes. That would be plural. Apparently my father is so sweet that she couldn't decide between bringing him her famous apple cake or her famous blueberry strudel cake. So she made both. I'm voting for her to win our version of *The Bachelor, Senior Citizen Edition*. Although there's some pretty decent Famous Chicken and Spaghetti and Famous Corn Bread Taco Bake in the running."

"Well, all right then. The video is uploading. Come around to the back door. It's unlocked."

Five minutes later, I heard a motorcycle roar down the alley then stop. I bolted out of my seat to race to the kitchen. No one I knew rode a motorcycle this loud, and the only person I was expecting was Lane.

After peering out the back door's peephole, I threw open the door and stared at my boyfriend, who was currently wearing a black leather jacket and sitting astride a shiny red Harley Davidson motorcycle.

I hate motorcycles. They're loud and dangerous. I know this because every one of my brothers owned one at one time or another, and every one of those idiots managed to hurt themselves riding it.

So, no way was I going to tell him how good he looked right now. Oh, but he did.

When I gathered my senses, I said, "Lane Bishop, have you lost your mind?"

He held up both hands. "It's not mine."

"Okay, well, whose is it?" I demanded.

Lane laughed as he pulled off his helmet and pocketed the keys then climbed off the motorcycle. "This beast belongs to my father."

"I didn't know Dr. Bishop rode a Harley," I said.

"Neither did I, but apparently the casserole ladies did. When I realized that I had several cars parked behind my truck, one of the helpful trio—the widow lady with the cakes—mentioned that maybe Pop would just let me take the Harley. That started a whole conversation between the ladies about which of them had been privileged to take a ride on said motorcycle and which of them did not wish to have their hairdos messed up by wearing a helmet."

I couldn't help but laugh.

"As you can imagine, my father turned several shades of red before he told me where he kept the keys. I suspect we'll be having a conversation about it after the church crowd leaves."

"Good luck with that." I held the door for Lane as he walked inside. "Grab a stool and join me. The video is ready to go."

Lane snatched up Roz's stool from its place in the corner and followed me into my office. Once he was settled beside me, I hit PLAY.

I watched in silence as the roaring sound of wind and rain combined with the image of swirling chaos to give a visual experience that I was glad I missed. Just as Bitsy described, a white flash of light filled the screen.

"According to Bitsy, we should be seeing a person on the screen any minute," I said, now on the edge of my seat.

"There he is." Lane reached across me to press PAUSE.

The image of a man filled the screen. True to Bitsy's word, it was plain that this person had red hair. It was also easily noted that he was wearing a black shirt embroidered with the Simply Eat logo on the pocket.

I sat back, unable to believe what I saw. Though the pelting rain obscured some of the face on the screen, this person was unmistakably Canon Ames.

"Now what?" I said on an exhale of breath, still reeling from what I saw on the screen.

Lane hit REWIND and watched the segment again. As before, he paused the video on the somewhat grainy close-up of Canon's face.

He studied the screen closely. Then he enlarged the image and sat back. "Is there any way this could be another person besides your waiter?"

"I don't see how that's possible," I told him.

"Then we have to turn this over to the authorities," Lane said.

"Bitsy is willing to do that. She just wanted me to see it first. I guess as a courtesy since I employed Canon." I paused. "I'm just stunned, Lane.

I never thought it could be him."

"Unless you can figure another reason that Canon Ames was in that alley in the middle of a tornado, then it is him who caused that fire, and he's running away from it."

I nodded. "No, you're right. There's no other explanation. But my gut says he's innocent even though I'm staring at the proof he isn't."

Lane wrapped his arm around me. "How about I call Jason? Maybe he can stop by and look at it and give us some advice."

I looked up into his eyes. "Yes, can we do that? I'd feel better if we talked to him about it before anyone else sees it. I know he's a game warden, but he's also state police, so that counts, right?"

"He's a licensed peace officer, so yes, it counts." Lane retrieved his phone and called the game warden. "I'm at Nora's restaurant. Do you have a couple of minutes to stop by and look at some footage from the night of the tornado?"

A moment later, he hung up. "We're in luck. He just left the clinic after dropping off an animal to be rehabbed and will be here in a couple of minutes."

I leaned against Lane's shoulder. The fact we'd found the person who caused the fire should have made me feel good. I'd have to work on that, because right now it only made me sad.

We sat in silence, both of us staring at the screen until Jason arrived. He crowded into the room, and I played the video from the beginning. When Canon's face came into view, Lane reached over to hit PAUSE.

Jason whistled under his breath. "Well, good work, you two. Looks like we've got our perp dead to rights. He's your waiter, right, Nora?"

I nodded. "His name is Canon Ames. His parents own Thistledown Farms."

"The wedding venue?" Jason said, his brows rising. "The location of the other explosion."

"Yes," I said softly. "Apparently Canon is the link between the two incidents."

"You don't sound sure," Jason said.

"She doesn't think he's guilty," Lane supplied. "She's got a gut feeling that Canon is innocent."

Jason nodded and stared at the screen for a moment. "Run it again, please."

Lane complied, leaving me to sit back and watch for the third time while the red-haired waiter ran down the alley in the middle of the night while a tornado was raging less than a hundred yards away. As before, he hit PAUSE when Canon's image appeared.

Silence fell between us. Then Jason shrugged.

"It looks pretty clear to me, Nora," the game warden said. "The movement of the debris and rain shows it had to happen during the tornado. I'm going to assume that the time stamp will confirm that. And we all recognize the man on the screen."

"We do," Lane said. "Don't we, Nora?"

I managed a nod.

"So, I can do this one of two ways. Either I go out tonight and quietly pick Canon Ames up for questioning, or I let the ATF and Brenham PD guys see this first and then let them handle it, likely with a lot of noise and guns drawn," Jason said. "Either way, we will need the chain of custody on the video."

"What does that mean?" I asked.

"That means we'll need access to the security camera and probably testimony from the camera's owner and the IT guy who pulled the footage and sent it to you."

"The camera belongs to Witt Sumner. His wife, Bitsy, is a friend."

Jason whistled under his breath. "Well, he's easy to find. And I assume he'll cooperate."

"You'd have to confirm that with him," I said.

Lane leaned closer. "I'm thinking we need to trust Jason with this. I don't think you want the feds or Brenham PD arresting Canon at work. Don't you agree?"

I nodded but without enthusiasm.

"Okay," Jason said. "I'll need you to email that video to me along with the contact information for Mrs. Sumner, since she's the one who initiated the conversation about the camera."

Another nod.

"I'll do that right now," Lane said, sliding the laptop keyboard in his direction. After forwarding Bitsy's email to Jason, he reached for my phone. "Do you have Bitsy's number saved?"

I shook my head. "No, but she's in the recent caller list."

After a few clicks, Lane had sent a screenshot of the number to Jason. "Okay, that should get you started."

"Before you go, I would like to say he's innocent," I told Jason, gesturing toward the computer screen. "But there's the proof he isn't. I can tell you that I never had any idea he might have this side to him. He's always been polite and helpful. And other than the two days he called in sick, he's been prompt and willing to take on extra work to get the job done. I feel like Roz will say the same."

"I'll be sure and ask her." Jason paused to give Lane a look. "Could I talk to Nora a minute?"

Lane nodded and squeezed my shoulder. Then he rose, allowing Jason to take a seat beside me.

"Nora, I understand about a gut feeling," Jason said. "So here's what I'm going to do. As a peace officer, I am bound by the laws of the State of Texas. You've shown me proof that a man may have committed a crime, and I am obligated to investigate that, even though I have the same impression of him that you do. Do you understand?"

"Yes," I said.

"But you are a private citizen. If you were to take an interest in proving me wrong and figuring out that someone other than Canon Ames caused that incident in your building, you are free to do that. As long as you follow the law while you're investigating."

I studied him for a moment. "Are you challenging me, Jason?"

He shrugged. "Hardly. I'm just making you aware of your rights, ma'am. How you spend your time is up to you."

"Right," I said slowly.

He gave me a look. I spied the beginnings of a smile. Jason was challenging me.

"So we have an understanding?" Jason said.

"We do," I told him.

"I need to warn you that your gut may be wrong. Mine has been on occasion." He paused. "Right now I have to do my job and take that young man in. I'm hoping you can find a reason for me to let him go."

I squared my shoulders and straightened my spine. "You've got a deal, Jason."

"I thought I might," he said.

CHAPTER TWENTY-TWO

LANE

Brenham, Texas
Tuesday afternoon

I walked with Jason out into the alley. "Thanks for talking her off the ledge. She really likes that kid, I guess. I've never seen Nora so upset about something. Well, that's not true," I admitted. "But I'm usually the cause of it."

Jason reached for the door handle of his truck and then paused. "Don't discount her gut feeling, Lane. She might be onto something. I'll be working on my end to get to the truth, but I've challenged her to do her own investigation."

I groaned. "Jason, I wish you hadn't done that. Nora is relentless when she wants to be. With Pop not yet recovered, I'm already stretched thin. Now I'll be chasing her around to make sure she's not getting into too much trouble."

He shrugged. "I may have made more work for you if you're planning to keep her safe, but that's what we do with the women we love, isn't it? Keep them safe, I mean, although I guess I could plead guilty to making more work for Cassidy on occasion. Anyway, Lane, listen to her, okay?

She's a smart lady."

I frowned as my temper threatened to rise. "Are you suggesting I don't appreciate Nora?"

Jason gave me a look. "Calm down, cowboy. I'm not suggesting anything of the sort. Cassidy says you're in town for another couple of weeks until the newlyweds return. I'm just saying don't waste the time you've got with her before you go back to your old life."

I let out a long breath then nodded. "Yeah. Okay, that's fair. I do tend to get wrapped up in my work."

"Cassidy might have mentioned that," he said. "But no judgment from me. I'm on call 24/7, so that pretty much is the definition of a workaholic. I just have to remember that while someone else can do my job, there's no one else who can love Cassidy like I can or was meant to." He gestured toward Pop's motorcycle. "Anyway, since when do you ride a Hog?"

"That belongs to my Pop." I told him how I came to find out about the motorcycle and why I was on it this afternoon.

"Your Pop has excellent taste in motorcycles," Jason said. "Cassidy would not be happy with me if I bought one of those."

"I got a similar impression from Nora. The first thing she did was ask me if I'd lost my mind." I grinned. "But it sure was fun to ride. Now that he's broken his leg, it's unlikely his doctors will let him get back on it, though."

"If I wasn't about to buy an engagement ring, I'd be making you an offer for it," Jason said. "Oh, and don't mention that to my girl or yours. Cassidy has no idea I've got plans to propose."

"Oh yeah? When?"

"Why?" Jason said with a chuckle. "Are you trying to get in a proposal to Nora before I pop the question with Cassidy?"

I laughed off the question. While I was happy for Jason and Cassidy, I knew that this engagement would up the pressure on me to do the same. Plus, there would be plenty of wedding planning going on.

"Your secret is safe with me," I told him.

Jason studied me for a moment. "And yours is safe with me."

"What are you talking about?" I asked.

He just smiled. "I'm having the ring custom designed. Her mother and grandmother each contributed diamonds from family pieces to include in the bands, so I can't propose until the ring is ready." Jason paused a beat. "I'd say you're probably safe for the next two weeks, maybe three."

We shook hands, and then I went back inside. I found Nora studying the computer screen.

"Sweetheart, how about you and I get out of here?" She looked up at me but said nothing, so I quickly continued. "We've got a couple of hours of daylight left. How about you and I go for a ride?"

She gave me the smile that always made my heart jump. "I would love that, Lane. But can I make a slight change to the plan?"

"Sure," I said as I watched her pick up her phone.

"Hey, this is Nora. Would you saddle Maisy Grace for me and another horse for Lane? He's a good rider, so give him one with some spunk."

Five minutes later we had exchanged Pop's motorcycle for my truck and headed down the highway toward Hernandez Ranch. Bypassing the house, I drove directly to the barn.

The ranch was known for their American quarter horses, and two of the finest of the herd were waiting for us when we arrived.

Nora was seated on hers in no time, but it took a few minutes for the feisty gelding, whose name I learned was Sizzle, to allow me to settle onto the saddle. When we finally left the barn and headed out toward the pastures, I let out a whoop.

"Enjoying yourself, Lane?" she called.

"I am, actually," I told her.

"Want to race?"

Before I could answer, Nora dug in and took off toward the horizon. "Challenge accepted," I called as I did the same.

We rode for an hour, although it seemed like much less. As the sun dipped toward the tree line, Nora finally slowed her pace to let me catch up. We rode side by side in silence until we reached the creek.

Nora climbed off her horse at the creek's edge. I held on tight to the reins as I wobbled to my feet. My horse lurched forward, leaving me standing there while he ducked his head toward the water.

"Should you be riding at that speed with a butterfly bandage on your forehead?" I asked her.

She patted her horse then released the reins. After walking toward a flat rock at the creek's edge, she sat down and stretched her legs out in front of her then looked off into the distance. "A month ago these pastures were filled with bluebonnets. It was absolutely gorgeous out here."

"Right. It was bluebonnet season," I said, "but did you hear what I said?"

Her attention shifted back to me. "I heard you just fine, Lane. I took the butterflies off this morning. They were about to fall off, and my doc said to go ahead and remove them."

I realized I hadn't noticed and didn't feel great about that. I really should have paid closer attention to the details, especially where they pertained to the woman I loved. "Okay, so bluebonnets, then."

"I wish you'd been here to see them," she said.

I let that statement hang between us in the evening air as I sat down beside her. "I wish I had too," I told her, and I meant it. "I was working. I'm always working, and that's a problem."

Her face softened. "I didn't say that."

"You didn't have to." I wrapped my arm around her. "It's true. And you're far more tolerant of that fact than I would be if things were the other way around. I'm not proud of that, by the way."

Nora leaned into my embrace then snaked her arm around my back. "I'm very glad you're here now, even if it's just until Kristin and Tyler return."

My phone buzzed with a text. I ignored it. Instead, I concentrated on how good Nora's cheek felt against my shoulder and how very much I wanted to have this moment go on indefinitely.

"I love you, Nora," I said, my lips pressed against the top of her head.

"I love you too, Lane," she whispered.

Jason was right. No one could love Nora like me. The problem was, I hadn't been very good at showing her how much I cared.

I couldn't imagine life without her, and yet I had prioritized other things over her. This was a problem that only I could fix.

Maybe I should pop the question right here and now. It just didn't seem right to do that without any planning or a ring. Nora deserved better than that.

Another text. I ignored it too. Then the phone rang.

I silenced it then gathered her closer and held her as we watched the sun sink lower. The moment might have been perfect if Nora's eldest brother hadn't chosen that particular time to drive up.

"Lane, your father's been trying to reach you."

I jumped up and headed toward Junior while fumbling for my phone. "What happened? Is he okay?"

"He's fine, but Pal is gone," Junior said.

"Oh no." Nora was beside me now. "Junior, you take the horses back to the barn. Lane and I will use the farm truck to drive to the barn and switch vehicles. If Dad or Mama call wondering why I'm not at the restaurant, tell them we're heading to Dr. Bishop's place. We need to find Pal."

Junior barely had time to nod before Nora had the keys in her hand and was heading toward the farm truck. "You drive," I told her, knowing she could find the most direct route to the barn faster than I could.

In what seemed like just a few minutes, we were in my truck racing toward Pop's place. By the time we got there, Pop was beside himself.

"He was great all the time you were gone," Pop said. "But then I guess he must have escaped when the pastor and the ladies all left. I've gone over this a hundred times in my head, and that has to be when it happened."

"Okay, Pop," I told him. "It's going to be fine. Slow down and tell me what happened. Start with when your visitors left."

He nodded. "Okay, well, I could hardly get up, of course, thanks to this busted leg. So I bid them goodbye from my chair. Thanks to that fancy lock that you put in, I could secure the front door from my phone. Pal had been right beside me the whole time. Then he wasn't."

My poor father looked like he was about to cry. "I'm so sorry. I just wish I'd done something different. Then Pal wouldn't be gone."

"We all have regrets, Dr. Bishop," Nora said, her tone soothing. "You didn't do anything wrong."

"That's right, Pop," I added. "Pal is smart. My guess is he's running around having a good time, and he'll be scratching at the front door any minute."

I exchanged a glance with Nora. Both of us knew that dog was too smart and well trained to just run off. If he was gone, there was a reason. Someone had taken him.

Nora looked over at Pop and nodded. "So how about your father and I stay here and wait for Pal while you take a stroll around the neighborhood and see if you can see him. Like you said, he's probably just running around."

"Right," I said. "Pop may be ready for dessert, but you're both going to have a hard time choosing which one."

While I snatched up the spare leash and a dog treat, Nora and Pop began discussing the pluses and minuses of the plethora of sweets in the kitchen. "I'll be back," I called then stepped outside and locked the door.

Before I moved from the front porch, I called Pal then waited. I repeated the process twice with no success. Then I tried whistling for him. This produced the same results.

"Okay, time to take this show on the road," I said, setting off down the driveway toward the street.

After I'd made a circle around the block, I paused to call Nora. It was pitch dark now, and I either needed another lead on the dog or a flashlight in order to keep looking. "Is Pal back yet?"

"No," she said, "but your dad did remember something. He thinks that Pal might have gone with Kirby."

"Why would he think that?"

"Hang on." I heard footsteps and a door closing. "Okay, I didn't want to say this in front of your father, but he took a pain pill after the pastor left. He said he remembers Pal curling up on the floor next to him, keeping watch. That's how he put it. Then he had this fuzzy recollection of someone asking if the dog needed walking. He thought it might be a dream, but I had a theory that I was about to check out with the pastor when you called."

"Go on."

"What if that guy who is doing the care for your father during the day happened by while all the guests were leaving? Might he strike up a conversation and even offer to see to the dog until you got back?"

It seemed possible. "Okay, well, you make the call. Meanwhile, I've got Kirby's address. I'll go see if my dog is there." I opened my contacts and took note of the address that Kirby had given me then headed in that direction. I was just turning the corner when Nora called back.

"Just what I thought. The pastor said a man who introduced himself as your father's caregiver came by to walk the dog."

I frowned. "Okay, I'm about to walk up the driveway and get my dog."

I knocked twice, but no one answered. Kirby's SUV was in the driveway, so I knew he must be there unless he truly was walking Pal. Though, if that was the case, I would most likely have run into them at some point in my search.

I walked around to the side of the house to look over the fence into the backyard. It was empty. Then I went back to the front door and knocked one more time. When there was still no response, I placed a call to Kirby.

He picked up on the second ring. Before he could say more than a greeting, I cut in.

"I want my dog. I'm at your front door."

The EMT muttered something I couldn't quite hear. "Give me a sec," came next. Then he hung up.

I stood there fully prepared to call the cops if he didn't open that door in a few seconds. Just as I was about to make that call, the door swung open. Pal came barreling out with Kirby hurrying behind him. I snapped the leash on my dog then scratched him behind the ear. "Good boy," I told him then retrieved the treat I'd grabbed along with his leash.

"Hey there," Kirby said. "I was just about to bring him home when you called."

"Why was my dog in your house?" I asked, keeping my tone even.

"Dude, I'm sorry," he said, his face flushed and both hands outstretched. I saw that your dad's visitors were leaving and thought I'd look in on him since your truck wasn't there. He told me I could walk Pal, so I did."

"Except that you walked him to your house, not mine." I was still trying to remain calm but just about to fail miserably.

"Just for a second. See, I was almost back at your place when, well, this is embarrassing." He shrugged. "I needed to use the facilities, and my home was closer than yours. So I was headed out to bring him back when you rang the doorbell. I thought it was those Girl Scouts who keep trying to sell me cookies. If I opened the door, I'd lose time and I'd end up buying more cookies than I need. Not that I need any, but you know what I mean."

I stood quietly waiting for Kirby to stop speaking. When he did, I gave him another minute of silence. I wasn't sure that he was telling the truth, but I had no proof that he wasn't.

"I don't blame you for being mad, Lane. I messed this up big-time. I should have contacted you. Though, in my defense, I got permission from your father before I took the dog out."

Okay, now he did look like he was telling the truth. I decided to let him off the hook.

"Yes, you should have," I said firmly. "Pop had taken a pain pill, so he barely remembers that you were there. He told Nora he thought it might have been a dream."

"Aw man, I'm really sorry. I promise this won't happen again," he said. "Am I still invited to stay with your dad tomorrow, or have I messed up too badly?"

I let out a long breath. I needed someone, and in truth he'd done nothing to show he wasn't trustworthy with my father.

"Yes, of course. Same time as today, okay. And no walking the dog, please. Backyard only for Pal, okay?"

Kirby prattled on with a few more apologies before I managed to walk away. I called Nora to let her know I was headed home with Pal.

CHAPTER TWENTY-THREE

Nora

Wednesday morning
Simply Eat

S o it's true then," Roz said, leaning against the entrance to my office. "Canon was arrested for bombing your building."

She wore sunshine yellow today with green striped pants and a set of neon pink bracelets adorning one arm. Shane stood behind her gaping at me as I gave them the short version of how their coworker had been caught on camera at the time the tornado hit.

"Why was he out in that weather?" Shane asked. "It was bad out there."

I shrugged. "It looks like he set the fire in the building. He may even have been living there, although it appears there wasn't much of the furniture left."

Shane glanced down at the floor then back up at me. "I just can't believe it. He was such a nice guy. Who knew he was a bomber?"

"No one is claiming that," Roz reminded him. "He was caught on camera running down the alley. There could be plenty of good reasons why."

As she said the words, she looked at me. Both of us knew there weren't many good reasons for being out in a tornado.

"Boss, do you want me to hire someone to replace Canon?" she asked. "We can't go on running this place with just Shane and me. Not on the weekend anyway."

I sighed. "I don't want to, but we can't be shorthanded for long, and we don't know what's going to happen with Canon. Go ahead and see if we can at least get someone in here part-time to make up for his absence."

Roz nodded. "And for the record, I don't want to replace him either. Canon was a good guy and a hard worker. Frankly, none of this makes sense."

She was echoing my thoughts. I nodded. "Agreed," was all I could manage to say.

I turned to my computer and clicked on my emails. Scanning my inbox, I spied something from Trent.

> *No news on the dog. Without a tattoo or chip and no patches on the vest, no one wants to talk about whether you've got an MWD. I've now seen the footage of your waiter. Not saying this is solved, but your case may have just gotten a little easier. This kid is the only connection between two locations that have had an explosion detonated in the past week. Pretty convincing stuff. That's off the record, of course. And I'm putting through paperwork to let you back into your building tomorrow.*

I sat back a minute then typed a response.

> *First the building—THANK YOU. Also thanks for checking on the dog. I've got my doubts about the video but no proof that he didn't do it. And I certainly cannot argue about the connection between the two locations. If any of this changes, I'll let you know.*

I hit SEND, then continued to scan my inbox. Just as I was about to click on an email from the grocer who'd been messing up our orders so much, I saw a response pop up from Trent. I opened it instead.

See that you do.

"Well that was short and to the point, Trent," I said under my breath as I opened the email from the grocer.

A knock at the back door distracted me. Roz opened the door, and I could hear her speaking to someone. I caught something about the grocery order, and then the door shut again.

I rose to investigate. Grocery bags were piled onto the counter, and Shane was helping Roz empty them.

"Did they get it right this time?" I asked as I leaned against the doorframe.

"Looks like it," Roz told me.

"Well, hallelujah," I said. "I guess my email worked."

"Email?" Roz made a face.

"Yesterday while you were at the catering event, I sent an email to the grocer asking him to be more careful with his orders. If he continued to mess up, I was going to have to replace him. That sort of thing." I shrugged. "I hate to be stern like that, but he needed to know that I am tired of him not getting everything to me."

"Oh," she said, offering a quick smile. "Right, of course. I'm sure he told you that he sent you everything we asked for that he was able to provide. That's what I keep hearing anyway."

"Probably," I said. "I haven't read it yet. Anyway, let me know when you start interviewing for Canon's job. Ideally we could have someone in training before the weekend shifts."

"Sure," she said. "I'll see what I can do."

I went back to my office and closed the door, then glanced at the email that was open in front of me. As Roz predicted, the grocer stated he'd provided everything we'd asked for in each order. It was the next sentence that confused me. I read it again, this time out loud.

"Considering the number of times recently when items have been canceled or substituted, I should be the one to warn you that there will be additional costs should this continue."

I picked up my phone and called the grocer. He answered on the first ring. "I see you've read my email."

"I have," I said. "And I'm confused."

"As am I," he told me. "But you go first."

"Okay, all I know is my chef has been having to make substitutions on almost every grocery order because items we've requested either don't show up or they're the wrong thing."

"Interesting," the grocer said. "Because I've been doing a whole lot of refunds against charges on your account. Have you looked at our latest statement?"

I glanced around on my desk. "It's not here yet," I told him after I determined it had not been in the stack of invoices I handled yesterday.

"I'll send you a link to access the online account. I see that you haven't signed up for that yet."

"Thank you. That's one of those things I was going to get around to in my spare time."

I heard the clatter of computer keys. "All right, I've sent the email. Look over the statement, then let me know if you still have questions."

"I'll do that," I told him.

"And Miss Hernandez, can I ask you something? Are you the only one who handles these orders?"

"No, my chef usually does it, although I have taken my turn at ordering if she's busy."

"Okay, well, that may be the problem. Just look over the statement and let me know if you still have questions," he said again. "I value your business and want to make this right, but only if it's something I'm doing. If the problem is on your end, I'll assume you'll handle it."

"Absolutely."

I ended the call and went back to the computer screen. After a few minutes, I was enrolled in the online account system and looking at my most current invoice.

My heart sank. Something was wrong, but I couldn't put my finger on exactly what it was. I navigated to last month's invoice. There were no returns and no change orders. Then I went back to the new statement. It was filled with returns, additions, and substitutions.

There was a crash outside my door, and Roz's voice rose. I could hear

Shane's voice as well, but I couldn't quite make out the words.

Rather than sit here and study the numbers on the page, I printed off the last three months of statements then closed out of the email. I would look over this when I had a chance, but with one waiter in jail and the other in trouble with the chef, it was not time to try and concentrate on numbers.

I placed a call to my insurance adjuster to let him know the building would be returned to me tomorrow, and together we made a plan for beginning the process of remediation. I hated to lose the merchandise downstairs, especially all of those books, but the adjuster gave me a whole bunch of good reasons for why it was a bad idea to try and clean them.

"Not knowing what burned except that it was likely a mixture of toxic chemicals means those fumes may have gone into the ventilation system. Do you want that on the items you sell?"

"Of course not," I had told him. "But it didn't smell smoky."

In the end, I agreed to listen to him—the expert—and allow the remediation to begin with a complete clean out of both floors. The one good thing that had happened with the theft of the furniture was there was almost nothing other than the items in the storage closet to remove from upstairs.

When I finished my call with the insurance adjuster, I sat back and viewed the mess that had become of my desk. Between the documents I'd just printed and the notes I'd taken on the process for remediating the building, I could easily spend another hour just handling what was semi-urgent.

But there was another crash and another round of yelling in the kitchen. The back door slammed, and through my window I spied Roz on her phone pacing the alley.

I pushed back from my desk and went out into the kitchen to see if order could be restored from chaos. At least out there the chaos was generally related to things that could be easily fixed like spilled food or fussy diners.

I found Shane sweeping up the remains of a broken plate. "Sorry, Nora," he said when he spied me watching him.

"It happens," I told him. "As long as it broke for some cause other than you throwing it at my chef."

A flicker of a smile appeared then faded as his spine straightened. "I wouldn't ever, I promise. It just slipped out of my hands while I was drying it."

I noticed he was wearing the gloves again. "Probably because those are slippery when they're wet. You only need to wear the gloves while you're handling food. You can go ahead and take them off now."

He nodded but made no move to do as I said.

"No, really. Wet gloves are dangerous. As soon as you get this swept up, remove them while you're working at the sink, please."

Shane ducked his head. "Would it be all right if I didn't, ma'am?"

I gave him an appraising look. "Shane, please take off your gloves."

Another reluctant look. I held his gaze with mine and refused to look away. Finally, he nodded and did as I asked.

To my surprise, his palms were fiery red and blistered in some places. In others skin was peeling.

"Shane, what have you done?" I gasped.

He looked down at his outstretched hands then mustered a smile. "Oh, they look good now. You should have seen them a week ago."

I edged closer and looked down to study his injuries. "What happened?"

"I was washing dishes and didn't realize how hot the water was, and I burned myself."

"Did you do that here? If you're injured at the restaurant, it's my responsibility to see that you're taken care of. A doctor needs to look at those burns."

"No, I didn't do it here, but thank you for your concern." He paused. "It's fine now. I got some cream to put on them that takes the sting out of it."

"How have you been working for a week with hands that look like this?"

"It's fine, Nora. Really. I haven't shown them to Roz, so if it's okay, I'll put the gloves back on before she comes in. She's already mad enough about that plate."

I hesitated a moment then nodded. He gave me a grateful look then donned the gloves and went back to clearing up the remains of the broken plate.

"That was the last one that needed washing," he told me as he put the broom and dustpan away. "The rest are in the dishwasher. We just had a couple leftovers that wouldn't fit."

Roz walked in, eyeing us both warily. "I've got two possible candidates for the temporary position," she said. "They'll be here in half an hour. Both recommendations came through friends in the business. The candidates have been told to arrive expecting to work. I'll see how they do on lunch prep. That means you're on serving, Shane."

"Roger that, ma'am."

The young waiter sounded so much like a soldier in that moment that I did a double take. He gave me a goofy grin then marched off to tackle his next assignment.

"What's with him?" Roz asked.

I shrugged. "Who knows? So tell me about these people we're interviewing."

The rest of the morning passed by in a blur of activity. Two new temporary employees with stellar recommendations were hired after completing a successful lunch shift. One would be coming in tomorrow morning to do prep and lunch shift, and the other in the afternoon to complete the remainder of the day.

After the new hires were dismissed for the day, I leaned against the counter and watched as Roz took Shane aside for a quiet talk. When the young man left smiling, I knew that whatever had transpired this morning between them was forgotten.

"He's a good kid," I told her after Shane slipped out the back door to take his break. "A little rough around the edges, but he seems willing to work hard."

She nodded. "I was skeptical of him, but he's proven me wrong. But so has Canon, only in a different way."

I ignored the temptation to set her straight on that whole innocent-until-proven-guilty thing in regard to Canon and debated whether to tell Roz about Shane's injured hands. By making her chef and giving her the responsibility of running the kitchen, Roz needed to know anything of importance in regard to her staff.

However, since Shane had been doing his work just fine all week—barring the mishap with the dish—I decided to keep that information to myself. At least for now.

I glanced at the clock then turned my attention to Roz. "Let's close up and go home. We're all tired, and I've got plenty to do in regard to getting the building next door back in shape. Tomorrow's another day."

Her brows rose. "Are you sure?"

I nodded. "It's the middle of the week, and you pulled off a catering gig with just Shane and my folks to help you."

"To be fair, your mother could run a kitchen better than any chef I've ever worked with or known. She's a culinary drill sergeant."

"True," I told her. "She's the inspiration behind this place, you know. We have these family dinners on Sundays, and I used to try to get in the kitchen and cook for her. My thought was that I'd be helping her by letting her sit and enjoy watching me work."

"But that didn't fly, I'm guessing," Roz said.

"Nope. She never once went for it. Instead, she'd tell me she only had one thing she wanted me and everyone else to do on Sundays in regard to dinner. Can you guess what it was?"

"Simply eat," Roz said, and I nodded. "I like that lady."

"Me too." I paused. "So, anyway, let's run a special on Thursday for anyone who wanted to dine with us tonight. If a diner presents a picture of themselves with our closed sign, dessert is free. Something like that. Can you come up with a dessert that would work with this scenario?"

Roz smiled. "I like it. And yes, absolutely. Maybe a Texas sheet cake?"

"Perfect."

My phone buzzed with a text from Lane. CAMERON IS TAKING THE AFTERNOON SHIFT, SO I'M FREE. PAL AND I THOUGHT WE'D STOP BY IN A FEW MINUTES. OKAY WITH YOU?

I quickly responded with a yes and a smile emoji. I was hitting SEND on my answer to Lane when another text came in. This one was from Bitsy.

BUBBA'S LOCKSMITH SERVICE COULDN'T COME UNTIL TODAY. HE'LL BE HERE IN A FEW MINUTES. WANT TO BE HERE WHEN WE OPEN THE DOOR?

I answered with a yes in all caps. Then I messaged Lane to let him know I might be down at the gym with Bitsy when they arrived. A thumbs-up appeared on my text.

"I'm just going to step out for a minute," I told Roz. "If you need to leave before I get back, lock up and go. I'll have my phone and keys with me."

CHAPTER TWENTY-FOUR

I arrived at the gym just as Bitsy and a man with a bright orange toolbox walked out of the building. Emblazoned on the toolbox was the image of a lock and the name BUBBA's LOCKSMITH SERVICE.

"Hey, Bubba," I said. "I didn't recognize you."

He grinned. "The wife's got me on one of those fasting diets. I'm starving all the time, but she likes the look of me, so I put up with it."

"Well, that's what counts, I guess," I told him.

"Oh, Nora," Bitsy said. "I'm so glad you didn't miss anything. I didn't know Bubba was already working on the interior lock when I texted you."

"That's 'cause skinny Bubba moves like a ninja," he said with a grin as he walked away. "I'm quiet as can be except for when my stomach is growling."

"So it's open already?" I asked Bitsy. "What was in the room?"

"Not yet," she told me. "It's the craziest thing. Bubba changed the lock, but the door won't open. He thinks it may be nailed shut from the inside. Who does something like that?"

"The plot thickens," I said.

"I guess so. Bubba is going to see if the exterior door works. I distinctly remember being told that the door was plastered over on the inside and wouldn't open. Something about a code violation if we were planning to use it for an apartment. Since we weren't, nothing was ever done about it. But if he can open it, maybe we can see if that's still true."

I fell in line behind Bitsy and Bubba. "Let me get this straight. Your upstairs apartment has one door that's covered by plaster and another that's locked from the inside?"

She nodded. "Looks like it."

"Okay, well, let's go solve this mystery." As I rounded the corner, I spied Lane's truck rolling up the alley with Pal in the passenger seat.

Lane parked and climbed out with Pal right behind him. The dog sat while Lane attached his leash.

"What's going on?" he said as he closed the distance between us. "Is that Bubba? He looks like he's lost weight."

"Yes. He's fasting or something." He leaned down to scratch Pal behind the ear. "We've got a locked room mystery to solve." I filled him in on the details while I watched Bubba and Bitsy chatting on the second-floor stair landing. "Want to join us?"

"Why not?" Lane followed me over to the metal staircase that traversed the back of Bitsy's building. With Pal at his side, they walked up the steps behind me.

"So it's an easy thing to change this lock," Bubba was saying as he knelt down and opened his toolbox. "The trick is whether we'll get it open once the lock situation is handled. If there's plaster on the other side, it won't budge. Even if they've put up Sheetrock or paneling, you're not going to get any swing to that door at all."

"Then what can we do to open it?" Bitsy asked.

"Well, you could blast it. Wouldn't need to use much." He slid me a look. "Sorry, too soon, Nora?"

"Carry on, Bubba," I said, shaking my head while Lane chuckled silently beside me.

The sound of power tools filled the air as Bubba worked on the rusted lock. Lane nudged me then gestured to Pal who was sniffing at the air.

"He's doing it again," he said.

"Weird," I told him. "I've never seen him do that."

"Okay," Bubba exclaimed. "We've got success with this old lock. She was rusty, but I got her fixed up. All you need to do, Miz Bitsy, is to turn that knob and see if we're in business."

Bitsy grinned as she reached for the doorknob. "This is exciting. One. Two. Three."

The door swung open easily, revealing an apartment that was clean and apparently occupied, given the grocery bags on the counter and a neatly folded stack of laundry in a white plastic basket on the floor beside them.

"Oh wow," I said softly, not believing what I was seeing.

Right there in front of me was every piece of furniture—at least as best I could recall—that had been missing from the apartment in my new building. Someone had actually moved Mr. Lazlo's furniture from his building—now mine—to this one.

But why?

"Don't move, everyone," Lane called just in time to keep us from barging in. "This is a crime scene."

Bitsy's hand flew up to her mouth. "Do you think so, Dr. Bishop?" Then her eyes widened. "Oh no. That means I'm a suspect, doesn't it?"

Bubba shrugged as he stowed his tools in the toolbox. "Your place, your responsibility. That's what I always say."

"You obviously didn't know this was up here, right?" I said, giving Bubba a withering look. "I can certainly vouch for that."

"Thank you, Nora." She nudged Bubba with her elbow. "You're the one who opened the door, Bubba. Does that make you my accomplice?"

"I am a paid contractor doing a job, Bitsy. You must not have read the fine print when you signed the work order. It says very clearly on page seven that the operator—that's me—is not responsible for the condition of the premises prior to—"

"Okay," Lane said. "Maybe you and Bitsy should go downstairs and discuss this. And Bitsy, you probably ought to call the cops to let them know what was found up here."

"Right." She gave Bubba a look. "Come with me."

"Yes, ma'am." He rose and gave her an exaggerated salute. "I don't guess either of you need any locksmithing done."

We both shook our heads. A moment later, Bitsy and Bubba disappeared around the corner of the building, leaving Lane and me alone with a most confusing crime scene.

"Any thoughts on what we're looking at?" I asked him.

I watched Lane's gaze sweep around the space. "Plenty of thoughts but no ideas. Mostly I'm thinking this is just plain bizarre. This is the furniture in the video your dad took before you bought the place, right?"

"Absolutely positive." I glanced down at Pal. "Lane, he's doing that sniffing thing again."

My phone buzzed with a text from my favorite ATF agent. "That was fast."

Lane gave me a questioning look.

"Trent Mendez with ATF. How could he know about the missing furniture so quickly?"

GOT A LEAD ON AN MWD THAT MIGHT BE LOCAL TO BRENHAM. HANDLER WENT AWOL SAME TIME AS DOG. IF YOU CAN IDENTIFY THE SOLDIER, YOU MAY BE ABLE TO IDENTIFY THE DOG WITHOUT A NUMBER OR CHIP.

I showed Lane. "Interesting."

"I'll ask him for a picture of the missing soldier."

Once I had sent the response, I tucked the phone into my pocket. "So what do we do now?"

"Stand guard until the cops come," Lane said. "It wasn't how I thought I'd be spending my afternoon, but it seems like the best idea given the circumstances." He looked down at Pal, who was still sniffing the air like someone was grilling a steak nearby.

"Seriously, Lane. What is wrong with him?"

"I don't know. Other than when Kirby is around, I haven't seen him do that."

He knelt beside the dog and scratched behind his ear then began to tie his shoelace. Pal nudged him then continued his odd behavior.

"You were home with your dad for lunch," I said. "Kirby was there too, right? Did he do that then?"

"The whole time," he told me as he finished tying his shoe and stood. "I finally sent Kirby home and told him I'd call him when I was about to leave. It drives me nuts."

"Do you think he's sensing a familiar smell?"

"That might be it," Lane said. "Maybe something that smells like his former trainer? A type of fabric softener or aftershave."

"I wish he could tell us. Because he's smelling it now, and there's just the two of us here." I paused as a thought occurred. "Oh, speaking of scents. I think I may have figured out why Pal alerted to the stairs at my building. Trent, the ATF agent, told me that Miguel was on the scene the night of the tornado and fire."

"Miguel?" Lane shook his head. "Are you sure? He's volunteer FD. I didn't think they were called out that night. If he was there, he was on his own."

"I keep forgetting to ask, but it's possible that there was residue on Miguel's boots that caused Pal to alert like he did at the ranch."

Lane frowned. "I don't know, Nora. The concentration would have had to be extra strong on the boots. These dogs are highly sensitive to scent, so it's possible, but remember—"

Without warning, Pal bolted into the apartment, making a beeline around the corner. A moment later, something thudded against the wall.

"Stay here," Lane said, stepping into the apartment. "I'll go get him. The less contamination of this scene, the better."

My phone buzzed with a text from Trent that said PIC OF AWOL SOLDIER. While I watched Lane follow the same path Pal had taken, I clicked on the photo it contained and waited for it to load.

A moment after he disappeared around the corner, I heard Lane shout something that sounded like, "What are you doing here?"

Ignoring the whole "watch out for the crime scene" thing, I raced toward the sound of Lane's voice. As I turned the corner, I stopped short.

Pal was practically slobbering over a person who'd curled up into a ball behind a stack of suitcases. The goofy dog jumped around like a puppy and acted absolutely giddy to see this person.

A man, I could tell from his size and what little of his features that were visible. But who?

"Sit," Lane commanded, and Pal immediately complied.

The person behind the suitcases unfolded from his position and stood. "Shane?"

My waiter held both gloved hands in front of himself, palms forward. "I can explain, Nora."

As I struggled to find the words to say something, I glanced down at the phone in my hands. The photo of the soldier, a man named Bowen West, had finally loaded.

And it was an exact image of the man standing in front of me.

"Bo," a woman called from the other room. "Are you here? Baby, I've warned you about leaving the door open. We need for people to think this apartment is empty. There's a truck parked just down the alley. If they see—"

Leigh Fraser walked around the corner and stumbled to a stop. I held up my phone in her direction, aiming the photo of the soldier at her.

"Anything you want to tell us, Leigh?"

The gym bag she'd been carrying fell out of her hands and landed on the floor with a thud. Her mouth opened as if she might speak, but then she closed it again.

"It's all right, sweetheart," Shane—or rather, Bowen—said. "The game is up. We're caught."

"No," she managed, tears threatening. "We worked too hard to have this happen. Can't we all just go on about our business and forget this just happened? No one's been harmed here."

Lane's chuckle held no humor. "You seem to forget that an entire apartment of furniture managed to leave Nora's building and arrive here in this one. That's theft. Your boyfriend here is AWOL."

I noticed he didn't mention Pal. But as I considered what was happening here, I had to also think about the fact that the dog that had gone missing from training was the same dog that Lane and I had fallen in love with.

"Neither of us wanted that," Bowen said. "An Army guy can sleep on a rock on the ground, and it doesn't bother them. Carpeted floors and a blanket were more than sufficient. We didn't do it."

"Right. And the groceries in there," I said, connecting the dots on more than one mystery. "Did you get those from Roz? Because it's funny how we kept getting our grocery order messed up, but only since you've been here."

"What? No. I bought those with my pay, fair and square," he protested. "The receipt is in the bag. It'll show I paid cash, and it'll also prove it's not even the same grocer, okay?"

"He's telling the truth," Leigh said. "And I'm not his girlfriend."

"No?" Lane said. "Then you've gotten yourself into a lot of trouble for a guy who you aren't in a committed relationship with. That doesn't make much sense, does it?"

"I'm not his girlfriend," Leigh repeated, her voice even and tight. "I'm his wife."

"Look," Bowen said. "Leigh didn't have any part of this. Not any of it, okay? She was surprised that I turned up. I'm the one who figured out there was an empty apartment up here that no one was using. I got myself set up here and then got hired on with you, Nora. I've worked hard and kept my nose clean."

"Yes, you've been a hard worker and a great employee. I just told Roz that not an hour ago. Considering the circumstances, you were taking a big risk serving a restaurant full of first responders for two days after the tornado," I told him.

"Hiding in plain sight," he said with a shrug. "No one would be looking for a soldier gone AWOL in a waiter uniform in the middle of a bunch of cops and firemen, would they? Besides, Canon had called in already. I might have bolted for those two days and come back when the coast was clear, but I couldn't leave you understaffed. You've been too good to me."

"Okay, fair enough. But one of you needs to tell me how the furniture got here," Lane said. "I mean, if you're cool with carpet, then there's no need for any of this fancy stuff."

Bowen looked past me to Leigh. Neither said a word.

Leigh shifted her attention from Bowen to me. "We don't know."

Footsteps pounded up the stairs, but it was Bitsy who came around the corner instead of the police officers I expected. "Leigh, what are you doing here?" she said, eyes wide.

Her gaze bounced around the room then landed on me. "We were supposed to stay out because it's a crime scene. The cops are literally at the door, and they are not going to be happy that we've trampled over the evidence. They stopped to take a call from someone important, or they would have followed me in."

"Actually, I'm the evidence," Bowen said.

"No, you're the waiter, and Leigh is my associate at the gym. I don't know why you're up here, but you can't stay."

"We're going to need everyone to come out single file," a deep voice called from the other side of the wall. "Mrs. Sumner, you were not supposed to go in."

Bitsy put her hands up and turned to leave. "We are all in big trouble now," she said over her shoulder as she left the room.

"After you," Lane said to Leigh. "Then Bowen. I'll be right behind your husband just to make sure you don't go anywhere. Nora, you'll be behind me. If anyone gets stupid, I don't want you in the line of fire."

"Wait," I said. "I need to ask Bowen a question." I turned to him. "I haven't known you long, but I'm usually a good judge of people. Or thought I was anyway. Why did you go AWOL?"

He sighed. "Tell him," Leigh said.

"I was Sarge's trainer. Part of the training team, actually, but he was special and it felt like he was mine, you know?" He paused to lean down and scratch Pal behind the ear. "When I heard he'd flunked out, it wasn't a complete surprise. He's as smart as they come, but really he's just a big teddy bear."

"I've noticed that," I said.

"So they fostered him out. I went to visit him when I had leave. And I didn't like what I saw. Sarge had landed in a bad situation. He was outside chained to a tree in the elements. I couldn't have that." He paused, seemingly unable to continue.

"So you took him?" I supplied.

He nodded. "I planned to bring him back and get him situated somewhere else. But then I just thought I'd come see Leigh, and then I didn't want to go back anymore. So I hid out here awhile, and nobody noticed. I figured they'd stopped looking for me."

"That's not how it works," Lane said. "They never stop looking for you."

"Yeah, I know that now. I landed in a cage of my own, I guess. When the wrong people find out something like this, they'll use it against you."

"Is that what happened to you?" I asked. "Did the wrong people find out about you and the dog?"

"Brenham PD," the man called. "I know there are others in there."

"Can I just do one thing before I go?" Bowen said. "I'd like to say goodbye to my dog."

"Dennison, is that you?" Lane called. "It's Lane Bishop." When the officer answered in the affirmative, Lane continued. "Give us just a second. I've got Nora here, Leigh from the gym, and Shane from the restaurant. Oh, and there's an MWD here with us. He's completely trained and under control. Understand?"

"All right, but whatever you're doing, you'd better not be messing with evidence, Lane."

At Lane's nod, the former waiter knelt down beside Pal. The younger man buried his face in the dog's fur and held him tight. "It was good while it lasted, Sarge. Be good for these folks, and take care of whoever you end up with."

Bowen climbed to his feet again and swiped at his eyes with the back of his hands. Then he looked over at Lane. "Thank you. You'll see that he's taken care of."

"I'll do my best," Lane said. "And you called him Sarge?"

"He's got a much longer name, but that's my nickname. He reminds me of an NCO I once had."

I frowned at Leigh. "You took this dog to your classes then lied to me when I asked questions about him."

"Yeah," she said. "I think you can see why I had to do that. I was just protecting Bo and the dog."

"If you were protecting this dog," Lane said evenly, "how did he end up running through a parking lot at a wedding venue?"

Bowen hung his head. "I have no idea."

"We don't," Leigh said. "Honestly. He was here, and then he was gone. The first I heard of him being found elsewhere was when Nora came into the gym to ask about a missing MWD."

"Dr. Bishop," Todd Dennison called. "You've got to come out now. ATF just pulled up, and they're not going to be happy that I've let you hang out at a crime scene. Come on out before the feds rat on me to the chief, okay?"

CHAPTER TWENTY-FIVE

All four of us—five including Pal—exited the building and were standing in the alley when Trent Mendez rounded the corner of the building. He immediately began barking orders, and a few minutes later the crime scene tape went up.

Bowen and Leigh were swiftly cuffed and loaded into the backs of two separate police cars. Bitsy's husband had arrived, along with what had to be a half dozen lawyers in a separate car. Witt Sumner had then spirited Bitsy away, and now the attorneys were speaking with one of the police officers.

Todd Dennison motioned for me to join him. "I wouldn't do this for just anybody, but that fellow who worked for you would like to talk to you. If you're willing to do that knowing I'll be standing there listening, I'll escort you over."

"Yes, absolutely."

I followed Todd over to the patrol car that held Bowen. Then Todd climbed into the driver's seat and rolled down the window. "Go ahead, West, but make it fast."

Bowen looked up at me, and it was almost impossible not to stare at the cuffs shackling his wrists. "Leigh was telling the truth. She doesn't know anything about how that furniture got moved and why the MWD went missing. Her only crime is loving me." He shook his head. "Man, that sounds like a bad country song."

"It does," was all I could think to speak into the silence.

Bowen stared down at his hands then looked back up at me. "I can't explain it, but that furniture just appeared there. I went to work, leaving an empty apartment, and came back to that."

"Didn't Leigh notice someone was furnishing her empty place?" I asked.

"Leigh didn't live there. She had her own place and was already working here when I showed up. I didn't want her associated with me until things cooled down."

"So you found a place to hide out," I supplied.

Bowen nodded. "Eventually we were going to make a life somewhere else. I was saving my wages, and so was she. We were going to take the dog and disappear. I already told you that, but it's the honest truth."

A thought occurred. "Did Canon know this?"

"He figured it out," Bowen admitted. "At least he figured out the part about me living here under another name. The rest of it? Nah, I don't think he knew about Leigh or the MWD."

"Time to wrap it up," Todd said.

"Who else knew you were in Brenham?" I asked Bowen.

Silence.

"What happened to the MWD's chip and tattoo?"

Silence.

"And those burns? How did you really get them? Were you there when Canon started the fire?"

Bowen still didn't answer.

"Time's up," Todd said. "Sorry about that, Nora, but I've got to get the prisoner to the jail now."

I leaned against Lane and rested my head on his shoulder. Two of my waiters were in jail, and I was witnessing the impending separation of the love of my life from his dog.

This was a lot to digest.

Once the sound of the sirens faded, I spied Trent Mendez heading our way. "I ought to confiscate that canine," he said before he'd even closed the distance between us. His expression was stony. He said nothing more.

In spite of the torrent of pleas begging to be released, I kept my silence as well. This was Lane's battle to fight, not mine.

One thing I had figured out during the time Pal had been with us was that this dog had made a difference in this man's life. So whatever happened right now, it needed to be Lane who handled it.

"I'd like to ask that you don't do that," Lane said evenly. "I'll sign whatever you'd like to make it happen, but I think we both know he's better off with a licensed veterinarian as his temporary custodian than putting him in a crate and shipping him off like evidence in a criminal investigation."

"Which he is," Trent said, his tone matching Lane's. "And he is the property of the US government."

Lane's spine was laser straight and his shoulders squared. He looked down at Trent, his expression unreadable. "I understand."

Trent nodded. "I'll see what I can do. In the meantime, the government thanks you for taking care of their dog. See that you report in and keep me apprised of the animal's condition."

"His name is Pal," Lane said. "I'll be at Lone Star Vet Clinic for another week and a few days. I'm staying with my father who is recuperating from surgery on a broken leg. I'll give you both addresses, but I won't be hard to find."

"No need." Trent turned his attention to me. "I noticed the yellow tape is off the building. I guess you'll be doing something with the building soon."

I sighed. "I hardly. According to my insurance company, the interiors are a total loss. I'm not sure what I'll be doing with the space, but at least they'll be paying for the cleanup and remediation."

"I have to ask. Did the suspect give you any information that will help us find out who set those fires?"

"Not a word," I told him. "His hands are burned, and he claims he stuck them in hot dishwater. He's been hiding them all week with gloves. He did tell me that Canon had figured out that he was hiding out in Brenham but said nothing else."

"Nora," Lane said, "let's think about this. Bowen is another link to the fires. He and Canon worked together. They took breaks together. Now you're saying that the Ames fellow knew that Shane wasn't who he said he was. That he was Bowen and he was hiding out here."

"And?"

"And all of that leads up to Bowen's involvement. Or at least the possibility of it."

Trent nodded. "I can't disagree."

"Right," I said.

"So, how are you doing with your belief that Canon Ames is innocent?" Trent asked. "Is your gut still telling you that?"

"It's getting harder to believe based on the evidence," I admitted.

"Indeed." Trent looked over at Lane. "I'll be in touch. Just know that returning the dog is never going to be off the table. He's got to go back eventually."

"I know," Lane said, his jaw clenched.

As Trent walked away, I wrapped my arm around Lane's waist. "It'll be okay."

After a moment, he nodded. "Yeah. It will. Can we go somewhere quiet? I need to think."

"The ranch?" I said.

"Closer to home." He paused to nod at his phone. "In case Pop needs me."

"Right, okay. Well, there's the restaurant, but we've got Pal with us." I paused. "You know what? If I get in trouble, I'll plead extenuating circumstances. Let's just make sure he stays out of the kitchen, or I'll be closed down for sure. Straight down the hall to my office, okay?"

We trudged down to Simply Eat in silence. I unlocked the door, and we filed inside, Lane first with Pal following at his heels then me. I locked the door behind me and went to fetch three bottles of water from the fridge and a bowl.

The dog was already sprawled out on the floor against the far wall. He perked up when I placed the bowl on the floor and filled it with water. While Lane settled on my desk chair, I retrieved Roz's stool and returned to my office.

We all fit—barely.

"This is cozy," I told him, taking a swig of water. "And I kind of like that right now."

The sound of Pal slurping water filled the silence. Then he burped, and we couldn't help but laugh.

"Thanks, Pal," Lane said, reaching down to scratch behind his ear. "We needed a little humor about now."

The dog stretched and then did that sniffing thing. "What now?" I asked then noticed the direction he was aiming his attention.

Just out of reach was the dog toy I'd retrieved from the building steps. I pulled the stuffed squirrel down and offered the furry thing to Pal. He sniffed then snatched up the toy and settled in the corner.

Lane watched Pal for a few minutes then leaned back in the chair and closed his eyes. "I'm trying to wrap my brain around what just happened, Nora, and I'm having trouble with it."

I nodded but otherwise kept quiet. This was a conversation that Lane needed to take the lead on. I was here to listen.

He reached for a notepad and pen. "May I?" When I nodded in agreement, he started scribbling what appeared to be a timeline.

"Okay. So the fire happened last Wednesday. We still don't know who caused it, but we have now figured out where the furniture went. Meanwhile, Canon is seen on Bitsy Sumner's security camera during the tornado. There's a bright light, presumably from the fire, and then we see him running, so he's got to be the one who set the fire. No one else is captured coming or going by that camera that night."

I frowned. "I don't know about that."

"What do you mean?"

"The video Bitsy gave me ends immediately after Canon is seen." I shifted positions on the stool. "If anyone else was in the area that night after Canon, it would be on the film."

"And unless that camera had malfunctioned," Lane said, "the camera is also going to show who moved that furniture."

"Right, but we don't have that video," I reminded him. "Just the part that I was given. But I can ask." I retrieved my phone and texted Bitsy.

"All she can say is no, right?"

"Okay, so now we've got the explosion out at the wedding venue. The tornado and building fire happened on Wednesday morning. Less than a week later, the building at Thistledown Farms is obliterated."

He noted these on the timeline. Then he studied the paper.

"So," Lane continued without looking up, "we can agree that the obvious connection is Canon Ames. He works next door to the building where the fire started, and his parents own the wedding venue. That's easy. But why the explosions? That's where it gets hard."

"Right," I said, watching him write notes under the dates.

"This kid is home from college for the summer. He's working, presumably to contribute to the expense of his education, and he isn't slacking off. He has parents who are obviously doing well for themselves."

"I met the father, and while he's not exactly a charmer, he seems like an okay guy," I said.

Lane nodded. "None of this leads me to think Canon has any reason to be involved in whatever was going on."

"That's what I've been saying all along, Lane."

I looked at his drawing then at him. "If not Canon, then who? And was he going there for another purpose then happened to witness the explosion? Maybe he was trying to stop it."

"Maybe. Who else knew about the apartment?" He tapped the pen against the paper. "Canon knew about Bowen. Would he have told anyone?"

"Why would he? Telling someone else would only hurt Bowen, and I got the impression the two of them weren't on bad terms."

"That leaves us with Roz," Lane said. "You told me she had suspicions about one of the waiters. Did she tell you that to throw off suspicion from her?"

I laughed. "Why would she do that? What benefit is that to her if either of the waiters is gone? It just makes more work for her."

"Then it has to be something else. Something other than whatever she gets out of working for you." He took a moment then continued. "What do you know about Roz, Nora? Is there something in her life that would make any of this seem like it makes sense?"

"There's nothing, Lane. I checked her out before I hired her." I paused to think a moment. "And when you add the uncertainty of what happened to cause the two explosions, it all adds up to nothing that makes sense. But I'm certain that it will eventually."

He nodded. "The problem is that time is not our friend right now, Nora."

"Then let's not waste it." I leaned over and kissed him.

His phone buzzed. "That'll be Pop."

I sat back on the stool while Lane talked to his father. "I'll be there in a few minutes," he said then hung up. "Sorry, sweetheart, but I need to get home to Pop."

"Go," I told him. "We're closed for the day, so I'm about to leave too."

"You surprise me. I figured you'd be heading next door to check things out now that the police tape is gone."

"Not today," I said. "I honestly don't have the brain power for it. And frankly I don't feel comfortable alone in there right now. Then there's the warning about toxic stuff that the insurance adjuster gave me. Long story, but it's all coming out starting in a few days."

"Then home sounds like the right place for both of us," Lane said. "Come on. I'll walk you to your car."

I snatched up the papers pertaining to the grocery issue and tucked them into my bag then followed Lane out. When I got home, I kicked off my shoes and padded to the kitchen with a fuzzy orange shadow at my heels. One bowl of kitty food for her and one bottle of water for me later, I was ready to tackle the grocery issue.

Only I really wasn't.

Instead, I called Cassidy and caught her up on everything that had happened. "That's quite a morning, Nora." She paused. "So if you're going to lose all the things in the building, what will you do with the place once the remediation process is finished?"

"I don't know," I told her. "There are lots of possibilities. I've had my mind elsewhere, so I haven't really thought about that."

"I understand," Cassidy said. "You know what would be cool?"

Agatha Kitty jumped into my lap and started purring. "What?"

"Why not break through the wall and enlarge your restaurant?"

"Actually," I said slowly, "I could look into that. It might be fun to have a bigger dining room. Of course that means more staff, and I'm sort of not doing great staff-wise right now."

"True, but you'd have plenty of time to fix that issue."

"I'll think about it."

We chatted a few more minutes before I hung up and opened my email program. A few minutes later, I pressed the SEND button on an email to the architect who had drawn up the plans for Simply Eat. He would know if it was possible to expand the restaurant into the other building.

Thinking about a bigger restaurant made me also think about a bigger menu. That thought sent me fleeing from the invoices. If I was going to add to the dishes we served in my enlarged dining room, I would need to get creative.

Lane called just as I had put away the last of the pots and pans from the day's experimental cooking session and was spreading out the invoices on my kitchen table. Agatha Kitty batted at the phone as I reached for it. I greeted Lane then put him on speaker. We talked about his day, his dad's progress, and the casserole they'd chosen for dinner.

"You missed out, Nora. The Famous Tuna Surprise was a winner," he said with a laugh.

"I'll take your word for it," I told him.

"How did you spend the rest of your day?"

"I did some recipe testing."

"Planning new dishes for the restaurant?" he asked.

"Actually, I may be planning an expansion to the dining room." I told him my idea.

"That sounds like a great idea. It's always busy, so why not make room for more people?"

"Now that I've finished with the creative part, I've just decided to tackle the office work I've been putting off." I told him what I'd been doing and why I was concerned about the invoices. "It makes no sense. I've got returns and changes and substitutions. I think he's got my account mixed up with someone else's."

"Check the account number. Is it yours?"

"Yes," I said testily. "I noticed that right away."

"What about the credit card number that the purchases are going to?"

I sighed. "Hang on. I'll grab my purse."

I retrieved my business account card and compared it to the number listed in the purchases section of the invoice. "It matches."

Then I went to the first batch of returns. "Lane," I said softly, "I'm being charged on the correct account, but the returns are being credited to a whole different number. And it's not mine."

"Well, there you go," he told me. "They have your account and someone else's mixed up. It should be a simple fix to have them straighten it out. If I were you, though, I'd go down there and speak with the owner personally. These things can be hard to explain over the phone."

"Yes," I said, folding the invoices and returning them to their envelope. "I'll do that. So, how was your dog thief today? I almost forgot to ask."

"Kirby was fine." He paused. "Apologetic but fine. And Pal did that thing again where he sniffs at the air when Kirby is in the room like he did when he was near Bowen."

Agatha Kitty nudged my arm. I picked her up and walked into the living room to settle onto my favorite chair. "Why do you think he's doing that with Kirby?"

"I don't know, but I don't think it has anything to do with breakfast burritos."

I chuckled then sobered. "To be clear, Pal isn't alerting to anything, right?"

"No, he's not. He's just, well, sniffing."

"Okay," I told him, yawning. "Maybe he thinks Kirby smells like Bowen. Same aftershave or something?"

"Possibly," he said.

"It's another mystery to be solved," I said, rubbing the purring cat's belly. "But not tonight. I'm tired. It's been a long day."

"I'm guessing it doesn't help that you're short on servers."

"Roz hired two temps, which will help. Canon will still have his job if he's released, but I can't wait for that to happen."

"And it might not happen, sweetheart," Lane said.

"I know," I answered softly.

"Tomorrow is another day," he said. "I have complete confidence that if Canon Ames is innocent, you'll find what you need to prove it."

"I hope so," I told him. "Right now there isn't much to go on. And it doesn't help that he's on camera at the scene of the crime. I wish I could talk to him. Do you think that's possible?"

"Probably not," Lane said. "I'd assume no one but his lawyers would be allowed to see him until he's released. Same with Bowen and Leigh."

We chatted for a few more minutes then hung up. I was almost asleep when I remembered to check my emails. If Bitsy had more footage, she might have sent it to me. I retrieved my laptop and opened my email program.

Unfortunately, she hadn't replied.

However, my architect had. My shoulders slumped as I read his brief response.

> There's no way to break through to the other building.
> The wall is load bearing, and it's unlikely you could get a
> permit considering the ages of the two structures. You could
> do a second restaurant next door and connect them through
> a patio up front, but that's about as close as you'll get to
> what you're wanting.

I sat back and read that again. Two restaurants.

Exactly what I had hoped to someday have, and here it was in black and white on the page. I began a deep dive into researching possible restaurant concepts that might work for a sister restaurant to Simply Eat. At some point, I closed my eyes just to rest them a bit. Then I was going to check on some darling dining chairs I'd seen at a restaurant supply site online.

I woke up during the night to a series of dings on my phone. I sat up and tried to figure out what was causing the noise. Then I remembered I'd taken my laptop to bed and forgotten to hit mute on the sound before I fell asleep.

As it turned out, the source of the sounds was a series of emails sent by Bitsy. Each of them said the same thing:

> I had to wait until Witt fell asleep to send this. I hope

it only goes out once, but I can't tell what I'm doing
in the dark.

I was smiling as I clicked on the video. Then I sobered as the familiar scene of the tornado filled my screen. I hit FAST FORWARD then paused when Canon's image appeared.

"Okay, Canon, let's see if I can find out who else was with you that night."

I watched the film for almost five minutes after Canon disappeared and never saw another human. To be fair, it was late—or rather, early, since the clock showed the time to be a few minutes before four o'clock—so I might have dozed off.

"Starting over," I muttered as I pressed PLAY. Again there was nothing new.

"Okay, slow motion this time. Maybe there's someone in the background who I'm missing." Beginning with one minute before Canon Ames' appearance, I watched frame after frame looking for any kind of anomaly.

Then I saw it. A spark of sorts.

And that's when I figured it out.

CHAPTER TWENTY-SIX

LANE

Thursday morning
Brenham, Texas

Today was supposed to be the day I left Pop alone all morning. The plan had been to see that he had breakfast, check on him midmorning, then come home for lunch. I would repeat the process in the afternoon and then leave work no later than four.

Pop was doing great. He was getting around just fine on his walker, and I knew that physically there was no need to have someone here with him all day. However, when it came to deciding to actually leave Pop alone, I just couldn't do it.

My father's arrangement with Kirby had only been for two days of care. I called the agency and inquired to see if it was too late to have someone come sit here for the day.

The woman on the other end of the line remembered my family and me immediately. "Mr. Ewing is free today. Do you want me to send him?"

Relief flooded me. "Yes, please do."

I made the arrangements then went in to tell Pop he'd have company for another day. Kirby arrived an hour later.

"Looks like you guys can't do without me," he said with a grin.

"I'm glad you were able to give him one more day. I'd feel more comfortable if he wasn't alone."

"Absolutely. E.B. and I can watch as many episodes of *Murder She Wrote* as he wants."

"Perfect. Thanks. I'll check in later and plan to be home for lunch," I told him.

"And Pal?" he said. "Is he staying with E.B. and me?"

Without going into the terms of my agreement with Trent Mendez, I said the dog would be coming with me. Kirby took the news just fine as Pal retrieved what had become his favorite dog toy—the grubby squirrel from Nora's office—and followed me to the truck.

I headed for work with yesterday still on my mind. As I was nearing the clinic, my phone rang. "Nora, you're calling early."

"You're not in surgery this morning, are you?"

"Just appointments and not for another half hour. What's up?"

"Can you stop by for just a few minutes? I have something to show you."

"Sure," I told her, turning left instead of right at the next stop sign.

Nora met me at the door and ushered Pal and me inside. "He really likes that toy, doesn't he?" she commented as I followed her into the kitchen where her laptop had been set up.

"I'm sorry to say there's nothing new in the rest of the footage from that night," she told me when I'd seated myself at the table. "Canon is the only person who walked down that alley for at least an hour before or after the storm."

"That's too bad."

"Yes, but watch this."

She pressed the button to start the footage. I watched until Canon appeared. She hit Pause and grinned. "What do you see?"

"Is this a trick question?" I looked again. "I see Canon Ames."

"Look again." She pointed to a spot on the image.

"What am I looking at?" Nora explained, and then I saw it. "Oh wow, that changes everything."

Nora

Thursday morning
Brenham, Texas

I sent Lane off to work then noticed that Pal had left his toy. I gathered the squirrel up and tucked it into my bag. Then I decided the thing probably should be freshened up before I turned it back over to Pal.

I threw it into the washing machine on a delicate cycle along with a few towels then went to the phone and called Roz. "How are things going?"

"Interesting morning so far," Roz said. "The two newbies are doing their best."

"Okay, so I just realized this morning that I hadn't posted anything about the promotion today, so let's forget about the Texas sheet cake and close for dinner again. Losing one waiter was bad enough, but losing two and trying to do a full dinner service just doesn't make sense."

"I agree."

"I've got to do a few things this morning, and then I'll be in. Is everything under control?"

"Everything's fine." She paused. "I still can't believe that Shane was arrested. And that he wasn't who he said he was. And Canon on top of that? I'm just shocked."

"You're not the only one."

I hung up with Roz and decided to try my luck with calling the grocer again instead of paying a personal visit. Once again he answered on the first ring.

"I've been wondering when you would call," he said once I identified myself. "What did you find out?"

"That I've got a mess," I told him. "I have more questions than answers, but the main question is I need to know who a credit card belongs to. I think you may have another account mixed in with my account."

"Not likely, but we can check on that. Let me pull up my records." I heard the sound of a keyboard, and then he returned to the line. "Okay, what credit card are you inquiring about?"

"The card that the purchases are going on is mine, but the returns are going to a card I don't recognize. It's new as of a month or so ago."

"Okay, well, that's the returns number I was given approximately five weeks ago. The instructions on the account state that purchases are on the card you say is yours and returns are on the other."

"Who gave that instruction?" I demanded. "Because it wasn't me."

"No, it was a woman who identified herself as your chef. Her name is Roz Holt. We have her on file as a person who can sign for invoices to the account. The name on the credit card where the returns are going is hers."

It was true that I had given Roz the power to buy whatever we needed in the way of groceries for the daily menu. I had signed the release and provided it to the grocery to be noted on my account.

However, I never expected this would happen.

"To be clear, Roz is ordering groceries on the store account, returning items, and having the amount of the return put on her own personal credit card?"

"That is correct," he said.

In that moment I had no words. I'd already been lied to by two of my employees. Now Roz? It was too much.

"Miss Hernandez? Are you still there? Have I answered your questions?"

"Yes," I said on an exhale of breath. "That answers everything. Just one more request."

"Anything, Miss Hernandez."

"Revoke all privileges for Roz Holt, and remove her from my account. Also, delete that second card. All purchases will be made only by me, and any returns will be made on the same card they were purchased."

"Yes, ma'am," he said. "It will be done immediately."

"And I'm sorry for accusing you of doing something wrong. Clearly it was my chef who caused all of this."

"This wouldn't be the first time I've seen something like this. Please don't worry," he said. "All is well."

"Not at Simply Eat," I muttered.

I hung up and placed the phone on the table. Then I rose and walked in to find my chef stirring a pot. The two new waiters were rolling silverware into napkins.

I returned to my office and printed a closed sign then went to the door and taped it on. Then I made sure the front door was locked before heading back into the kitchen.

"Roz," I told her. "What did you do with all the money you stole from me?"

She froze. "I don't know what you mean."

"Stop," I said. "I know all about the credit card scheme and the money you got for returning food before I saw it. It would be an easy matter to add up that amount and call the cops. But I'm going to give you a chance to explain first." I paused to let that sink in. "Oh, and before you do, send those two home and tell them I'll pay them for a full day of work. They can call tomorrow to see if we'll be open, because we're closed for the rest of today."

She did as she was told. Once the employees had filed out and we were alone, Roz's defiant pose went soft. "I didn't want to do it."

"Do what?" I demanded. "I need you to explain."

"Okay, so I figured out the first week I was working here that something was off about the building next door. That guy was always there, and I don't think the old man or the contractor who did some odd jobs had a clue what was going on. Anyway, I got caught climbing the stairs to try and see what was happening. There were. . ." She paused, tears now threatening. "Well, let's just say there were threats made. I was scared. Considering what he was doing up there, I knew he would make good on them."

I didn't bother to ask who she was talking about. I'd seen the proof in the video. "What was he doing?"

"Making pills," she said.

My heart slammed against my chest. "He was making meth? That would explain why it exploded."

"No, Adderall. Apparently it's easy to cook up in a kitchen and it isn't as dangerous to make. There's a smell, and it can cling to anyone who's in there when the cooking is happening. I noticed it in the alley a few times but didn't know any of that until I did some research. Anyway, there was a full lab set up in that kitchen. When the building went up for sale, he needed another place to go. I don't know where it was, but he was back as soon as the old man left town."

"Even though I bought it," I said.

"Yeah," Roz told me, studying the floor. "I felt bad about that too. I wanted to warn you, but I was afraid."

"What else do you know, Roz? If this drug isn't dangerous to make, what caused that fire?"

"I had just told him I was done. No more. He told me he'd blow up my house, but first he'd take out the apartment next door just to show that he could. Oh, and the furniture? He told me he had it moved to Bitsy's place to incriminate Shane. All he had to do was call the cops and say Shane stole it and he'd be arrested. Then they'd figure out he was AWOL and he was a goner." She paused. "He's the one who took Shane's dog to the wedding venue and dropped him there. It was to get back at Shane for not agreeing to be his errand boy and distribute what he was making."

My anger rose. "You knew about Shane?" Roz winced as I paused to take a breath. "And the apartment was ruined to prove a point. Well, that's just great."

Roz nodded. "He told me that he'd blown up the building at the venue just to show me what he could do if I stopped paying him."

"Well, there's no need to be afraid. He'll be arrested today."

Relief flooded her face. "Really?"

"Yes, the proof has been uncovered. He's caught."

"That takes care of one problem," Roz said. "But it doesn't fix what I have done."

"No," I said firmly. "It doesn't."

She removed her chef's apron and placed it on the counter. "I'll save you the trouble of firing me by leaving voluntarily."

I stood firm and didn't immediately respond. "I think that's for the best," I said after a moment. "I'll expect anything with my logo to be returned before you get whatever wages you have coming to you, minus what you've stolen from me. And as long as you don't give me any trouble and don't come back here ever again, I won't turn this into a police matter."

She nodded then gathered up her knives into their case and picked up her purse. A moment later, she was gone. I locked the door and exhaled a long breath.

Now it was time to call Trent Mendez to give him the news that the case was solved. "I'll get him today," the ATF agent said after I'd told him what I knew. "You'll testify?"

"Of course."

We hung up, and I placed another call. This one was to my favorite game warden and my best friend's boyfriend, Jason Saye.

"Hey, Jason," I said, "remember when you asked me to find a reason to let Canon Ames go? I've found it."

"I'm listening," he said. "What've you got?"

"Are you where you can watch Bitsy's video?" I asked.

"I can pull it up on my phone," he said. "Just give me a minute to find a place to park. Okay, go ahead."

"I want you to fast-forward to the spot where you first see Canon's face. When you're there, I want you to watch carefully then pause it when his hand comes up into the frame. Let me know when you're there."

"I'm there," he said. "Now tell me what I'm looking at."

"You're looking at a man with a wedding ring on, Jason. And if those are what I think they are on that band, they are diamonds. They match the band that Canon Ames' father was wearing the day after the explosion. I went out there to look at the remains of the building I'd just been in on Saturday at the wedding, and he stopped to see what I was doing. The sun caught the diamonds in his wedding band as he was adjusting his hat." I paused. "Just like in the video."

"So we've got the wrong Ames," he said.

"Well, all I can say is the man in that image is Canon's father, not him. What he was doing in the alley is your department, as is whether or not his son is involved."

I texted Lane to let him know it was done. I also briefly filled him on what happened with Roz. He called immediately.

"So she knew and said nothing?" he said.

"She was afraid of Pat Ames. On one level, I get it. I can't say what I would do to be safe as a single woman in a new town. It must have been frightening."

"I'm not going to argue about this, but I will say that I doubt you would make the choices she did." He paused. "I need to check in with Pop. Can I call later?"

"Sure," I said. "With the restaurant on pause until I hire new staff, I've got plenty of time. Let me know if you'd like me to go check on him."

"I hired Kirby for today. I'll let you know about tomorrow."

Just as I hung up with Lane, I heard a knock at the door and walked in that direction. It was Roz. I pressed record on my phone just in case she'd returned to cause trouble, and then I tucked my phone into my pocket and opened the door.

"I'm sorry. I forgot my whetstone for the knives. It's in the drawer."

"Sure, come on in." I watched her go to the kitchen and retrieve the stone, and then she retraced her steps. As she reached the door, I said, "Remember, you don't have to fear Pat Ames anymore."

She gave me a confused look. "Who is Pat Ames?"

"The guy you've been talking about," I said. "Canon's father."

Roz shook her head. "Canon's father isn't the man I'm afraid of. I've seen him over there a time or two, but he never paid any attention to me. I know he was there the night of the fire because Shane told me he'd burned his hands trying to put it out."

"Shane was there too? That's impossible. He's not on the video."

"There's a blind spot," she said. "If you stay up against the wall, the camera can't see you. He knew about the camera because he watched it being put in. So Shane went in and out the side door, not the stairs. After Shane met you, he was done with letting those people use your building like that. So he went to confront him. There was an argument, as you can imagine."

"Wait, I tried that door after the tornado. It was almost impossible to open."

She shrugged. "Shane said he'd made it look like it hadn't been open. Something he'd learned how to do. He didn't say where. But I saw him go in there more than once by that way, so I know it's true."

I sighed. Could things get any worse?

"It was the other guy who scared me," Roz continued. "Do you know why that dog your boyfriend has doesn't have a tattoo or chip? He put the dog under general anesthesia and removed the tattoo then dug out the chip. Nice guy, huh? Just to make sure he had control of Shane, he hid the chip and told him he'd bring it to the cops if he didn't cooperate. That's what he's like, Nora. I'm still pretty shocked about that."

"Roz, it's Canon's father. That's shocking, to be fair, but just because Canon is nice, that doesn't mean his father is."

"No, Nora. His name is Kirby something-or-other, and he's a part-time EMT with the city. Most of the time he's just scamming people, threatening folks, or making drugs to sell." She paused. "Great guy."

"Kirby Ewing?" I barely managed to get the words out.

"That's the guy." Then she described him. "Do you know him?"

I managed a nod. "He was on scene when I was injured after the tornado."

Roz nodded toward the door. "I'll go now. I'm really sorry."

After Roz left, I called Jason again and told him what I knew. "I'll let Brenham PD know he needs to be picked up. Do you have any idea where he might be?"

My heart lurched. "Oh, Jason, he's with Lane's dad today."

We hung up, and I called Lane. "You need to go home, Lane. Right now. I'll explain why once you're in your truck. And I'll meet you there."

Lane and I arrived at the same time. Jason's truck and two cars from Brenham PD were parked outside.

I raced inside on Lane's heels only to have him stop short. "Good work, Pop," he said as I looked around him at the scene in the den.

Kirby Ewing was tied up to a chair with Dr. Bishop grinning at him. "This guy thought I was old and useless. Do you know he was trying to set up an Adderall lab in the potting shed outside? I guess he thought I wouldn't figure it out."

"How did you figure it out? And for that matter, how'd you get him tied to the chair, Pop?" Lane asked.

"I'm feeling good enough to wander," he told me. "Out to the yard anyway. I was out there with Pal, and he started doing that strange sniffing thing he does. Then next thing you know, out of the shed comes my caretaker."

"Great," Lane said under his breath.

"I'm not proud of giving medication to someone it isn't prescribed to, but I figured it'd be safer for me if I mixed a couple of pain pills into Kirby's iced tea. He'll wake up just fine, but he won't be happy about it."

"There are a lot of things he won't be happy about," Lane said. "I'll tell you all about it later, Pop."

"Okay," Pop said. "So it's nearly lunchtime, and I've got a house full of people. I say we bust out the casseroles and celebrate. Then I'll have to put a word out on the casserole ladies' grapevine about my adventures in crime fighting today."

"Adventures in crime fighting?" Lane echoed with a groan.

"It ought to at least get me a few cakes, don't you think?" he said with a smile. "I've put a moratorium on casseroles, at least until next week."

Later, after the stock of casseroles was slightly diminished and Kirby Ewing had been hauled off to jail, Lane set his father up in the den with a marathon of *Murder She Wrote* episodes then walked me out to my car.

"Well," he said slowly, "it's been quite a day."

"It has," I said.

"Tomorrow will be better," he told me. "I'll still be here, and it won't be today."

"I like both of those things," I said, snuggling into his embrace. "And no more mysteries, at least not tomorrow."

"None," he said. "I promise."

CHAPTER TWENTY-SEVEN

LANE

Two weeks later
Hernandez Ranch

I drove all the way back from Fort Cavazos with a smile on my face. Pal had spent most of the journey snoring loudly on the carpeted floor of my truck. As we were nearing Brenham, he'd perked up and was on the passenger seat leaving slobber marks on the window.

"How am I going to get Nora in here if you're going to wash the window with your tongue?" I said. "Have some consideration, please. This is a big day for me."

It was a big day for a lot of reasons. Just that morning I'd been given temporary custody of my furry copilot, pending the outcome of Bowen West's court-martial. An investigation into Bowen's allegations against the fosters had already uncovered enough evidence to back the soldier's story.

Bowen's testimony would likely knock some time off whatever sentence he received. Even better, once he was released he could apply to become Pal's owner. In the meantime, the pup would hang out with me.

It wouldn't be easy to give up my canine companion when the time came. For that reason, I had applied for a dog of my own. Because of my expertise, my military training, and the fact that I'm a veterinarian, I was assured I'd have a dog sooner rather than later.

I was pretty happy about that.

There was something else I was happy about, though, and it involved Nora. I patted my shirt pocket where I had stashed the ring box after I picked it up from the jeweler's. My original plan had been to do something like Jason and get a ring designed for Nora.

Then Pop had offered up Mom's ring.

We'd both cried over that. And if I wasn't careful, I'd start crying all over again.

I sniffed and then gave Pal the side-eye. He was staring at me, and I swore it looked like he was smiling.

"Cut it out," I told him. "We're almost to Nora's."

I hurried to move the ring from my pocket to the pouch on Pal's newly made vest. "Remember the plan, okay, soldier?"

Pal reached over the distance between us to press his massive paw onto my arm. I nodded my approval, and we drove the rest of the way to Nora's in silence.

When I got there, Nora was waiting outside. She climbed into the truck and shooed Pal off the seat.

"Sorry about the slobber on the window," I told her as I reached over and kissed her. "You look beautiful, sweetheart."

Her smile was radiant. "Welcome back. Did everything go okay?"

"It's official. He's mine until Bowen can qualify for him."

"And if that doesn't happen—because we don't know how long he'll be in jail?"

"If that doesn't happen, then he stays with me."

She smiled. "That makes me happy, Lane."

NORA

Same day
Hernandez Ranch

"I thought we were going to celebrate," I told Lane when I noticed he was going the wrong direction to leave the ranch.

"We are. I just thought we'd go back and finish the conversation we were having two weeks ago."

"Two weeks ago?" I tried to remember but drew a complete blank. "We've had a lot of conversations since then, and I'm pretty sure we finished all of them."

"Just tell me where the bluebonnets were pretty. Remember, we rode horses out there, and you told me you wished I'd seen the bluebonnets."

"Oh yes." I gave him directions then held on while we bounced down the ranch roads until we'd reached the spot. He climbed out, and I followed. Pal bounded from the back seat and joined us.

"We were sitting over there," Lane said, pointing to the rocks. "Let's go back to that spot."

Something was up. I just couldn't decide what that was.

The job at the clinic had ended last week and he was back in College Station at his research job. We'd talked about my plans to build a second restaurant next door to Simply Eat, but he hadn't said anything about his.

Apparently his decision to fix the issue with too much work and too many miles between us had been postponed.

We settled on the rock, and then Lane checked his watch. Off in the distance, I heard the drone of an engine.

"So we were here and you were telling me about the bluebonnets," Lane said.

"Yes, that's right. They're the prettiest right here."

"Every year?" he asked me.

"Yes," I said slowly as the sound of the engine grew louder. "What are you up to, Lane? You're acting weird."

"I need to tell you something." He moved closer. "I've wanted to marry you just about from the first time I saw you. I knew you were the one, but I couldn't do it. So I stayed busy, and I never told you why. So I want to tell you." He paused. "War changed me, Nora. The sleep, the fireworks, and other things. . ."

"I know," I said softly. "Or at least I had an idea."

"I couldn't bring you into my life as a wife to someone who had so many issues."

I opened my mouth to speak, and he pressed his finger to my lips. "Let me get all of this out.

"Since Pal came into my life, he's helped me see that I'm broken but not so broken that I can't be fixed. I've been seeing a counselor for a while. I'm feeling good about things, and I wanted you to know that my hesitancy about proposing has never been about you. It's always been about me. I'm so sorry for not telling you sooner or trusting you with what I've been dealing with, but I just didn't have the words."

Tears threatened. I wrapped my arms around him. "I'm so glad you found the words, Lane."

"I love you, Nora. You're the most patient woman I know. If you'll have me, I want to. . ."

He leaned back and held me at arm's length. "I need to do this properly."

Before I knew what was happening, Lane had slipped off the rock and was down on one knee. As if it all had been planned, Pal came to stand and then sit beside him.

Lane reached for my hand. Pal placed his paw over the top of Lane's hand. The growl of the engine was almost a roar now. It was, I realized, an airplane that was nearly overhead.

"Right on time," Lane said, nodding toward the sky. "How else does an Air Force guy ask the most important question of his life? Look up, Nora."

I glanced up to see a very familiar crop duster airplane flying low enough to reveal that the pilot was my brother Tony. At that moment, a banner unfurled from behind the plane with the words WILL YOU MARRY ME? emblazoned on it in Aggie-maroon letters.

My breath caught. Tears clouded my vision. I looked down in time to see Lane retrieve a black velvet box from a pocket on Pal's vest.

"Nora Hernandez, will you do me the honor of becoming my wife?" Pal let out a quiet yip. "And Pal's foster mom, of course."

Somehow I managed to say yes. I was blubbering like a fool and ruining my makeup, but I didn't care.

Lane opened the box and presented it to me. "This was my mother's, Nora. I've had it sized to fit you, but Pop and I are totally fine if you want to use the stones to design something that's more your style."

"It's perfect," I somehow said as he slid the ring onto my finger. I held out my hand to admire the beautiful oval diamond with the cluster of smaller round diamonds surrounding it. "It's just so very perfect."

Pal must have agreed, because he took the opportunity to cover the ring with a big slobbering lick.

"Pal," Lane chastised. "What have I told you about slobbering?"

"It's fine," I said, leaning over to take both my fiancé and my new dog into my embrace. "Make no mistake, we will be going back to the house so I can wash my hands, but it is totally fine."

We sat there for a few more minutes, letting the quiet settle between us. Finally, I grinned. "How did you manage to convince Tony to do that?"

"I told him there were a lot of Aggies getting engaged and no one filling the niche market of airplane proposals in the College Station area. It's certainly a decent side hustle to fill in between crop-dusting gigs. From what I understand, he's already got a lot of interest. End of school year is apparently the time to get engaged."

I leaned my head against his shoulder. Pal settled at my feet.

"Speaking of jobs, I quit mine at the university. Well, I gave my notice. I'll be sticking around to transition in whoever takes over for me. And I put my house on the market two days ago. I've already got three offers, so that's an encouraging sign."

"Wow," I said. "My head is spinning. You'll actually be close?"

"As close as Lone Star Vet Clinic," Lane said. "Tyler and Kristin are in agreement that we need more than two full-time vets if we're going to keep up with the demand. They offered me the spot, and I took it. Pop may even come in and help out when he feels up to it. That's kind of a full-circle moment."

"Oh, Lane. That's great news."

"I agree. So about those bluebonnets," Lane said. "We never talked about it, but if we were to build a house right here, where would it need to go in order to get the best view of them?"

I looked up at him. "Excuse me?"

He held up both hands. "Hey, if you don't want to live here, that's fine, but your dad wants to give this plot of land to us as a wedding present, so you'll have to take that up with him."

"You talked to my dad?"

He gave me a look. "I know it's old-fashioned, but it matters to me that we have your parents' blessing. I talked to both of them. Oh, and act surprised when your mother pitches her concept for the restaurant at the party she's throwing for us tonight."

"Okay, wait," I said, my brain spinning. "Restaurant concept? Party? Explain."

"While we're out here, your family and our friends are waiting for us to arrive at our engagement party. That's what we're celebrating, although we can also celebrate Pal's adoption."

At the sound of his name, Pal's ears perked up. We both laughed.

"At the party, your mother will tell you all about her idea to do a family-style restaurant at the new building, with meals that are based on the ones she's served to her family over the years."

"Really?"

"It would be a companion to Simply Eat with more of a Sunday-dinner any-day-of-the-week kind of vibe. I have it on good authority that the lasagna will be considered a menu item staple." He grinned. "She's been thinking about this awhile but never said anything. I told her she ought to give it a shot and see what you thought. Anyway, I just wanted you to be prepared in case you need to let her down gently."

"I love that idea, Lane. It's so cool. I'll act surprised, but I love it. And I love you. And oh my goodness, I love this dog that is leaning against me, presumably telling me it's time to kiss you."

I looked down and could have sworn that Pal was grinning at me. Then I kissed the man I would be marrying very soon in the spot where I would be watching bluebonnets grow for many years to come. Because he—and the happiness he brought—was worth the wait.

Kathleen Y'Barbo is a multiple Carol Award and RITA nominee and bestselling author of more than one hundred books with over two million copies of her books in print in the US and abroad. A tenth-generation Texan and certified paralegal, she is a member of the Texas Bar Association Paralegal Division, Texas A&M Association of Former Students and Texas A&M Women Former Students (Aggie Women), Texas Historical Society, and is a board member of American Christian Fiction Writers. She would also be a member of the Daughters of the American Republic, Daughters of the Republic of Texas, and a few others if she would just remember to fill out the paperwork that Great-Aunt Mary Beth has sent her more than once.

When she's not spinning modern-day tales about her wacky southern relatives, Kathleen inserts an ancestor or two into her historical and mystery novels as well. Recent book releases include bestselling *The Pirate Bride*, set in 1700s New Orleans and Galveston, its sequel, *The Alamo Bride*, set in 1836 Texas, which features a few well-placed folks from history and a family tale of adventure on the high seas and on the coast of Texas. She also writes (mostly) relative-free cozy mystery novels for Guideposts Books.

Kathleen and her hero-in-combat-boots husband have their own surprise love story that unfolded on social media a few years back. They make their home just north of Houston, Texas, and are the parents and in-laws of a blended family of Texans, Okies, and three very adorable Londoners.

To find out more about Kathleen or connect with her through social media, check out her website at www.kathleenybarbo.com.

GONE *to the* DOGS *Series*

Grab a lapdog to cuddle and relax into a
fun small-town Texas mystery series.

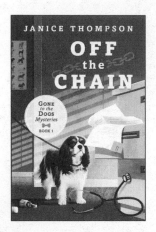

OFF THE CHAIN
(Book 1)

BY JANICE THOMPSON

Marigold and her coworkers at Lone Star Vet
Clinic only want to help animals, but someone
is determined to see them put out of business.

Paperback / 978-1-63609-313-0

DOG DAYS OF SUMMER
(Book 2)

BY KATHLEEN Y'BARBO

Country music star Trina Potter is back in
town to help her niece start a dog rescue,
but more than one person wants to send her
packing back to Nashville.

Paperback / 978-1-63609-394-9

BARKING UP THE WRONG TREE
(Book 3)

BY JANICE THOMPSON

Veterinarian Kristin Keller is determined to
figure out why her star patient is suddenly acting like a very different dog just days before his
next big agility competition.

Paperback / 978-1-63609-451-9

THE BARK OF ZORRO
(Book 4)
BY KATHLEEN Y'BARBO

Someone is spray-painting local dogs with the letter Z. The cops blame pranksters while pet owners are blaming each other.

Paperback / 978-1-63609-517-2

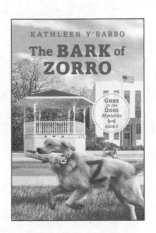

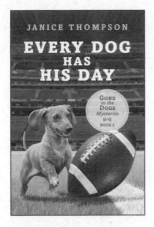

EVERY DOG HAS HIS DAY
(Book 5)
BY JANICE THOMPSON

A dog is lost, rescued, reunited with her owner, and missing again. Who is behind this high-profile case with a high-dollar reward?

Paperback / 978-1-63609-587-5

Find this series and more great fiction wherever books are sold and at www.barbourbooks.com